Richard Hughes is a UK-based crime thriller author from Essex. Born in London, he developed a passion for crime novels early on, which has since shaped his writing. *Secrets of St Mary's is* his debut novel and the first in an anticipated series. Hughes' work delves into the gritty side of crime fiction, blending suspense and realism inspired by his lifelong interest in the genre.

I would like to thank my family for their continued support. Without them, this would not have been possible.

Richard Hughes

SECRETS OF ST MARY'S

AUSTIN MACAULEY PUBLISHERS
LONDON * CAMBRIDGE * NEW YORK * SHARJAH

Copyright © Richard Hughes 2025

The right of Richard Hughes to be identified as author of this work has been asserted by the author in accordance with sections 77 and 78 of the Copyright, Designs and Patents Act 1988.

All rights reserved. No part of this publication may be reproduced, stored in a retrieval system, or transmitted in any form or by any means, electronic, mechanical, photocopying, recording, or otherwise, without the prior permission of the publishers.

Any person who commits any unauthorised act in relation to this publication may be liable to criminal prosecution and civil claims for damages.

This is a work of fiction. Names, characters, businesses, places, events, locales, and incidents are either the products of the author's imagination or used in a fictitious manner. Any resemblance to actual persons, living or dead, or actual events is purely coincidental.

A CIP catalogue record for this title is available from the British Library.

ISBN 9781035892167 (Paperback)
ISBN 9781035892174 (ePub e-book)

www.austinmacauley.com

First Published 2025
Austin Macauley Publishers Ltd®
1 Canada Square
Canary Wharf
London
E14 5AA

Introduction

The village of St Mary's was a place where time seemed to stand still. Nestled among rolling hills and ancient woods, it was a picture of tranquillity, where the only sounds that disturbed the peace were the distant toll of church bells and the gentle rustling of leaves in the breeze.

The villagers went about their lives with a quiet predictability, their routines as steadfast as the old stone cottages that lined the narrow lanes. It was a place where everyone knew each other's name, where secrets were whispered but rarely spoken aloud.

Yet, beneath the serene surface, shadows lingered. Secrets, long buried and carefully guarded, simmered just out of sight, threatening to unravel the fragile calm that enveloped the village. St Mary's was not immune to the darkness that crept into the lives of its residents, no matter how hard they tried to keep it at bay.

John Bailey, the village vicar, was a man who had found solace in the quiet life St Mary's offered. To his congregation, he was a pillar of strength, a beacon of faith in a world that often seemed lost. But John carried his own burdens, ghosts from a past he had worked tirelessly to leave behind.

To the villagers, he was a man of God, but behind closed doors, he wrestled with the demons of his former life—a life that was slowly catching up with him. In a small cottage on the edge of the village, an elderly woman sat in her attic, her sharp eyes trained on the world below.

She had watched over the village for decades, her notebooks filled with the comings and goings of its residents. To some, she was just a harmless old woman, but she knew more than anyone could imagine. Her secrets were like threads in a web, each one connected to another, forming a complex tapestry that could unravel the lives of those she observed.

Then, there was Sam—a young man caught in the crossfire of his own mistakes and the manipulations of those around him. Desperate for redemption,

Sam found himself entangled in a web of deceit and fear, each choice he made pulling him deeper into the darkness that threatened to consume him. His path would lead him to the doors of the church, seeking salvation from a man who might be the only one who could save him—or damn him.

As the villagers went about their daily lives, unaware of the storm brewing on the horizon, the stage was set for a reckoning. In the quiet corners of St Mary's, where secrets were kept and sins were hidden, a chain of events had been set in motion.

The past, long buried, was about to resurface, bringing with it consequences that no one could foresee. In the end, when the truth finally emerged from the shadows, St Mary's would never be the same.

The Unknown

A single bulb flickered weakly in the dimly lit room, casting a hesitant glow that barely pierced the oppressive darkness. Shadows clung to the walls, shifting and whispering like forgotten secrets, as if the room itself were alive with hidden intent.

The air was thick, suffocating, as if the darkness had taken on a life of its own, coiling tightly around everything within. In the centre of the room, a figure stood over a body sprawled across the floor. The figure's features were lost in the gloom, obscured as if the shadows themselves were conspiring to erase its identity.

Its breath came in shallow, ragged gasps, each exhale stirring the heavy silence that gripped the space. The body lay unnervingly still, a dark pool spreading beneath it, seeping into the floor and merging with the surrounding shadows.

It was impossible to tell whether the body was alive or dead—only the unbearable quiet hinted at the grim reality. The figure hesitated, its hand twitching by their side as if caught in a silent debate. The oppressive silence seemed to press down on it, urging action, demanding resolution.

Yet, it remained frozen, suspended in a moment that stretched like the shadows around them. Outside, the wind howled, rattling the windows with a ferocity that mirrored the turmoil within. The figure glanced around, its eyes sweeping the room as if searching for answers that eluded it.

The space was achingly familiar, yet alien—memories and secrets lay buried beneath layers of darkness, just out of reach. Was this the church, with its cold stone walls that had witnessed countless prayers? Or the summerhouse, once a sanctuary, now a prison for the secrets it held?

Perhaps, it was Jock's flat, a den of despair where shadows danced in time with the flickering light. The figure couldn't be sure—the lines between places and memories were blurred, distorted by the darkness. Its mind raced, each thought a tangled thread in a web of confusion.

It knew the body on the floor, knew the face shrouded in darkness. But the truth was elusive, slipping through its grasp like smoke, leaving only questions in its wake. *Who am I in this moment of reckoning?* The figure's thoughts spiralled. *Am I the protector or the aggressor? The saviour or the destroyer?*

The lines between these roles blurred, leaving only a fractured sense of self that threatened to unravel. The scent of iron and fear hung heavy in the air, mingling with the suffocating darkness. The figure's heart thundered in its chest, a relentless drumbeat that echoed through the silence.

A decision loomed before it, the weight of choice pressing down like a physical force. In the distance, the mournful howl of the wind pierced the night—a haunting sound that reverberated through the room, reminding it that time was slipping away, each moment a chance lost to indecision.

The figure took a step back, the shadows shifting with its movement, whispering secrets in a language only it could understand. The room seemed to close in, the walls tightening around it, holding the truth just out of reach. Then, as if waking from a dream, the figure turned and slipped into the shadows, its silhouette melting into the darkness that swallowed the room whole.

The flickering bulb cast one final, feeble glow before succumbing to the void, leaving only the echo of retreating footsteps to fill the silence. The body remained on the floor, a silent witness to the secrets that lingered in the air. The room was still, the darkness settling like a shroud over the unknown, a mystery waiting to be unravelled.

As the night deepened, the shadows whispered promises of what was to come—a tale of deception and redemption, of choices made and paths untaken. And in the silence, the truth lay waiting, hidden beneath the layers of darkness that had swallowed it whole.

Chapter 1
A Broken Sanctuary

The sun hung low over the village, casting a soft golden hue across the ancient stone walls of St Mary's church. It was a perfect Sunday morning, the kind that made Mrs Wilson especially grateful for her quiet, close-knit community. In her late fifties, with a firm Catholic faith that never wavered, Mrs Wilson had never missed a Sunday service.

Today, she stood just outside the entrance, her usual handbag slung over one arm, greeting Reverend John Bailey with her characteristic smile. "Such a lovely service today, Reverend," she said, her voice brimming with sincerity. "We're blessed to have you in our community."

Reverend John, a man in his late forties, recently assigned to the parish, returned her smile, though there was a flicker of distraction in his eyes. "Thank you, Mrs Wilson. It's always a pleasure to see you here," he replied, his tone warm yet distant, as though his thoughts were elsewhere.

Mrs Wilson, always perceptive, caught the shadow that crossed his face as he glanced towards the other parishioners. They were filtering out of the church, exchanging their goodbyes, but John's attention seemed to slip, his gaze unfocused.

She leant in slightly, her voice dropping to a whisper, "Is everything alright, Reverend?"

The village itself was peaceful, as it usually was on a Sunday morning, with the gentle hum of life carrying through the narrow streets. But beneath John's calm exterior, something stirred—a creeping unease that he couldn't shake. Something in the air had shifted.

St Mary's, with its towering stone arches and weathered statues, had stood for centuries as a symbol of hope and faith for the villagers. Yet, for John, the church no longer felt like the sanctuary it was meant to be. There was an unsettling presence within its walls, something dormant that felt as though it were awakening.

"Reverend, any news about the break-in?" Mrs Wilson asked quietly, her brows furrowed with concern. "I've been thinking about it ever since it happened. It's unnerving, to say the least."

Reverend John's jaw tightened ever so slightly. "No significant leads yet," he said, his voice lowering to match hers. "The police are still investigating. Whoever did it, they were careful. Too careful."

"They took the collection plate, didn't they?" She asked, the lines on her forehead deepening with worry.

"They did." John nodded, his eyes shifting briefly towards the vestry, where the worst of the damage had been done. He could still picture the scene—the toppled candlesticks, the faint scent of burnt wax lingering in the air, and most disturbingly, the strange symbols scrawled hastily on the vestry walls.

The police had dismissed them as random graffiti, but John knew better. He had seen those markings before. They weren't random. But he hadn't told the authorities that—not yet.

Mrs Wilson sighed, clutching her handbag a little tighter. "It's dreadful. Our church, violated like that. It makes you wonder what kind of world we're living in. Is there anything I can do to help?"

John gave her a tight smile, though it did little to mask the tension in his eyes. "Your prayers are always appreciated, Mrs Wilson. But if you see or hear anything unusual, please let me or the authorities know."

Mrs Wilson's expression hardened with resolve. "We must protect our church and our community, Reverend."

"We will," John replied softly, though his mind was already drifting back to the vestry, to those symbols. He knew what they meant, and it wasn't just a simple act of vandalism.

Their conversation was abruptly interrupted by the growl of a car engine—a sound out of place on such a quiet morning. Reverend John's head snapped towards the road. A small red car, its modified exhaust roaring, sped past the church.

The blacked-out windows gave it an ominous, almost predatory feel. John's pulse quickened as the car slowed, just enough for the driver to look directly at him. James Parsley. Even from a distance, John could see his familiar grin, the challenge in his eyes unmistakable. There was something too knowing, too deliberate about the way James stared at him, as though he were silently mocking the reverend's unease.

For a brief moment, time seemed to slow. The village faded into the background, and John's mind was thrown back to a darker time—before he'd come to St Mary's, before he'd taken up the mantle of reverend. The last time he had seen James, it had been under very different circumstances, ones he had tried to bury deep within himself. But now, James was back.

John swallowed hard as the car disappeared around the bend, leaving only the echo of its engine in the air. He clenched his hands to steady himself, forcing his expression to remain neutral. He couldn't afford to let this show, not in front of Mrs Wilson or anyone else. The break-in had already stirred whispers among the villagers, and James's sudden reappearance threatened to unravel everything.

"That's James Parsley," Mrs Wilson said, her voice sharp with disapproval. "Released from prison, and now he's back—bold as brass. Some people never change."

Reverend John nodded slowly, still staring after the car. "Yes, I've heard he was released."

"It had to have been him, Reverend," she continued, her voice rising with conviction. "Who else would break into the church? He's been trouble his whole life."

"We don't know that for sure, Mrs Wilson," John replied evenly, though the thought of James being involved had already crossed his mind more than once. "The police are still investigating."

She scoffed, frustration colouring her tone. "But he's done it before! Don't you remember? The post office burglary. He spent eighteen months in prison for that."

"We'll have to wait for the police to uncover the truth," John said, though something about the situation didn't sit right with him. There was more to James's story than village rumours suggested. "What do you know about him?" John asked, steering the conversation away from assumptions.

Mrs Wilson let out a weary sigh. "James Parsley. He's been trouble since he was a boy. His parents—such lovely people—salt of the earth. But James? He was always different. They moved here, hoping for a fresh start, but it didn't take long for his reputation to catch up with him."

She glanced around, lowering her voice even further. "There was one incident. He must've been twelve, maybe thirteen. He got his hands on an air rifle, would hide in the woods, and take shots at anything that moved. One day, he shot another boy in the eye. Nearly blinded him."

John's brow furrowed. "I hadn't heard that."

"Most people prefer not to talk about it," Mrs Wilson said with a shake of her head. "But it only got worse as he got older. His parents tried everything, but nothing seemed to work."

"And now?" John asked, his voice steady but probing. "Has he changed at all since he's been back?"

Mrs Wilson hesitated. "I haven't seen much of him. But from what I hear, he's still the same. Angry. Withdrawn. And some say he's been hanging around the church at night."

John remained calm outwardly, though his mind was racing. He'd heard similar whispers from other parishioners, and now that James had made himself visible again, the unease gnawing at John's gut only intensified.

"People don't act out without reason," he said slowly. "There's always something deeper driving it."

Mrs Wilson gave him a sceptical look. "You think it's more than just him being bad?"

"I do," John replied, his voice firm. "I've learned over the years that people often have unseen struggles. James may have made mistakes, but I don't believe we know the whole story. There's something more here."

She shook her head, clearly unconvinced. "The village doesn't forget easily, Reverend. Especially not after all the trouble he's caused. But maybe you're right. If anyone can reach him, it's probably you."

John offered her a thin smile. "Thank you, Mrs Wilson. But this isn't just about helping James. It's about uncovering the truth."

She studied him for a moment, as if trying to read something in his face. Slowly, she nodded. "I trust your judgment, Reverend. But be careful. Not everyone's as forgiving as you."

"I understand," John said, rising from the pew and offering her his hand. "But sometimes, the truth is worth the risk."

As Mrs Wilson made her way out of the church, John lingered, the weight of his thoughts pressing down on him like a physical force. The church was nearly empty now, only the creaks of the old pews and the faint whisper of the wind remained.

The stillness felt oppressive, as though the air itself carried the burden of secrets that had yet to be uncovered. *There's more to this than meets the eye,* John thought, his resolve hardening. *And I'm going to find out what it is, no matter the cost.*

Once alone, the calm, benevolent mask he had worn all morning began to slip. Beneath it, tension simmered just below the surface. This wasn't just about the break-in. There were personal reasons driving his interest in James Parsley—reasons he had kept hidden from Mrs Wilson, and from everyone else in the village.

Taking a deep breath, John inhaled the familiar scent of old wood and incense. The church, once a place of sanctuary, now felt more like a place of reckoning.

Secrets had a way of festering, of clawing their way to the surface when left too long in the dark. The time for passive waiting was over. Whatever lay hidden in the shadows, John was determined to bring it to light. No matter the cost.

Chapter 2
Echoes of the Past

James Parsley sat in the driver's seat of his small red car, the engine's growl loud enough to vibrate the windows of the village shops as he cruised through the narrow streets. The blacked-out rear windows gave the car a sinister look, fitting for the man behind the wheel.

His gaze was fixed straight ahead, but his mind wasn't on the road. It circled back to Reverend John—the way the man had looked at him earlier, James's face broke into a slight grin, the corners of his mouth twitching. It wasn't just a simple glance; the reverend's reaction had been laced with something else.

Recognition. Fear. Beside him, Sam slumped in the passenger seat, barely awake, his eyes half-lidded. The tension between the two men and the quiet village outside seemed lost on him. He glanced at James, then out the window again, his mind preoccupied with thoughts he didn't want to confront.

James gripped the steering wheel tighter. The encounter with John bothered him—not because of the past they shared, but because there was something about the reverend that felt unfinished. He had always known when someone was hiding something, and John was hiding something.

As they reached the edge of the village, James pulled the car into a narrow side street, parking just outside a rundown block of flats where Jock lived. The building, covered in grime and graffiti, looked as though it had given up on itself a long time ago.

James killed the engine, the sudden silence making the air feel thick and oppressive. Sam stirred, blinking heavily. "We're just here for a minute," James muttered, irritation creeping into his voice. "Stick with me, yeah?"

Sam nodded, though his focus remained elsewhere, his movements slow and robotic as they climbed out of the car. The stairwell inside reeked of decay—

urine, rotting garbage, and something else James didn't want to think too much about. He hated this place, but Jock had what he needed.

As they ascended the stairs, their footsteps echoed through the narrow space, growing louder with each step. On the third floor, a young man with hollow eyes and shaky hands passed them without a word, slipping past like a ghost. James barely gave him a glance as he reached Jock's flat.

The door creaked open, revealing a familiar scene. The room was thick with smoke, the air heavy with the smell of stale cigarettes, sweat, and something worse. The curtains were drawn tightly, blocking out any hint of daylight. James spotted Jock sprawled on the couch, his grin widening as he saw them enter.

"What brings you here on this fine day?" Jock asked, his Glaswegian accent thick with mockery.

"Business," James replied curtly. He pulled a crumpled £20 note from his pocket. "For both of us."

Jock didn't bother with small talk. He took the money, disappearing into the kitchen and returning with a small tin that clinked as it hit the table. Inside were the familiar tools—needles, an elastic strap, and the small brown wraps of heroin. The ritual was practiced, familiar, and mechanical.

James and Sam settled on the floor, backs against the peeling wallpaper. Jock heated the heroin over a gas flame, dividing the liquid into two needles. The couple on the sofa, deep in their addiction, barely stirred as James wrapped the elastic cord around his arm. He caught a flicker of hesitation in Sam's eyes.

"You alright?" James asked, his voice low, though his attention remained on his own arm.

Sam nodded, though the faraway look in his eyes remained. "Just tired."

James grunted in response, turning his attention back to the needle. The familiar rush of warmth spread through him, dulling the edges of the world, softening the sharpness of his thoughts. But even in the haze, Reverend John's face floated in his mind, unbidden and unwanted.

There was something about the man that gnawed at him, something too familiar, too unsettling. He needed to know more about John. There was a reason the reverend had reacted the way he did, and James wasn't the kind of man to leave questions unanswered.

Back at the Church

Reverend John sat in the vestry, the quiet of the space offering no comfort. His thoughts circled endlessly around James Parsley's reappearance. It couldn't have been a coincidence. James had deliberately driven by the church— he had wanted John to see him. But why?

John had tried to dismiss it, telling himself that James was just passing through. But that look in his eyes—the recognition—had been unmistakable. And it was connected to the break-in, of that John was sure. The strange symbols left on the vestry walls haunted him.

The police had dismissed them as graffiti, but John knew better. He had seen those symbols before. Rising from his chair, John began pacing, his footsteps echoing softly in the stone-walled room. His mind drifted back to his conversation with Mrs Wilson.

She had been quick to blame James for the break-in, but she didn't know what John knew. She didn't know what was at stake. Pouring himself a small whiskey, John settled into his favourite chair by the window, a book resting on his lap.

The scent of old wood and incense lingered in the air, but for the first time, the comfort of the church felt distant. There was more to James than the villagers knew. More to him than the gossip that circulated in hushed whispers. And there was more to Reverend John than anyone realised. The phone rang suddenly, jolting John from his thoughts. He glanced at the clock—9:25 pm. Too late for a casual call.

"Hello?"

"Reverend, it's Mrs Wilson," came the familiar voice. "I'm hosting a coffee morning on Wednesday. Eleven sharp. Some of the others haven't been attending church as regularly, so it would be good for them to meet you. Make sure you come."

Before he could respond, the line went dead. John sighed, replacing the phone on its cradle. He scribbled the event into his diary, but his mind remained elsewhere. Was James behind the break-in? And if so, why? There had to be more to it.

John stood, moving towards the window. The church loomed across the street; its stone facade bathed in the glow of the streetlights. But even in the stillness, something felt wrong. He drew the curtains and readied himself for bed, though he doubted sleep would come easily.

Later That Night

James and Sam left Jock's flat under the cover of darkness. The high was starting to fade, leaving James restless, his thoughts gnawing at him. As they descended the stairwell, Sam trailed behind, still groggy. At the bottom floor, a group of teenagers loitered near the entrance.

James squared up to the tallest of the bunch, locking eyes with him. The lad sneered, muttering something to his friends, but James didn't take the bait. He wasn't in the mood for a fight—not tonight. They reached the car in silence, and James turned to Sam.

"I'm not taking you all the way home. I don't have enough petrol."

Sam shrugged, used to James's unpredictability. "Just drop me at the bottom of the road."

James didn't argue. The car ride was spent in tense silence. When they reached the edge of the lane leading to Sam's aunt's house, Sam stepped out, the cool night air brushing against his skin. He watched as James's taillights disappeared into the darkness.

Sam's thoughts drifted as he made his way to the small summerhouse at the bottom of his aunt's garden. It was cramped but liveable—a far cry from the life he'd once imagined for himself. His dreams felt distant now, buried under layers of regret and addiction.

He fumbled for his key, slipping inside the darkened room. The fleeting remorse he had felt earlier vanished as he collapsed onto the bed. Sleep came slowly, his mind racing with thoughts he couldn't quite pin down.

The Next Day

Reverend John woke early, the weight of the previous day still hanging over him. He went through the motions— dressing, preparing breakfast, reviewing his notes for the service—but his mind kept circling back to James.

The church was quiet when he arrived. He lit a candle, his eyes lingering on the vestry door. The symbols had been scrubbed clean by the police, but John could still see them in his mind. They meant something—something only he seemed to understand.

As he prepared for the service, he made a silent vow; he would find out what James wanted. He would uncover the truth, no matter how deeply buried it was.

The village hid many secrets, but John knew that the time for silence was drawing to an end.

Chapter 3
Redemption's Path

The Past

John Bailey was not born into the world under that name. He had entered life as Lorcan McNally, a name that carried weight and history on the border between northern and southern Ireland. His family was devoutly Catholic, deeply rooted in the traditions of the church.

His father was a Lector in the church, his uncle and brothers were both priests. In the McNally family, the path of religious devotion was well-trodden, and young Lorcan was expected to follow suit. Growing up in the shadow of the Troubles in Northern Ireland during the 1980s, Lorcan's beliefs were forged in the crucible of conflict.

His childhood was marked by the sounds of unrest and the fear that permeated the air. Though his family provided a haven of faith, the external world was fraught with violence and division. As he navigated adolescence, Lorcan fell in with the wrong crowd, forming close ties with sectarian bosses.

The allure of their power and influence was undeniable, and before long, he found himself entangled in a web of crime. Despite his involvement in numerous illicit activities as a Loyalist, Lorcan was never convicted. His ability to evade justice became almost legendary among those who knew of his past.

Yet, as the years passed and the weight of his actions began to press upon him, he realised he could not continue down this path. The Good Friday Agreement brought a fragile peace to the region, and with it, an opportunity for Lorcan to escape the clutches of his former life.

Determined to leave the Troubles behind, he moved to the England, seeking refuge with relatives whose family name was Bailey. Embracing this fresh start, he legally changed his name to John Bailey, adopting his middle name to further distance himself from his turbulent past.

As John Bailey, he was reborn—a man with a second chance at life. John's intellect and education paved the way for him to pursue a new path. He applied to study theology, determined to follow in his father's footsteps and seek redemption through faith. He excelled in his studies and upon graduation, was accepted into the church, soon becoming a reverend.

A New Life

His past, however, was not so easily left behind. The Bishop who had guided him on his journey was well aware of John's history. Though he disapproved of Lorcan's former associations, he believed in the possibility of redemption. The Bishop offered John a position as a chaplain at a prison, seeing it as a place where he could seek closure and atone for his past.

He told John that this was his 'sentence'—five years of service before he could be considered for a parish position. John accepted the Bishop's terms and embraced his role as chaplain, taking services and providing spiritual guidance to the inmates.

It was here, in the cold, grey walls of the prison, that he first encountered James Parsley. James Parsley was part of a new intake of prisoners, a man whose reputation preceded him. He had requested to see the chaplain, and the meeting was arranged.

For John, James was just another soul in need of guidance—a stranger with no ties to his past. But destiny had other plans. Shortly after, another prisoner requested a meeting with the chaplain. This time, the encounter was far from routine.

As the prisoner was escorted to the chapel, John felt a chill run down his spine. The guard introduced the man as Shane O'Brien, but John recognised him instantly as a figure from his past who knew him as Lorcan McNally. Shane's eyes widened in surprise, then narrowed into a hard glare.

"Lorcan?" He said, his voice tinged with disbelief and something darker—betrayal. John's heart skipped a beat.

"You must be mistaken," he replied, forcing his voice to remain steady. "My name is John Bailey."

Shane's laugh was cold and devoid of humour. "Don't play me for a fool, Lorcan. I'd recognise you anywhere. You've been running from your past, haven't you? Thought you could just leave us all behind?"

John's mind raced as he glanced at the guard, who was standing a few feet away, oblivious to the tension between the two men. "I'm Chaplin John Bailey," John said, his voice low. "I'm not the man you think I am."

"Not the man I think you are?" Shane stepped closer, his voice dropping to a dangerous whisper. "You turned your back on us. You left Ireland, left everything we fought for. You betrayed us, Lorcan. And now, you think you can hide behind a new name and a collar? You think that makes it all go away?"

Shane's voice grew more intense, his eyes never leaving John's face. "You disappeared, Lorcan. Under the cover of darkness, no word, no explanation. Just gone. We fought side by side for years, and you abandoned us like we were nothing. Your parents?

"They told everyone they didn't know where you were. Didn't even know if you were dead or alive. Some thought you were killed, others thought you had just gone underground. But here you are, living a comfortable life in England of all places. England? Seriously? The very people we spent our lives fighting against, and you sided with them over us?"

John could feel the weight of Shane's words pressing down on him, but he kept his face impassive, though his heart was racing. He knew this moment would come eventually, but not like this. Not here, where everything he'd built was on the line.

"You walked away from everything, Lorcan. Left us all in the dust, pretending you didn't owe anyone an explanation. Your family, your friends, the cause. We were left to pick up the pieces while you made yourself a new life. You think we didn't suffer?

"You think we didn't bleed after you left? Every day, we wondered if you were dead in a shallow grave, or living it up in some foreign land, and it turns out, it's the latter."

Shane took another step closer, his voice low and dangerous. "But to live here, with the Brits? What kind of sick joke is that? After all we did, after all we sacrificed. You spat on our loyalty, on the cause we bled for. And now, you've become one of them."

John swallowed hard, his palms sweating as he clasped his hands together. "Shane, you don't understand. I—"

"Don't understand?" Shane cut him off, his eyes blazing with fury. "I understand perfectly. You ran. You took everything you knew with you. You think we wouldn't notice? The bosses, Lorcan. They were asking questions, talking to everyone they knew trying to find out where you were or what had happened.

"They'll be very interested to know you're still alive. You've got secrets. You think you can just walk away and hide behind a collar? No, mate. That's not how this works."

John clenched his jaw, trying to remain calm, but Shane's words cut deep. His past had caught up to him in ways he never anticipated. "I left because—"

"You left because you were scared," Shane snapped. "Coward. You left Ireland with secrets that don't belong to you. You betrayed us all and now, you're a dead man walking. They'll tear you apart. Do you understand? They'll come for you, Lorcan. You should've stayed gone, but now, you're just living on borrowed time."

Shane's bitterness deepened with every word, each accusation like a dagger to John's heart. "You think you can hide forever? You think England will protect you? You're more of a fool than I thought."

John remained silent, his mind racing. He had long known that his past could one day resurface, but the venom in Shane's voice made it clear—there would be no running this time. John took a deep breath, trying to steady his voice. "The Good Friday Agreement was an opportunity, Shane. An opportunity for everyone to start making peace.

"And that's what I've been trying to do—make peace with my past. I know I left everyone behind, but you have to understand, I had no choice." Shane's eyes narrowed, his posture rigid as he listened, but said nothing. "The bosses, my uncles—they're the reason I left. They refused to change.

"They wouldn't hand over their arms, even when it was clear the fight was coming to an end. I couldn't be part of that anymore. I had to go, to escape the violence, the blood on my hands. Yes, I left under the cover of darkness, but that was the only way. It was as if I had been kidnapped, Shane. I disappeared just like the people we took, those who were never seen again."

John's voice trembled slightly at the confession. "I vanished like them. But not because I wanted to betray anyone—I was trying to save myself."

Shane's face twisted into a bitter smile. "Your uncles, they may not be active in the streets anymore, but they haven't changed. They're still involved, one way or another, and they'd be grateful to me for handing you over to them."

John shook his head, his hands tightening into fists. "No, Shane. It doesn't have to be like this. They don't need to know I'm here. You don't have to do this. We've all moved on—or at least, we should have."

Shane's gaze hardened. "Moved on? You may have moved on, Lorcan, but the rest of us? We're still paying for the choices you made. And don't think for a second that your uncles will forgive your betrayal. They'd still like to see you pay for what you did."

John's pulse quickened. He had expected this, but it still stung. "Look, Shane, this isn't how things should be. If you give me up, it won't change anything. The fight's over. We need to let go."

Shane leant closer, his voice sharp and biting. "Let go? You of all people, hiding here in England, think you have the right to talk about letting go? You've been hiding behind a new name, behind that collar, while the rest of us had to live with the fallout."

John stood his ground. "Shane, you can walk away from this too. You don't owe them anything. Just leave it."

But Shane's expression remained cold, unforgiving. "Leave it? No, you don't get to tell me what to do. Besides, why are you so concerned about staying hidden? Why England? Why this prison?"

John frowned, trying to change the subject. "I'm not the one on trial here."

"That's rich," Shane spat. "You think you can just—"

"That's fine," John interrupted, his voice suddenly calm, but with a hint of threat. "I'll ask the prison officers. It seems like you've got your own secret, Shane. Why are you here, really?"

Shane's face went pale for a brief moment, the mask of anger cracking just enough for John to see the fear lurking beneath. Shane quickly recovered, but the damage was done. The balance of power had shifted, even if only slightly.

John felt a subtle but undeniable shift in their interaction. He had regained a measure of control, but he could sense the turmoil in Shane's mind. Was Shane also a deserter? Was he, too, running from their shared past? What had brought him to England, and why was he here, locked up in this prison?

John could find out easily enough, but he wasn't sure he wanted to. Engaging further might only pull him deeper into the web he had fought so hard to escape. He exhaled slowly, trying to maintain the calm he'd managed to regain.

"Shane," he began carefully, "you're clearly hiding something. I don't care what it is. I don't care what you've done, or why you're here. But I'm not going to discuss this—our reunion—with anyone. I hope you can extend me the same courtesy."

Shane's eyes narrowed as he studied John, or Lorcan, as he still thought of him. The tension lingered in the air, thick with unspoken threats and the weight of their shared history. Shane wasn't used to being on the back foot, and the idea of John holding even the smallest piece of leverage over him clearly didn't sit well. But he knew he had no choice, at least for now.

After what felt like an eternity, Shane gave a small, begrudging nod. "For now," he agreed, his voice still laced with resentment.

John met his gaze, unflinching. "Good."

The room fell into an uneasy silence, both men measuring each other, their pasts hanging between them like an unresolved storm. John's mind raced—he had no idea what Shane had been involved in since he'd left Ireland, but whatever it was, it had brought him here, to this prison, and it couldn't be good.

Shane's face darkened, the tension in his body shifting from anger to something more dangerous. "You don't want to dig too deep, Lorcan," he warned, his voice barely above a whisper. "You may not like what you find."

John held his gaze for a moment longer, then stepped back, feeling the weight of Shane's unspoken threat. "I'm not looking for trouble, Shane," he said quietly. "But I won't let you drag me back into something I left behind."

Shane said nothing, but the look in his eyes made it clear that this conversation wasn't over. Not by a long shot. John turned and gestured to the guard that the meeting was over. As Shane was led away, he couldn't shake the feeling that this encounter had only opened the door to something far more dangerous than he had anticipated.

Shane was returned to his cell, he took a deep breath as he stepped inside. He paced for a moment, still seething from the encounter with John, when he heard footsteps approach. Turning, he saw James Parsley lingering in the doorway, a sly smile tugging at the corner of his mouth.

Without invitation, James stepped inside and leant against the wall, eyes gleaming with curiosity. "So, who was that you were talking to earlier? Looked like something more than your average confession."

Shane's back tensed, but he didn't turn to face James. He clenched his fists, trying to steady his breathing, the anger still simmering. "None of your business, Parsley. Walk away."

James chuckled, taking a step closer, ignoring the warning in Shane's voice. "Oh, come on. You and the good reverend seemed like old mates for two blokes who just met. I heard something—caught a name. *Lorcan*, or something like that? Doesn't sound very 'John Bailey' to me."

Shane clenched his fists, but he didn't react immediately. Slowly, he turned to face James, his eyes narrowing, voice low and dangerous. "You're playing with fire, James. The man you think you met as Reverend Bailey? He's not what you think. He's got a past that could fuck you up. Do not get involved."

James raised an eyebrow, his smile widening. He was not intimidated—yet. "A past, eh? What, was he some kind of bouncer at the church convention?" James laughed to himself.

Shane stepped forward, his face inches from James, his voice dropping to a growl. "You think you're fucking clever, don't you? Think you've found some meat on the bones. But I'm telling you, James—whatever you think you want to know, you don't. And whatever you're planning? Forget it. He is not a man to cross. You don't want to get involved, James."

James's eyes flashed with a mix of curiosity and greed. The mention of John's darker past only fuelled his ambitions. "So, he's got secrets? Sounds like an opportunity to me. Maybe he'd be open to a little arrangement. Maybe he'll owe me a favour or two."

"You're a fucking idiot! You think you can bribe him? Manipulate him? John Bailey might be wearing a collar now, but the man he used to be, he was fucking dangerous. You go sniffing around where you don't belong, and you'll end up in a ditch somewhere, with no one even remembering your name."

"Come on, Shane. You're overreacting. He's a priest, what's he gonna do?"

Shane's face was filled with cold menace, his voice dropping to a deadly whisper. "The man you think you can control? He's been hiding, lying low for years. But he's still got blood on his hands. Blood he's trying to wash away with all that preaching and salvation talk. But deep down, he's still *Lorcan*. And if you push him, if you back him into a corner—he'll remind you who he really is. And when that happens, you'll wish you'd listened to me."

"I don't care about his past, Shane. I'm not scared of him. If he's got secrets, then he's vulnerable. And I'll use that. You might be afraid of him, but I'm not. He's just another man with something to lose."

Shane shook his head slowly, his voice filled with dark finality. "You don't get it, do you? You're walking into a world you can't handle. Stay out of it,

James. I'm warning you—stay out. This isn't some game where you get to pull the strings. You get involved with him, and you won't be coming back. So, don't ever ask me about this again. And don't ever mention this to me, or anyone else."

Shane stepped closer, towering over James, his eyes cold and unblinking. "And if you think you're smart enough to get in on this, to use him for your little schemes—let me be clear. You'll be the first to get buried. I'm not going to warn you again."

For the first time, James felt the full weight of Shane's words. But stubborn as he was, the glimmer of opportunity still lingered in his mind. He forced a smirk, though it didn't reach his eyes. "We'll see about that, mate." Without a word, James slipped out of the cell, leaving Shane in silence.

Shane's eyes tracked him as he departed, his face hardening with a mix of frustration and dread. He knew James wouldn't heed the warning—that stubborn arrogance made him a liability.

"You bloody fool, Parsley," Shane muttered under his breath. Shane stood in the centre of his cell, the air heavy with the weight of his warning. As the sound of James's retreating footsteps faded into the distance, the silence that followed felt suffocating.

He could feel the storm brewing—one that James, in his arrogance, would never see coming until it was too late. Shane's mind raced with possibilities, each darker than the last. He knew what men like Lorcan were capable of when cornered, and James was too blind to recognise the danger he was stepping into.

Shane let out a long, slow breath, his fists unclenching. It was only a matter of time before the past came crashing back, pulling them all under. He crossed the room and sat on the edge of his bed, staring at the cold, concrete wall. Shadows shifted in the dim light, their shapes twisting like the ghosts of his past.

"Trouble's coming," he muttered to himself, his voice barely a whisper. "And no one's walking away from it unscathed."

As the night closed in, the prison's distant hum seemed to grow louder, pressing in on Shane from all sides. The past wasn't just a ghost—it was a reckoning. And if they weren't careful, it was coming for all of them.

A Few Days Later

John had tried to push the encounter with Shane to the back of his mind, focusing instead on his duties at the prison. But the unease gnawed at him, refusing to let go. He had just finished leading a service in the chapel when James Parsley approached him, a knowing look in his eyes.

"Interesting service, Father," James said, leaning casually against the doorway.

John forced a smile, though his nerves were frayed. "I'm glad you think so."

James's smile was all teeth, predatory. "You've got quite a history, don't you? Seems like there's more to you than meets the eye."

John's heart sank. "What are you talking about, James?"

"I'm talking about that little chat I overheard between you and Shane, and what Shane told me," James said, his voice dropping to a conspiratorial whisper. "You see, I've got good ears, and I heard enough to know you're not just some run-of-the-mill reverend. You've got secrets."

John felt the ground shift beneath him. "That conversation was private, James. You shouldn't have been eavesdropping, and Shane shouldn't be speaking out of turn."

James chuckled. "I wasn't eavesdropping. I just happened to be in the right place at the right time. And now, I think it's in my best interest to make sure you look after me."

John's eyes narrowed. "What do you want, James?"

James shrugged; his expression nonchalant. "For now? Just keep me on your good side. I'm sure I'll think of something specific down the line. But until then, I expect you to take care of me. I'm not asking for much—just a favour here and there."

John's mind was spinning. Shane's threat was bad enough, but now, James was trying to leverage the situation for his own gain. "This isn't a game," John repeated, his voice barely above a whisper.

James's smile grew wider. "You're right, it's not. But you've got something to lose, Reverend, and that makes you vulnerable. So, I suggest you start thinking about how you're going to keep me happy."

John felt the walls closing in around him. He knew he couldn't afford to have James as an enemy, especially not with Shane already holding a knife to his throat. What had Shane told him, was he telling the truth or just saying anything that came to mind?

"I'll keep that in mind," John said, his voice tight.

"You do that," James said, pushing off the wall and straightening his jumper. "And remember—I'm your friend, Reverend. Let's keep it that way."

John watched James walk away, his stomach churning with a mix of fear and anger. He knew he was in deep, and the only way out was to play the game—for now.

A Fresh Start

One morning, as John prepared for another day at the prison, the phone on his desk rang, its sharp tone cutting through the quiet. It was the Bishop, the man who had guided John with a firm yet compassionate hand. John picked up the receiver, feeling a mix of anticipation and apprehension.

"Good morning, Bishop," John greeted, his voice steady.

"Good morning, John," the Bishop replied, his tone warm and reassuring. "I have some news for you. We've found a parish for you—a small village in need of a steady hand and a guiding presence. This is your reward for the service you've given at the prison."

John felt a rush of emotions at the Bishop's words. This was the moment he had been waiting for—a chance to truly start anew. A fresh start, a blank page. "Thank you, Bishop," John said, trying to keep the tremor of excitement from his voice. "I'm grateful for the opportunity."

"The parish is in a quiet village," the Bishop continued. "It's a community struggling for parishioners, but I believe you have the skills and the heart to bring them back together. A new chaplain is already in place at the prison, so you're free to begin your new journey."

After the call ended, John sat in his small office, absorbing the news. The past few years had been a time of reflection and redemption. He had faced old ghosts and worked tirelessly to help those in need, but now, he could finally leave behind the shadows of his past and embrace a future that he could shape.

But as he packed his belongings, the weight of Shane's threat and James's demands hung heavily over him. He knew that leaving the prison wouldn't be the end of his troubles—it might just be the beginning.

Within weeks, John had packed his belongings and made the journey to the village, a quaint place nestled in the rolling hills. The church was a beautiful old stone building, its spire reaching towards the heavens. It stood at the heart of the village, surrounded by lush gardens and centuries-old trees.

As he arrived, the sound of birds singing, and the gentle rustling of leaves greeted him—a stark contrast to the harsh sounds of the prison. This was a place of peace and renewal, a haven where he could truly be himself.

Upon his arrival, John was immediately introduced to Mrs Wilson, a pillar of the community and a woman known for her kindness and dedication to the church. She was waiting for him outside the church, her warm smile a welcome sight.

"Reverend Bailey, I presume?" Mrs Wilson greeted, extending her hand. "Welcome to our little village. We're so pleased to have you here."

"Thank you, Mrs Wilson," John replied, shaking her hand with genuine gratitude. "I'm honoured to be here and to serve this community."

Mrs Wilson showed him around the village, introducing him to key members of the community and sharing stories of the church's history. As they walked through the cobblestone streets, John felt a sense of belonging he hadn't experienced in years.

The village was charming, with its stone cottages, colourful gardens, and friendly faces. The people were welcoming, albeit curious about their new reverend. John sensed their hope that he could breathe new life into the church and the village itself.

As the days turned into weeks, John settled into his role with enthusiasm. He organised community events, visited parishioners in their homes, and worked to restore the church to its former glory. He preached sermons that resonated with the villagers, drawing more people to the pews each Sunday.

For the first time in a long while, John felt truly at home. He was no longer Lorcan McNally, the man with a troubled past, but Reverend John Bailey, a man of faith and conviction. The village was his sanctuary, a place where he could continue his journey of redemption and help others find their path.

But even in the peaceful surroundings of the village, John couldn't shake the feeling that his past would catch up with him. Shane's threats and James's demands were a dark cloud on the horizon, and he knew that sooner or later, they would have to be dealt with.

In the quiet moments, as he sat in the church alone, John reflected on the road that had brought him here. The decisions he had made, the lives he had touched, and the redemption he sought all led him to this place. But he also knew that the shadows of his past were never far behind, waiting for the right moment to emerge.

Mrs Wilson became a trusted confidante and friend, her unwavering support a source of strength for John. With her by his side, he felt confident in his ability to guide the village and its people towards a brighter future. The village, with its peaceful charm and resilient spirit, was where John Bailey would finally call home.

He knew that while the shadows of his past might never fully disappear, he had found a place where he could shine a light strong enough to banish them—or at least keep them at bay for a little while longer.

Late-Night Confession

One particularly restless night, John found himself unable to sleep. The weight of his past was pressing heavily on his mind, and he decided to take a walk to the church, seeking solace in its quiet, sacred atmosphere. As he unlocked the heavy wooden door and stepped inside, the familiar scent of incense and old wood greeted him.

The flickering candles cast long shadows on the stone walls, and for a moment, John felt a sense of peace. But that peace was shattered when he heard the door creak open behind him. He turned to see Mrs Wilson standing in the doorway, her face etched with concern.

"John," she said softly, "I saw the light on and thought I'd check if everything was alright."

John forced a smile. "Just couldn't sleep, Mrs Wilson. Sometimes, the quiet of the church helps to calm my mind."

She nodded, but there was something in her eyes that told John she wasn't entirely convinced. "May I join you?" She asked, stepping inside without waiting for an answer. They sat together in one of the front pews, the silence between them filled with unspoken thoughts.

After a while, Mrs Wilson broke the silence, "John, I've lived in this village for a long time, and I've seen a lot of people come and go. But there's something different about you. You carry a weight that most people don't. And I can't help but wonder, is there something you're not telling me? Something that's troubling you?"

John hesitated, his mind racing. He had never spoken about his past to anyone in the village, and he wasn't sure if he was ready to start now. But there was something about Mrs Wilson—her kindness, her understanding—that made him want to open up.

"Mrs Wilson," he began slowly, "we all have things in our past that we're not proud of. Things that we wish we could forget. But those things. They have a way of sticking with you, don't they?"

She nodded, her expression softening. "Yes, they do. But sometimes, sharing those burdens with someone else can make them a little easier to carry."

John looked at her, his eyes filled with a mixture of fear and hope. "I wasn't always a reverend, Mrs Wilson. There was a time in my life when I was someone else. Someone I'm not proud of."

She reached out and placed her hand on his. "We all have our demons, John. But what matters is who we choose to be now. And from what I've seen, you're a good man. A man who's dedicated his life to helping others."

John swallowed hard, the lump in his throat making it difficult to speak. "I try to be. But sometimes. Sometimes, it feels like no matter how hard I try, my past is always there, lurking in the shadows."

Mrs Wilson squeezed his hand gently. "The past is a part of who we are, John. But it doesn't have to define us. You've made a new life for yourself here, and you've brought hope to this village. That's something to be proud of."

John looked into her eyes, seeing the sincerity in her words. "Thank you, Mrs Wilson. Your support means more to me than you know."

She smiled warmly. "You're not alone, John. And if there's ever anything you need to talk about, I'm here. We all need someone to lean on from time to time."

John nodded, feeling a sense of relief wash over him. He wasn't ready to share all his secrets just yet but knowing that Mrs Wilson was there for him made the burden a little lighter.

As they sat together in the quiet church, John realised that he had found not just a parishioner, but a true friend. And for the first time in a long while, he felt a glimmer of hope that maybe, just maybe, he could finally find peace.

Chapter 4
Crossroads of Faith

The sun began to rise over the village, casting a warm glow on the July morning. The villagers were starting their day, with some making their way to the train station to catch the first train into London.

The local farmer, Jeff, was in his truck, delivering produce to the village shop as he had done for as long as he could remember. Today, he had fresh eggs, milk, and cream loaded in the back. The shopkeepers, Irene and Ben, had run the village shop for the last 40 years.

Born and bred in the village, they had met at the local school and were married in the village church. The shop was more than just a business; it was the heart of the community, a place where everyone knew each other's names and stories.

"Morning, Jeff," Ben called out as Jeff entered the shop. "What have we got this morning?"

"Five dozen eggs, some milk, and cream," Jeff replied, setting down the crates. "Has my magazine arrived yet?"

Ben went behind the counter and handed Jeff a magazine wrapped in a brown paper bag. Irene, who was stocking shelves nearby, glanced over with disapproval as Jeff rolled it up and placed it in his pocket.

"How did you do last week? Did you sell everything?" Jeff asked, changing the subject.

"Yes," said Irene, opening the till and pulling out an envelope. "We sold the lot." She handed the envelope to Jeff, who kissed it with satisfaction.

"Lovely," he said, bidding the couple goodbye before leaving the shop. Jeff approached his truck, which still had the engine running. He opened the door, climbed in, and drove away, ready to continue his day's work.

Inside the shop, however, tension lingered. Ben did his best to avoid mentioning the magazine, but Irene wasn't one to let things go easily. "Why do you have to order that 'publication' for Jeff?" She asked, her voice laced with irritation. "I don't like it, and I don't like it showing up on our account each month."

Ben sighed, already weary of the argument. "It costs us £3.50, and we sell it for £6. We make money on it, which is the main point of business."

Irene responded sarcastically, "You're right, that £2.50 profit each month that £30 profit annually, certainly keeps us in the high life. Have you ever thought we should list our business in *Tattler*?"

"Irene, does it really matter? You're lactose intolerant, but we still sell full-fat milk."

"It's not the same, and you know it, Ben," Irene replied, her voice rising. "There's a difference between selling milk and selling smut."

Ben held up his hands in surrender. "Can we just move on? We have a lot to do, and the bickering is getting in the way."

Irene huffed but relented, turning her attention back to her work. The couple began preparing the shop for the day ahead, a routine they had perfected over the decades. Ben stood next to the wine and beer fridge, rearranging the bottles when he noticed something was missing.

"Irene, did you sell any wine yesterday?" He called out.

"I don't think so. Why do you ask?"

"We have a gap where the Sauvignon is, and I don't remember selling any. When we do, we always put another in its place from out back."

Irene frowned, walking over to inspect the shelf. "Are you sure?"

"I'm quite sure," Ben replied, a hint of concern creeping into his voice.

"If you're worried, check the CCTV," Irene suggested, though she sounded more dismissive than helpful.

Ben muttered something under his breath and decided to drop the matter, but a seed of doubt had been planted.

Meanwhile, the church caretaker, Henry Thompson, had just arrived for work. His old black bicycle was locked against a lamppost in the church grounds, adorned with a front and rear light and a wicker basket on the handlebars. In his seventies, Henry had been working as the caretaker since he took early retirement from the post office years ago. Living in the village all his life, Henry knew everyone.

It was early morning, and the sun was just beginning to rise over the village. The churchyard was bathed in a soft, golden light, the dew on the grass shimmering like a thousand tiny diamonds. Henry was out in the garden, tending to the flower beds. He moved methodically, pruning the roses with careful precision, his weathered hands steady despite the years of labour they had seen. Each snip of the secateurs was deliberate, almost meditative, as Henry's mind wandered through the events of the past few weeks.

"They say the devil finds work for idle hands," Henry muttered to himself, the words barely audible in the stillness of the morning. "But this place, it's always been a sanctuary. Never thought I'd see the day when someone would violate it like that."

He straightened up, wiping the sweat from his brow with the back of his hand. His gaze drifted towards the church, its stone walls standing resolute against the backdrop of the waking village. The memory of the recent break-in still gnawed at him, a violation of the sanctity he had spent years preserving.

Inside the church, Henry went about his day, cleaning, sweeping, and mopping the floors. Once finished inside, he went out the rear door into the church grounds. As he approached the shed that housed the lawnmower, grass trimmer, and other tools used to maintain the grounds, he stopped to inspect the broken side door, which had been forced open during the burglary.

"If I got my hands on those that did this," he muttered under his breath, the early morning sun highlighting the damage, a stark reminder of the violation the church had suffered.

Henry shook his head in frustration and went about his work, determined to restore some sense of normalcy to the sacred grounds. As he worked, he noticed Reverend John approaching from the rectory. The reverend, always an early riser, seemed to carry the weight of his thoughts in the furrow of his brow.

"Good morning, Henry," Reverend John greeted him warmly. "How are things this morning?"

"Morning, Reverend," Henry replied, straightening up. "Just getting on with it. The break-in's still a bit of a mess, but we'll have it sorted soon enough."

Reverend John nodded, his eyes scanning the grounds. "It's a shame, what happened. We're all hoping the police will find whoever did this."

"Aye," Henry said, his tone noncommittal. "We'll see."

The reverend paused, as if considering whether to say more. "You know, Henry, if you hear anything, anything at all, please let me know. Even the smallest detail could be important."

Henry nodded, but there was a flicker of something in his eyes—something that made John uneasy. "Will do, Reverend."

With that, Reverend John continued on his way, leaving Henry to his thoughts. Henry watched him go, sensing there was more to the reverend's interest in the break-in than met the eye. But as always, Henry kept his suspicions to himself.

Returning to his work, Henry couldn't help but think about James Parsley and the rumours surrounding him. He had seen the boy grow up, witnessed his descent into trouble, but he had never voiced his thoughts. It wasn't his place, and he believed in keeping the peace, even in his own mind.

Meanwhile, Reverend John's mind was also active. The coffee morning at Mrs Wilson's was approaching, and he intended to use it as an opportunity to learn more about the village's undercurrents. He needed to understand the dynamics and the hidden stories, and Henry's silent presence, along with the villagers' chatter, could provide valuable insights.

As the village bustled with morning activity, the paths of its inhabitants continued to intertwine. The break-in at the church was a small event in the grand scheme, but it had set off ripples that would affect many lives.

Henry, Reverend John, James Parsley, and others were all part of a story slowly unfolding, each playing their part in ways they might not yet understand. John, although an honest, hardworking man, had kept a small part of the break-in to himself.

He didn't want his parishioners to know the full extent of what was actually stolen. He had told Mrs Wilson it was just the collection tin. Mrs Wilson would indeed spread the word of the break-in to everyone, and if she knew the full list of items taken, she would have even more to say.

John looked at Henry, who just got on with his work, avoiding involvement. John could sense Henry's discomfort with his presence, almost as if he was willing a conversation to start. After a few seconds, John made his excuses to leave.

He thanked Henry and began to walk towards the rear open door of the church. When he reached the door, he turned to Henry and called out, "Can you please get some additional locks for all the doors? I don't want this to happen again."

Henry glanced up from the flower bed he was tending, nodded to John, and carried on. John went inside. The church was cool, a nice shelter from the July sun. John wandered through the church towards a curtain. Behind the curtain was a door that had been forced open. The lock around the handle had been battered many times, likely with a hammer and chisel.

Behind the door was the office, with wood panelling covering the old stone walls. The office was lit by a single light hanging from the ceiling. There were no windows, just a large oak desk and a green leather wingback chair, both over a hundred years old.

It was suggested that both the chair and desk were made in the room, as they were too large to fit through the door. John walked over to the desk and sat down. Across from where he was sitting was a glass display cabinet, now broken and dusted with forensic powder in an attempt to lift fingerprints.

The cabinet, about 1.5 meters tall and half a meter wide, had four shelves. Other than a few old framed pictures, the cabinet was empty. John frowned, shook his head, and stroked his beard with his left hand. His other hand was clenched into a fist on the table, his knuckles turning white.

John got up from his chair, walked over to the filing cabinets, opened a drawer, and thumbed through the files until he found one marked 'Inventory'. He removed it from the cabinet and took it back to his desk. From the top drawer of the desk, he pulled out a notepad.

He opened the file and flicked through until he came to the section marked 'Office'. There was a photograph of the cabinet before the break-in, showing it housed a number of valuable items, including candlestick holders, a chalice, a pall, and other historical artefacts.

John wasn't sure what value these would have to anyone unless they were melted down. They couldn't be sold as they were, too many questions would be asked. The realisation that these centuries-old items would likely be melted down for scrap filled John with a rare, seething anger, an emotion he hadn't felt for many years, long before he joined the church.

There was a call he had been putting off for a couple of days, a call he didn't want to make but knew he had to. He finished noting the items that were missing and with the photograph for support, placed them in an envelope provided by the police.

He picked up the phone and called the Bishop to break the news. The call lasted around 20 minutes. At the end of the conversation, the Bishop said he would come to St Mary's to see the damage for himself and to offer his support. As John hung up the phone, he felt a mixture of relief and dread.

The Bishop's visit would bring some much-needed attention to the break-in, but it also meant more scrutiny and more questions. He sat back in his chair, trying to calm the storm of emotions within him. The theft had not only violated the sanctity of the church but had also stirred something deep and unresolved within him.

John finished up in his office, picking up the envelope before closing the door behind him. He headed out of the side door into the church grounds where Henry was busy working.

"Dear Henry," John said, "would you please clear up the mess in the office? The police have done what they need to do. I'm off to the police station now. If you need anything, please call."

Henry looked up from his work, nodded, and returned to his tasks. John walked across the road to his cottage, got into his car, and drove away from the village towards the police station, about a mile away in the main town. Normally, he would walk, but today, he was in a hurry and didn't know how long it would take at the station.

The police station was on the main road, with limited parking down the side of the building. John found a space, parked, collected his bag from the back seat, locked the car, and walked up the ramp into the station. Entering the reception area, he saw a sign saying, 'Please ring the bell for assistance'.

Voices from the office behind the partition could be heard. John pressed the bell and waited. A young lady, newly qualified and still on probation, greeted him.

"Hello, Reverend. How are you?" She asked. John knew Chloe and her family well.

"I'm very well, thank you. How are you, Chloe?" John replied.

"I'm good, just busy with shifts. I haven't had time to come to church, but I will soon. Are you here to see Mike?" Chloe asked, referring to Sergeant Mike Porter, the investigating officer.

"Yes, he is expecting me," John confirmed.

"Take a seat, I'll tell him you're here. Would you like tea or coffee?" Chloe offered.

"Yes, please. Tea, white, no sugar," John said.

Chloe nodded and disappeared into the office. Moments later, Sergeant Porter appeared at the door.

"John, nice to see you, though I wish it were under better circumstances. Please, come this way," Mike said.

John followed Mike into an interview room. Mike held the door for Chloe as she brought in their drinks.

"Tea for you, John, and your coffee, Sarge," she said, placing the drinks on the table before leaving.

"Do you have any updates, Mike? I've only mentioned the donations that were taken, nothing else," John said, his frustration barely concealed.

Mike sighed, running a hand through his hair. "We didn't find any prints; they were wearing gloves. CCTV hasn't shown anything either. We think they came from the back, through the graveyard, and forced entry at the side door."

"Yes, I thought the same," John replied, his voice tightening with anger. "But Mike, this is more than just a break-in. These items have been part of St Mary's for centuries. They're not just objects; they're part of our history, our identity."

Mike leant back in his chair; his expression serious. "I understand, John, but we have to work with what we have. Whoever did this knew what they were after, and they're good at covering their tracks."

John's frustration bubbled over. "This is a church, a place of worship, peace, and love. It shouldn't be violated in this way."

"I agree," Mike said, his tone firm. "But there are people out there who don't share the same values. They'll do whatever it takes to make a quick buck, and they don't care about the damage they leave behind."

John clenched his fists, trying to control his rising anger. "You have to do more, Mike. I want whoever did this to face justice. These items are irreplaceable, and I won't rest until they're returned."

Mike nodded slowly. "We'll do our best, John. But justice doesn't always come swiftly, and sometimes, it doesn't come at all. You need to be prepared for that."

John's voice softened, his frustration giving way to a weary resolve. "I know, Mike. But I can't give up hope. This church means too much to the community."

Mike placed a hand on John's shoulder. "We'll keep looking, John. And if there's anything more we can do, we will."

John sighed, feeling the weight of the situation. "I know, Mike. I just, these items mean so much to the church and the community. We need them back."

"We'll do our best, John," Mike said, his voice firm. "But we need to work within the system. If we can gather more evidence, we'll take the necessary steps. For now, try to stay hopeful."

"Mike, I shall talk to the Bishop, but I want to go public with this. I want people to know what's missing and what to look out for. If someone is selling my property, I want to know," John insisted.

Mike just nodded. "Thanks for coming in and bringing these bits. I'll be in touch," he said, opening the door for John.

The two men shook hands, and John left the station, feeling a mix of frustration and determination. As John drove back to the village, his thoughts swirled around the missing artefacts and the potential suspects. He needed answers, and he was willing to go to great lengths to get them.

John arrived at his cottage, parked, got out of the car, and walked towards the church. He looked down the side to see if he could spot Henry. The shed was open, so Henry must still be around, John thought. He wandered into the garden and saw Henry pruning some bushes.

John called out, "I'm back, Henry."

Henry looked over, waved, and continued pruning. John knew Henry preferred to avoid conversations about such matters, so he decided not to push it. Instead, John headed into the church through the side door. "Well, someone has been busy," John said to himself as he noticed a new lock had been fitted on the door behind the curtain.

The padlock was open, with two keys attached. John felt a wave of relief and gratitude. He rushed back out to the garden and called out to Henry, "Good work, well done. Thank you!"

Henry, without looking up, raised his hand to acknowledge the reverend. John returned to the church, taking a moment to appreciate the new security measures. He then made his way to his office to gather his thoughts and plan his next steps.

The events of the day had been draining, but John felt a renewed sense of determination. He knew that finding the stolen items and bringing the culprits to justice would not be easy, but he was resolved to see it through. The church was more than just a building; it was a sanctuary for the community, and he would do everything in his power to protect it.

As he sat at his desk, John thought about his conversation with Sergeant Porter. The frustration and anger he felt were still fresh, but he knew he needed to channel those emotions into productive actions. He would talk to the Bishop about going public with the theft, hoping that someone in the community might come forward with information. John picked up the phone and dialled the Bishop's number. After a few rings, the Bishop answered.

"Hello, Bishop, it's John," he began. "I wanted to discuss the recent break-in at St Mary's."

"Ah, John, I was just about to call you," the Bishop replied. "I've been briefed on the situation. How are you holding up?"

"I'm managing, but it's been a challenge. The stolen items are irreplaceable, and I believe going public with the theft might help us recover them," John said.

The Bishop was silent for a moment before responding. "I understand your frustration, John. If you think this will help, I support your decision. We must do everything we can to protect our church and its history."

"Thank you, Bishop. I'll begin preparations to make a public announcement. I appreciate your support," John said, feeling a weight lift off his shoulders.

"Stay strong, John. We're with you in this," the Bishop replied before they ended the call.

John hung up the phone, feeling a renewed sense of purpose. He knew the road ahead would be tough, but with the support of the church and the community, he was confident they would find a way to restore what had been lost.

As the sun began to set over the village, John stepped out of his office and into the quiet serenity of the church. The events of the day had taken their toll, but he was ready to face whatever challenges lay ahead. The church and its community were worth fighting for, and he would not rest until justice was served.

John sat at his desk and stared at the telephone. He knew he needed to make a call but felt uneasy. This call could open up something much bigger. He hesitated, thinking it over. Finally, he put his hand on the phone and began to dial a number. He got halfway through and hung up.

The consequences weighed heavily on him—the life he once knew could come back to haunt him for the wrong reasons. He looked at the phone, then put his elbows on the table, his face in the palms of his hands, and rubbed his face vigorously.

"Fuuuuucccccckkkkkk," he shouted, the sound echoing in the quiet office. John leant back in his chair, trying to gather his thoughts. The frustration and anger bubbled inside him, but he knew he needed to stay composed. There was too much at stake.

As night fell, the village settled into a quiet slumber, the day's tensions fading into the background. But in the stillness of the church, a storm was brewing, one that would soon shake the foundations of the sanctuary that Reverend John had worked so hard to protect.

Henry locked up the tool shed, his hands steady despite the thoughts swirling in his mind. As he walked past the church, he paused, his eyes lingering on the stone walls that had stood the test of time. He had seen much in his years, and though he kept his thoughts to himself, he knew that the village was on the brink of something. The break-in was just the beginning.

"Things are changing," Henry muttered to himself as he headed towards his bicycle. "And not necessarily for the better."

With one last glance at the church, Henry mounted his bicycle and pedalled away, the night closing in around him. The village slept, but the undercurrents of tension and secrets continued to stir, waiting for the right moment to surface.

Chapter 5
Whispers of the Village

The evening sun dipped below the horizon, casting a warm, golden glow over the village. The streets were quiet, with only the occasional rustle of leaves in the gentle breeze. Inside the village shop, Ben and Irene were winding down for the day, their silhouettes moving against the backdrop of shelves lined with goods.

"Ben," Irene called from the stockroom, her voice carrying a hint of fatigue, "have you managed to cash up yet?"

"Doing it now," Ben replied, glancing at the till as he counted the notes with practiced precision.

The rhythmic sound of coins clinking into the drawer was the only noise in the shop, a familiar routine that brought a sense of closure to the day. Irene busied herself in the stockroom, preparing to restock the shelves for the next day. The comforting scent of fresh bread lingered in the air, a reminder of the bustling day that was slowly coming to an end.

They continued to work for another hour, their routine familiar and unhurried. With a flick of her wrist, Irene turned the sign to 'Closed' and dimmed the lights, casting a soft shadow over the now-quiet shop. Meanwhile, across the village, a very different scene was unfolding at Sam's house.

The cramped room was thick with the stale odour of cigarettes and unwashed clothes. Sam and James sat hunched over a worn-out table, their heads close together as they whispered conspiratorially.

"So, we're going through with it, then?" Sam asked, his voice wavering with uncertainty. He avoided James's eyes, focusing instead on the chipped paint of the table beneath his fingers.

"Of course we are," James replied, his eyes gleaming with a dangerous excitement. "We hit the shop tonight, take anything of value." His tone was casual, almost as if they were discussing the weather rather than a crime.

Sam swallowed hard, glancing at James with apprehension. "And how are we splitting this up?"

James leant back in his chair, the faintest hint of a smirk on his lips. "I'll take care of the cigarettes. You focus on the vodka, whisky, and brandy. Those sell fast, and we'll make a killing."

The plan was reckless, a threadbare scheme woven with desperation and greed. But for James, it was business as usual. He spoke with an air of confidence, outlining the details with the ease of someone who had done this countless times.

"The back door's weak," James continued, tapping the table for emphasis. "We can use a crowbar to force it open, break the locks. It's simple."

Sam didn't share James's confidence. He shifted uncomfortably, feeling the weight of impending doom settle in his stomach. "What if we get caught?" He asked, voicing the fear that had been gnawing at him all evening.

James's demeanour darkened, his eyes narrowing into slits. "If you get caught," he said, his voice dripping with menace, "you don't bring me into this. Got it?"

Before Sam could respond, James lunged forward, grabbing a fistful of Sam's hair and yanking it back sharply. "But if I get caught," James sneered, his grip unrelenting, "you're going down with me."

Sam winced, nodding to appease James. The pain shot through his scalp, but it was the cold, calculating look in James's eyes that terrified him. He felt trapped, ensnared in a web of criminal intent spun by a man who had nothing to lose.

James released Sam with a shove, chuckling darkly as he settled back into his chair. "You worry too much," he taunted, a cruel smile tugging at the corners of his mouth. "It's easy money, Sam. Just do as you're told."

Sam's mind was a whirlwind of conflict. Irene had been kind to him in the past; she was a friend of his aunt, and he couldn't bear the thought of betraying her trust. But backing out wasn't an option—not with James calling the shots. Sam was in too deep, his involvement a foregone conclusion.

As they continued to plot the break-in for Friday evening, Sam couldn't shake the feeling of dread that clung to him like a second skin. He knew James had been to prison before and seemed almost indifferent to the prospect of going back. For James, incarceration was a temporary setback, a place where he could bide his time and plot his next move. But for Sam, it was a nightmare.

He didn't want to end up behind bars, caught in a cycle of crime and punishment. The thought of it made him sick to his stomach. He stared at the cigarette butts piled in the ashtray, each one a testament to the stress of the past few hours.

"What if—?" Sam hesitated, his voice barely above a whisper. "What if we don't go through with it?"

James's eyes flashed with anger, a dangerous glint that sent a chill down Sam's spine. "Don't be stupid, Sam. We're doing this."

The room fell silent, the tension palpable. Sam sat quietly, his mind racing with thoughts of escape. Life would be better without James, he mused, the idea forming like a seed in his mind. If James disappeared, maybe Sam could finally break free from the chains that bound him.

For a fleeting moment, hope flickered within him—a glimmer of a life beyond the shadow of crime. But the reality of his situation quickly snuffed it out. Sam was trapped, his fate intertwined with that of a man he feared and despised. If only his heart would just stop beating, and he was less alive.

As the evening deepened, Sam resigned himself to his role in the scheme. He would do what was required of him, if only to keep James at bay. But in the quiet corners of his mind, a plan was taking shape—a plan to reclaim his life and leave the darkness behind.

***

John had a restless night's sleep, tossing and turning with a sense of unease that clung to him like a shadow. He glanced at the clock: 4:58 am. Too early to be awake, but sleep was elusive. He gathered his thoughts, threw back the duvet, and got out of bed. Stumbling like a zombie, he made his way to the shower, hoping the hot water would bring him to life.

The shower did its job, and soon, he was dressed and downstairs. He put the kettle on and made a cup of tea. Settling into his favourite chair, he sipped his tea and watched the morning break. The birds sang their dawn chorus, flitting about the garden in search of the early worm. Feeling somewhat better, John managed to calm his uneasy sense of anger.

He finished his tea and walked over to his desk. He opened his diary to see what the day had in store; a hospital visit at 11, a hospice visit at 1:45, and a meeting with a young couple at 5 to discuss their wedding plans. But the list of tasks did little to soothe his mind.

The church's recent troubles weighed heavily on him, and he couldn't shake the feeling that the village was holding its breath, waiting for something to happen. John left the house and walked over to the church. It was still early, 8:20 am.

He unlocked the large wooden doors and let himself in, a familiar sense of unease settling over him. Yet, he pushed forward, walking down the aisle to his vestry. As he approached the altar, he stopped, bowed his head, made the sign of the cross on his body, and kissed the crucifix before him.

He walked around the back, stood at the altar, and looked out over the empty church. The quiet and peace filled the air, but it did little to soothe his troubled mind. He looked up towards the ceiling, muttering something to himself as he held the cross hanging from a chain around his neck.

He stepped down and walked to the vestry. As he put the key in the lock, anger churned in the pit of his stomach. He let go of the door handle, took a step back, and gathered his thoughts before approaching the door again. Grabbing the handle, he opened the door and went inside.

Henry had cleared up the mess left on the floor. The pictures were arranged neatly on the shelves in the cabinet. John smiled to himself, thinking, *Henry is a good man*. John sat at his desk and noticed a note on a scrap of paper.

It read, 'Dear John, I have measured the cabinet doors and will go to town to see if I can get the glass cut to size. Henry.'

This gesture filled John with a renewed sense of purpose. He hadn't asked Henry to do this; it was out of Henry's way to go to town on his bicycle. John set about his day, opening his Bible and making notes for the meetings he had later.

Time passed quickly, and soon, it was time to leave. John gathered the things he needed, placed them in his bag, and locked up the church before heading out. John crossed the road to his cottage, unlocked his car, and got in. He started the engine and drove off towards town, determined to face the day with a sense of resolve.

John drove to the hospital with a heavy heart, his thoughts still lingering on the events of the past few days. As he parked his car and made his way to the hospital entrance, he braced himself for the unknown challenges he might face. His Monday mornings at the hospital were always unpredictable, but today, he sensed it would be particularly difficult. Entering the hospital, he greeted the receptionist with a warm smile. "Good morning, Janet."

"Good morning, Reverend Bailey," Janet replied, her voice tinged with the weariness of the early hour. "They're expecting you in Ward 3."

John nodded, making his way to the lift. As the doors closed, he took a deep breath, steeling himself for what lay ahead. When he arrived at Ward 3, the familiar sounds of beeping machines and hushed conversations greeted him. He entered the room where a family was gathered around an elderly woman lying in bed.

The woman's frail body was a stark contrast to the vibrant life John knew she had lived. Her daughter, a middle-aged woman with tear-streaked cheeks, looked up as he approached.

"Reverend Bailey," she whispered, her voice breaking. "Thank you for coming."

John placed a comforting hand on her shoulder. "I'm so sorry for your loss, Margaret. Your mother was a wonderful woman."

Margaret nodded, tears flowing freely. "She was. She always spoke so highly of you."

John spent the next hour with Margaret and her family, offering words of comfort and praying with them. He listened as they shared stories of their loved one, memories that brought both tears and smiles. His presence provided a small measure of solace in their time of grief.

After leaving the family, John visited other patients, offering prayers and support where needed. Each encounter reminded him of the fragility of life and the importance of compassion. Later, John made his way to the hospice for the daily service in the chapel.

The small room held only a handful of people, most of them regular attendees. He led the service with a gentle, reassuring tone, reading passages that spoke of hope and peace. As he left the hospice, the weight of the morning's experiences pressed heavily on him.

He drove back to the village, stopping at the home of Mrs Clarke, an elderly parishioner who had recently been unwell. Knocking on the door, he waited for a moment before it opened to reveal Mrs Clarke, her face lighting up with a smile.

"Reverend Bailey, what a pleasant surprise!" She exclaimed.

"Good afternoon, Mrs Clarke. I wanted to check in and see how you're doing. Is there anything you need?" John asked, his tone warm and inviting.

"Oh, I'm managing, but it's so kind of you to come by," she replied, stepping aside to let him in. They settled in the cosy living room, the smell of freshly brewed tea wafting through the air. Mrs Clarke poured them each a cup, her hands trembling slightly with age.

"How have you been feeling?" John enquired, taking a sip of the tea.

"Some days are better than others," Mrs Clarke admitted. "But I'm grateful for the good days. The doctor says I need to rest more, but it's hard to sit still when there's so much to do."

"I understand. But it's important to take care of yourself," John said gently. "Is there anything I can help you with? Groceries, perhaps? Or anything around the house?"

Mrs Clarke shook her head. "No, no, you've done so much already. Just having you here is a great comfort. How are things at the church?"

John hesitated for a moment, not wanting to burden her with his troubles. "We're managing. It's been a challenging few days, but we're getting through it."

Mrs Clarke reached out and patted his hand. "You do so much for all of us, Reverend. Remember to take care of yourself too."

John smiled, touched by her concern. "Thank you, Mrs Clarke. That means a lot." They continued to chat for a while, the conversation light and comforting.

As John prepared to leave, Mrs Clarke walked him to the door. "Thank you for stopping by, Reverend. Your visits always brighten my day," she said.

"It's my pleasure, Mrs Clarke. I'll see you at church on Sunday," John replied, giving her a warm smile before heading back to his car.

As he drove home, John reflected on the day's events. Despite the challenges and the sadness he had encountered, he felt a renewed sense of purpose. The support and gratitude of his parishioners reminded him of the importance of his work, and he resolved to continue facing each day with strength and compassion.

John arrived back at the church, feeling the weight of the day's emotions pressing on him. The church stood silent and still, a comforting presence against the backdrop of the village. He noticed that Henry had already left for the day; the grounds looked immaculate, a testament to Henry's dedication.

Unlocking the heavy wooden doors, John stepped inside and made his way to the vestry. He sat down at his desk, allowing himself a moment to breathe and gather his thoughts. The stillness of the vestry offered a brief respite from the turmoil of his mind. He opened his Bible, letting the familiar passages bring him some peace as he awaited the young couple scheduled to meet him.

The minutes passed, and soon, the echo of footsteps approached the church door. John stood up, smoothing his clerical collar, and walked to greet the couple. As they entered, the sun cast a warm glow through the stained-glass windows, illuminating their faces with vibrant colours.

"Welcome to St Mary's," John greeted them warmly, extending his hand. "I'm Reverend John Bailey. You must be Emma and Dean?"

The couple nodded, smiling. "Yes, that's right," Emma said. "Very nice to meet you, Reverend."

John shook their hands firmly. "It's a pleasure to meet you both. I don't believe we've met before. Do you live in the village?"

Emma shook her head. "No, we live in town, but we love this church and its grounds. We'd like to have our wedding here."

John's smile widened. "I'm delighted to hear that. St Mary's has a special charm. When is your wedding? Have you set a date?"

Dean nodded. "Yes, we've set the date for July 24th next year."

"Wonderful," John replied, his tone enthusiastic. "Let's see if we have space in the diary for you. Please, follow me." He led them down the aisle towards a set of pews near the front of the church. "Let's sit here and discuss the details," he suggested.

The couple sat down, looking around at the church's intricate architecture and the beautiful stained-glass windows. "I'll just retrieve my diary from the vestry," John said. He walked back to his office, the sense of purpose driving away the earlier fatigue. He returned with his diary and settled into the pew opposite the couple.

"Now," John began, flipping through the pages. "July 24th next year. Yes, we have that date available." He made a note in the diary, then looked up with a warm smile. "St Mary's will be delighted to be part of your special day."

Emma and Dean exchanged a look of relief and happiness. "Thank you so much, Reverend," Emma said. "We were really hoping it would be possible."

"It's our pleasure," John replied. "Let's talk a bit about your plans. Do you have a theme in mind, or any particular traditions you'd like to include in the ceremony?"

Emma and Dean glanced at each other, their faces lighting up. "We're thinking of a classic, traditional ceremony," Dean said. "Emma has always dreamed of a wedding with a lot of floral arrangements and candles."

"That sounds beautiful," John said. "We can certainly accommodate that. Our florist, Mrs Harper, does wonderful work with flowers, and we can arrange for plenty of candles to be placed around the church."

Emma beamed. "That sounds perfect. Also, we were wondering about the music. Is it possible to have a choir?"

"Absolutely," John said. "Our church choir is quite talented. I can arrange for them to perform during your ceremony. Do you have specific hymns or songs in mind?"

"Can we have a think about it, or could you make suggestions?" Emma said.

"Certainly," John replied. "Is there anything else you have questions about or need help with?"

Dean hesitated for a moment before speaking, "We were also hoping to have a small reception in the church hall afterward. Is that possible?"

John nodded. "Yes, our church hall is available for receptions. It's a lovely space, and we can help with the arrangements. How many guests are you expecting?"

"About fifty," Dean replied. "We want to keep it small and intimate."

"That's a perfect number for the hall," John assured them. "I'll make a note of that as well. We're here to support you every step of the way. If you need anything, just let us know."

Emma and Dean looked at each other, gratitude shining in their eyes. "Thank you so much, Reverend," Emma said. "This means a lot to us."

"It's my pleasure," John said, standing up. "Thank you for choosing St Mary's for your wedding. We're honoured to be a part of your special day." He led them to the church door, shaking their hands warmly as they left. "I'll be in touch with more details soon," John promised. "Take care, and God bless."

As they walked away, John locked the church doors behind them, feeling a sense of accomplishment. The day's earlier weight began to lift as he made his way back to his cottage, grateful for the moments of joy and connection that balanced the challenges he faced.

The next day was the day of Mrs Wilson's coffee morning. John wasn't exactly looking forward to it, knowing that Mrs Wilson had her nose in most things. She was a lovely, thoughtful lady, but someone who took it upon herself to be aware of everything happening in the village.

John was woken by his alarm, feeling refreshed, and the events of the last few days seemingly fading away. He began his usual routine; a hot shower, a cup of tea, and a quiet moment in his favourite chair, gazing out the window at the garden.

The morning song of the birds landing in his garden provided a peaceful backdrop. Leaving the chair, John walked to his desk, sat down, and began to check his diary for the day's events. His eyes landed on the entry for 11 am. 'Coffee Morning at Mrs Wilson's. 11 am. Sharp!' The added exclamation mark seemed to emphasise its importance.

He worked at his desk for a while, organising his thoughts and tasks until it was time to leave for Mrs Wilson's. He pondered whether he could address her less formally, but the thought quickly evaporated. John checked the address he had scribbled next to the event and left the house, deciding to stop by the shop to purchase fresh flowers. Mrs Wilson would appreciate the gesture.

As he entered the shop, Irene greeted him with a warm smile. "Good morning, Reverend," she said. "Are you ready for your coffee morning with Mrs Wilson?"

"How do you know I'm going for coffee with Mrs Wilson?" He asked, surprised.

"It's Mrs Wilson," Irene replied with a knowing grin. "She has told everyone in the village that you're going to her coffee morning. As far as she is concerned, you're something of a celebrity in the village."

John, a little confused, questioned the comment. "What do you mean?" He asked, feeling a bit nervous about the answer.

"Nothing, she just mentions you in every possible conversation. It reminds me of a schoolgirl crush!" Irene said, laughing it off. John smiled at this. He selected a bunch of flowers from the small display. "Are those for Mrs Wilson?" Irene asked.

"Yes," John replied.

"I suggest you put those back and take these instead," she said, coming over to where John was standing. Irene pulled out a bunch from another bucket. "These are better; she likes these."

John laughed and made a small joke. "My prom date," he said, and they both chuckled. He paid for the flowers, said goodbye, and left the shop. The morning was pleasant, with the sun high in the sky and the flowers fragrant. The village seemed to be bathed in a warm, golden light, making everything look picturesque and inviting.

John walked briskly to Mrs Wilson's house, the flowers in hand, feeling a mixture of anticipation and mild apprehension about the impending coffee morning. John arrived at Mrs Wilson's house, walking up the neatly kept driveway towards the door.

He paused for a moment before ringing the bell, feeling a slight twinge of nervousness. Within seconds, the door swung open, revealing Mrs Wilson with a broad smile.

"Reverend Bailey, welcome!" She exclaimed, her eyes sparkling with warmth. She made small talk for a moment or two before asking, "Reverend, would you mind if I call you John?"

"Not at all," he replied, hoping she might reciprocate with her first name. Of course, she didn't. Instead, she simply invited him in and asked him to go through to the conservatory. She closed the door and followed him. As they entered the conservatory, John was met with the sight of four other ladies already seated and engaged in animated conversation.

Mrs Wilson stepped in front of him, commanding attention with a raised hand. "Ladies, may I have your attention, please? This is Reverend John Bailey," she announced with an excited lilt in her voice. She then introduced her friends: Mrs Gilbert, Mrs Davey, Mrs Marchant, and Mrs Beaumont. "Ladies, this is John," she said, emphasising his first name in a way that made John feel slightly out of place amidst the formality.

Mrs Wilson invited John to sit next to her, placing a delicate bone China cup and saucer in front of him. She picked up a teapot and began pouring tea. "Help yourself to milk and sugar," she offered with a gracious smile. On the table before them was an array of homemade cakes, their sweet aromas mingling with the scent of freshly brewed tea.

The ladies continued their conversations, seamlessly incorporating John into their circle. They quizzed him about his life, his background, and what led him to join the church. John answered candidly, sharing glimpses of his journey and his faith.

His responses seemed to satisfy the group, and they nodded approvingly. The conversations ebbed and flowed, with John contributing thoughtfully. After a couple of hours, he glanced at his watch and realised it was time to move on. He made his excuses, standing up to leave.

"I have another appointment to get to," he said apologetically.

Mrs Wilson stood with him, her expression one of sincere gratitude. "Thank you for coming, John. And thank you for the wonderful flowers; they are my favourite. See you on Sunday," she added as she walked him to the door and closed it behind him.

As John walked away from the house, he couldn't shake a feeling of oddness about the afternoon. It felt as if he had been subjected to some kind of test or initiation. He chuckled to himself, trying to dismiss the thought. Upon returning to the church, he spotted Henry in the garden, diligently attending to the flower beds.

"Hello, Henry," John called out.

Henry straightened up and nodded in acknowledgment. "Hello, Reverend. The diggers will be arriving tomorrow; we have a funeral on Friday. All in hand, John, all in hand," Henry reassured him, his tone confident.

John nodded, feeling a sense of comfort in Henry's reliability. "Thank you, Henry."

With that, John entered the church, ready to continue with the rest of his day's duties. Despite the strange feeling left by the coffee morning, he felt a renewed sense of purpose. The community depended on him, and he was determined to be the pillar of support they needed, come what may.

Chapter 6
Shadows of the Past

John had known from the moment he saw James driving past the church that trouble was close at hand. The memory of their brief encounter years ago hovered like a dark cloud, threatening to rain down the secrets he had worked so hard to bury.

As he watched James's car crawl slowly past, an uneasy feeling twisted in his gut. Did James remember him? Did he recognise the man behind the clerical collar? James Parsley had recently been released from prison, where he had served a 3.5-year sentence for wounding with intent.

The village was still buzzing with the details of the incident— how James, in a fit of rage, had forced his way into his neighbour's home over a debt. A knife had been involved, blood had been spilled, and James had been sent away, leaving behind a reputation that preceded him wherever he went.

As John went about his duties in the church that day, the familiar peace of St Mary's felt fragile, as if it could shatter at any moment. He was tidying the altar when the heavy wooden door creaked open. A sliver of morning sunlight sliced through the dim interior, and John felt his breath hitch in his throat as a shadowy figure blocked the light.

"Hello, John," a voice called out, thick with sarcasm. The emphasis on his name sent a chill down John's spine. "How are you, John?" John stiffened, recognising the voice before he even saw the face. He forced himself to remain calm, though his heart was hammering in his chest.

"Who is it?" He asked, struggling to keep his voice steady. "Come inside."

The figure stepped forward, and there he was—James Parsley, standing in the doorway with a smirk playing on his lips. The glint in his eyes was unmistakable, a predator toying with its prey. This was not the place where one would expect to find James, yet here he was, a dark spectre in the hallowed church.

John straightened his back, forcing himself to maintain composure. "What do you want, James?" He asked, his voice more controlled now, masking the turmoil roiling within.

James sauntered closer, his steps slow and deliberate, each one echoing in the silence of the church. "I hear you've been asking about me," he said, his voice low and taunting. "Asking the good folks of this village all sorts of questions, trying to pin that little break-in on me."

John's heart pounded, but he refused to give James the satisfaction of seeing him flinch. "I'm simply looking for the truth, James," he replied, his tone firm. "The church is a sanctuary, and I intend to keep it that way."

James chuckled, the sound dark and menacing as it echoed off the stone walls. "Sanctuary," he repeated, as if the word amused him. "You think you can keep your little sanctuary safe, do you? You think you can keep your secrets safe?"

John's composure wavered, a flicker of doubt creeping into his voice. "I don't know what you're talking about, James. If you have something to say, say it."

James leant in closer, his breath hot against John's ear. "We all have secrets, John. You've got yours. I've got mine. And some of them, well, some of them have a way of coming to light, don't they?"

John's mind raced. How much did James know? How much did he remember? The weight of his own past pressed down on him; a suffocating pressure that made it hard to breathe. "Whatever you think you know, James, it's in the past," John said, though the words felt hollow. "We're both different men now."

James pulled back, studying John with a look that sent a shiver down his spine. "Are we? I wonder about that, John. I really do. But here's the thing—I may have seen something that night. Something you might want to know about."

John's heart skipped a beat. "What do you mean?"

James smirked, enjoying the control he held over the situation. "I may have seen someone that night. Someone slipping away, someone you might recognise. But why should I tell you anything? What do I gain from this?"

John felt a surge of desperation, knowing he had to keep James from using whatever he knew as leverage. "James, I would be very happy to take confession with you," John said, taking a step forward, trying to regain control of the conversation. "Let me help you. Whatever it is, you can unburden yourself. You don't have to carry this alone."

James's expression hardened, the mocking amusement vanishing from his eyes. "Confession? You think I want your help? You think I need your absolution? Not going to happen, John. Not going to happen." His voice was resolute, a wall that John could not break through.

The tension between them was palpable, the air thick with unspoken threats and unresolved grievances. John felt the weight of his own secrets pressing down on him, the fear that James might know more than he let on gnawing at his mind. James turned to leave, a cruel smile on his lips.

"I'll be in touch, John," he said over his shoulder, his voice dripping with mockery.

"Don't come back, James," John called after him, his voice ringing with authority. "You're not welcome here. Don't come back if the door is open or locked. Don't darken my doorstep again."

James paused at the door, looking back with a smirk that made John's blood run cold. "We all have secrets, John," he repeated, his voice echoing through the stone chamber as he walked away, laughing to himself.

The door swung shut with a heavy thud that reverberated through the empty church. John stood alone in the silence, the shadows seeming to creep closer as his mind spiralled into a storm of worry and anger. He began pacing up and down the aisle, his concern turning to rage. His fists clenched at his sides, and he muttered angrily under his breath.

"James has to go," John said aloud, the words a promise and a threat. The fear of his past catching up with him was a noose tightening around his neck, and he couldn't let James tighten it any further. He stared at the altar, the flickering candles casting a warm glow that felt both comforting and accusing. "James has to go," John repeated, the determination in his voice solidifying his resolve.

He couldn't let James threaten everything he had built, everything he had worked for. Whatever it took, he would ensure that James Parsley would no longer be a shadow over St Mary's or his life.

***

Later that evening, Sam lay sprawled on the narrow bed in the cramped summerhouse at the bottom of his aunt's garden. The space that had once been a cheerful retreat was now more like a prison, filled with the faint musty smell of old wood and mildew.

A single window was partially open, letting in the cool evening air that carried the scent of freshly cut grass and damp earth from the garden beyond. The room around him was cluttered with the remnants of a life lived on the edges—empty bottles, scattered clothes, ashtrays overflowing with cigarette butts, and the occasional used syringe.

The dim light cast long shadows across the wooden walls, amplifying the feeling of confinement. Sam was nursing a hangover from a bottle of wine he had stolen from the village shop a few days earlier. It was cheap wine, enough to blur the edges of his reality, if only for a while.

As he lay on the bed, staring up at the low ceiling, he tried to ignore the dull throb in his temples. He replayed the theft in his mind, the thrill of taking something without getting caught, the brief escape it provided from the bleakness of his existence.

Suddenly, a loud bang against the window shattered the quiet, making Sam jolt upright. His heart leapt in his chest as he squinted against the dying light, trying to make out the figure outside. James's face appeared, pressed against the glass, his eyes burning with an intensity that sent a shiver down Sam's spine.

"Are you going to let me in, you fucking loser?" James barked, his voice cutting through the air like a knife. There was a sneer on his lips, a look that told Sam he was nothing more than a pawn in whatever game James was playing. Sam hesitated, his mind racing with a mix of dread and resignation.

James was the last person he wanted to deal with, especially now. He felt the familiar weight of dread settle over him as he reluctantly pushed himself off the bed. His body protested with each step as he made his way to the door, his feet dragging across the worn carpet.

He glanced back at the disarray of his room, the bed unmade, the remnants of his stolen indulgence scattered around him. It was a reflection of his life, chaotic and without direction. He unlatched the door slowly, hoping to delay the inevitable confrontation. But before he could fully open it, James shouldered his way inside, the force of his entrance causing Sam to stumble backward.

James brought with him an air of menace that filled the small space, making it feel even more claustrophobic. The door swung shut with a dull thud, cutting off the outside world and leaving them alone in the dim, tense atmosphere.

"What the fuck is up with you?" James snarled, his gaze raking over Sam with a mixture of contempt and impatience.

Sam swallowed hard, trying to muster a semblance of calm. "What do you mean?" He replied, his voice betraying his nervousness. He hated how small he felt under James's scrutiny, like a bug about to be crushed underfoot.

"You look fucked, Sam. What have you been doing?" James's tone was accusatory, each word a jab that chipped away at Sam's fragile composure.

"Nothing, just had a drink, that's all," Sam mumbled, avoiding James's piercing gaze. The truth was, he had tried to drink away the reality of his situation, but it never worked. The problems were always waiting for him when the haze cleared.

"Are you drunk?" James demanded, his voice rising with irritation.

"No!" Sam protested, though he knew it was a weak denial.

The truth was, he was still feeling the effects of his stolen indulgence. He had tried to escape the weight of his reality through the wine, but it had only left him feeling more hollow and ashamed. James's eyes narrowed, a dangerous glint flickering within them.

"You better not be, because we're hitting the shop this evening."

Sam's heart sank at James's words, a mix of dread and disbelief knotting his stomach. He met James's gaze, his voice barely above a whisper. "Seriously?"

The question seemed to provoke James, who responded with a sudden burst of violence, slapping Sam hard across the head. The impact sent a sharp jolt of pain through Sam, leaving him reeling. His vision blurred for a moment, and he stumbled back, clutching his head in shock.

"What the fuck did you do that for?" Sam asked, anger and humiliation battling for dominance within him. The slap was a reminder of his place, a stark affirmation of his powerlessness against James.

"You're a fucking loser, Sam. A fucking joke," James spat, his words dripping with contempt. His presence was suffocating, a dark cloud that threatened to engulf everything in its path.

Sam looked at James, feeling the weight of those words. He had heard them so many times before, from so many different people, that they had almost lost their sting. Almost.

"Then why do you hang around with me?" Sam asked, the question escaping his lips in a tone more sheepish than defiant. Deep down, he already knew the answer, but he needed to hear it again, to understand why he was stuck in this toxic orbit.

James leant in closer, his eyes locking onto Sam's with a predatory gleam. "Because I can control you. You'll do what I say. If you don't like it, Sam, make me stop. I dare you. Go on, have a swipe, have a pop."

He pointed to his chin, goading Sam, daring him to fight back. The challenge hung in the air, a taunt that felt both hollow and dangerous. Sam's hands clenched into fists, his mind a whirlwind of conflicting emotions. He had one chance—to hit James hard, to reclaim a scrap of dignity. But as he stood there, heart pounding, he realised the futility of it all.

James was stronger, more vicious, and he thrived on intimidation. As James taunted him, Sam's mind flashed back to moments of fleeting strength. The idea of standing up for himself, of throwing a punch and maybe, just maybe, changing the balance of power between them. But fear held him back, the fear of what James might do, of the retaliation that would surely follow.

Instead of striking, Sam took a shaky breath and unclenched his fists. He couldn't bring himself to act on the impulse that flared within him. Defeated, he asked quietly, "What do you want?"

James smirked, the expression of a man who knew he held all the power. "We're going to make some money, Sam. And you're going to help me do it." The words hung heavy in the air, a binding contract signed under duress.

Sam felt the last vestiges of his autonomy slip away, swallowed by the shadow that was James Parsley. As James outlined his plan, Sam nodded along, his mind trapped in a cycle of fear and resignation.

The summerhouse, once a haven from the outside world, now felt like a cage, its walls closing in with every word James spoke. Sam's heart ached with a longing for freedom, but he knew it was a distant dream, eclipsed by the reality of his current entanglement.

As James left, the door slamming shut behind him, Sam sank back onto the bed, staring at the ceiling as despair settled over him like a suffocating fog. The path ahead was shrouded in uncertainty, and Sam could only hope for a future where he might one day escape the darkness that held him captive.

Later that evening, James returned to Sam's place, the weight of the night's plan heavy on his shoulders. Sam was waiting in anxious anticipation, his mind racing with the knowledge that James would be coming back for one reason, and one reason only.

James had been scheming for weeks, the plan forming and solidifying in his mind like a jigsaw puzzle. He had meticulously studied every detail of the small convenience store they were about to rob. The shop was situated on a quiet street, the kind where people thought nothing exciting ever happened, which made it the perfect target.

James was convinced it would be an easy hit, and he needed Sam to make it happen. "We're doing it tonight, no fucking about," James declared as he stepped into Sam's cramped living room, the dim light casting shadows on the walls. Sam sat on the edge of a worn-out couch, feeling a knot tighten in his stomach.

"The shop is being done, and you're coming with me. I've been casing it for weeks. We smash open the back door, run in, I take the cigarette counter, and you grab as many bottles as you can."

Sam nodded, but his heart wasn't in it. He couldn't shake the feeling of dread that clung to him like a second skin. James had always been the one with the plans, the one who never seemed to fear the consequences. Sam, on the other hand, was riddled with doubt.

He knew James well enough to understand that backing out wasn't an option. If he hesitated, he risked James turning on him, and that wasn't something he could afford. James had a way of making his intentions clear, and Sam had learned long ago not to test his patience.

"We go through the back, straight in, grab and out," James continued, pacing the room with a feverish energy. "We run down the towpath next to the canal. It's dark, and there are no cameras. I've walked the dog along there many times. We'll be ghosts."

James' confidence was intoxicating, and Sam could feel its pull, even as his instincts screamed at him to stop. "I'll park my car at the bottom," James said, his voice steady and assured. "We load it up, and I'll drive to yours. We offload the stuff there. Agreed?"

With that, the plan was born, and Sam found himself nodding, though every fibre of his being told him to refuse. He glanced at James, seeing the determination etched on his friend's face. James was a force of nature, a whirlwind of ambition and recklessness, and Sam was caught in his wake.

"James, are you sure this is going to work? Are we really going to get away with it?" Sam's voice wavered as he voiced his concerns, hoping against hope that James might reconsider.

"You're a fucking pussy, Sam," James snapped, his eyes narrowing with disdain. "Just do as you're told. Besides, my next plan could see us earn some big money."

James didn't elaborate further, but the slight grin on his face told Sam everything he needed to know. James was always thinking two steps ahead, his mind forever plotting the next big score. As darkness fell, the boys fortified themselves with alcohol and weed, the substances dulling their nerves and heightening their bravado.

The small summerhouse at the back of Sam's property became their sanctuary, the air thick with smoke and the acrid scent of whiskey. James was full of confidence, his bravado bolstered by the substances coursing through his veins.

Sam, on the other hand, felt his anxiety deepen with each passing minute. Dressed in dark clothing, they left the confines of the summerhouse, stepping into the cool night air. The sky was overcast, the stars hidden behind a blanket of clouds.

James moved with a purpose, his strides long and confident, while Sam trailed behind, his mind a tumult of fear and uncertainty. As they made their way towards the store, Sam couldn't shake the feeling that this was a turning point.

The choices they made tonight would ripple through their lives, altering the course of their futures. But as he looked at James, his friend's determination was unwavering, and Sam knew he had no choice but to follow. The night was silent except for the soft rustle of leaves and the distant hum of traffic.

The canal loomed ahead, a dark ribbon cutting through the landscape. James was right—there were no cameras, no prying eyes to witness their crime. It was the perfect setting for the heist, but Sam couldn't help but wonder if the darkness would truly conceal them or if it would only serve to swallow them whole.

As they approached the rear of the shop, James motioned for Sam to stay behind a tree and keep low. Sam watched as James moved with precision, staying in the shadows and surveying the area like a predator stalking its prey. After a tense moment, James gestured for Sam to join him. Sam crept forward, his heart pounding in his chest. He kept low, just as James had instructed.

"Where's your phone?" James whispered sharply.

"At home, where you told me to leave it," Sam replied, his voice barely audible.

"Good," James said with a nod. "At least you listened this time."

With James's back turned, Sam glanced at the crowbar on the ground. A dangerous thought flitted through his mind—one good blow could free him from James's grip forever. His eyes lingered on the crowbar, contemplating the weight of his decision. But the moment passed as James bent down, picking up the crowbar with practiced ease.

James wedged it between the door and the frame, working with steady confidence. With a final grunt, he forced the door open. They waited, ears straining for the sound of alarms or sirens. When silence prevailed, James grinned.

"Remember, Sam; vodka, whiskey, and brandy. No fizzy pop, and don't stop for a pick 'n' mix." He chuckled.

James entered first, moving like a shadow through the stockroom towards the main shop. Sam followed, nerves jangling. He was more afraid of James than of getting caught, his feet dragging with reluctance. James made quick work of the cigarette cabinet, sweeping cigarettes, tobacco, and cigars into his bag with swift, greedy motions. Just then, the shrill alarm pierced the silence.

"Run!" James barked.

Sam grabbed the bag of booze and bolted after James, adrenaline fulling their flight. They dashed down the lane, clinging to the shadows. Both were unfit, but fear kept them running. Back at Sam's house, they headed for the tool shed at the bottom of the garden.

Inside, Sam's heart thundered in his chest as he moved an old lawnmower and garden tools. He knelt, removing loose floorboards to reveal a shallow hole in the ground. Quickly, they stashed the stolen goods and their dark clothes in the hole, replacing the floorboards and repositioning the lawnmower with meticulous care.

They crept to the summerhouse, their sanctuary. Sam rolled a joint with trembling hands and lit it, taking a long drag to steady his nerves. He cracked open a can of beer, but James snatched it from him, his gaze unyielding.

"That's mine," he said with quiet menace. In the distance, faint police sirens wailed. Sam's heart skipped a beat. "Chill out, Sam," James said, unfazed. "If they come here, they've got no proof."

Despite James's assurance, Sam's nerves were frayed. He smoked another joint, sinking further under James's control. *No going back now*, he thought, resigned to his fate. He lay on his bed, bracing himself for the inevitable knock on the door, fear twisting his gut into knots.

Chapter 7
Crossroads of Redemption

A few weeks had passed since the break-in, and a tense quiet had settled over the village. The once-vulnerable shop now stood as a fortress, its newly installed security measures—alarms and iron gates covering the rear doors and windows—gleaming in the morning sun like a warning.

The memory of the two rogues who had violated its sanctity lingered like a bad dream, prompting Ben to ponder the possibility of selling the shop and moving to the coast, seeking a quieter life away from the lingering sense of violation. But Irene had no such intention.

The village was her home, and the shop, inherited from her parents when they retired, was her legacy. She envisioned passing it on to their children, just as her parents had done. Despite her soft-spoken demeanour, Irene was a pillar of strength, keeping her opinions private and refraining from indulging in the village gossip.

On this morning, the familiar rumble of the local farmer's truck heralded the arrival of fresh produce. "Good morning, Irene," Jeff called out as he entered the shop, his voice as hearty as ever. "How are you on this fine morning?"

"I'm well, thank you, Jeff. How are you?" Irene replied, a genuine smile on her face.

"Fair to middling, fair to middling," Jeff answered with his customary response, a twinkle in his eye. He handed over a box of vegetables, leaving it on the counter. "I've got more in the truck," he said, turning to fetch the rest. As Jeff returned with more boxes, he glanced around. "Is Ben around?" He asked.

"Yes, he's in the back room. I'll get him," Irene said. She made her way to the back room, where Ben was busy with stocktaking and arranging shelves. "Jeff's here, Ben. Can you please go and see him?" Irene said.

Ben looked up, a trace of annoyance in his eyes. "You won't burn in hell for handing over an envelope to a customer, Irene," he said sarcastically.

"How dare you, Ben. I've told you I don't agree with this," Irene replied, her voice firm. "Just go and see him."

Ben muttered something under his breath as he made his way to Jeff, extending a hand for a handshake. "Any news? Have they caught the buggers?" Jeff asked, his voice low.

"No," Ben replied with a shake of his head. "I don't think they will, but we all have our suspicions."

Irene's voice came from the back, a note of warning in her words. "You don't have any proof, Ben. You can't keep telling people what you think. This could land you in trouble."

Ben exchanged a look with Jeff, their shared suspicions hanging in the air like a dark cloud. "If I had my way, I'd sell the shop and move to the coast," Ben mused, his thoughts drifting to dreams of a quieter life. "Set up a tea room or something. Maybe a coffee shop."

Jeff listened as Ben spoke of his dreams, but their conversation was interrupted by the sharp clang of the door opening.

James strolled in, his presence like a cold wind cutting through the shop. Ben stiffened, muttering under his breath to Jeff, "Makes a change for him to use the front door." James began to roam the aisles, his eyes scanning the shelves with a calculating gaze. Ben kept a close eye on him, his heart pounding in his chest. "Can I help you with something?" Ben asked, trying to keep his voice steady.

"No, I know what I want," James replied, his voice dripping with defiance. He picked up some tins of beer and made his way to the counter, Ben trailing closely behind. "You got a problem?" James snarled, his eyes narrowing as he fixed Ben with a challenging stare.

Ben's heart raced; his palms sweaty with anxiety. "No, no problem," Ben replied, forcing a smile. "Just offering a service." Ben went behind the counter, scanning the beers and cigarettes. He kept the items close, wary of James's unpredictable nature. "£15.85, please," he said, his voice tight with tension.

James handed over the cash, snatched his items, and left the shop, the door swinging shut with a finality that left the air heavy.

Jeff watched James go, a newfound bravado in his voice once James was safely out of earshot. "I was this close to confronting him," Jeff said, holding his thumb and forefinger close together. "That's the first time I've seen him," Jeff continued, emboldened by James's departure.

The two men exchanged tales of bravado, imagining what they would do if they ever caught the culprits. "I'd string him up," Jeff declared.

"I'd cut his fingers off," Ben added, their words more bark than bite.

Irene emerged from the stock room, her expression stern. "Haven't you got work to do, Jeff?" She chided gently.

"Yes, of course. Bye, Ben. Irene," Jeff said, tipping his hat as he left the shop.

As the door closed behind Jeff, Ben and Irene were left in the silence of the shop, the echoes of their encounter with James lingering like a shadow. The village may have seemed quiet, but beneath its serene surface, tensions simmered, waiting for the next spark to ignite the flames.

James's mind was ablaze with thoughts as he walked away from the village shop, the sound of the door slamming behind him echoing like a gunshot in his mind. He could feel Ben's eyes burning into his back, and it only fuelled his anger.

He clenched his fists, the familiar itch of violence tickling his skin. He needed a fix, something to take the edge off, and he knew exactly where to get it. But for now, the beers would be a start. He made his way through the winding lanes, the weight of his anger propelling him forward.

As he approached the shed at the back of Sam's aunt's garden, the familiar scent of damp wood and earth greeted him. It was a reminder of the world he had carved out for himself, a world of shadows and secrets. Pushing open the door, James found Sam already there, crouched over the loose floorboards.

Sam looked up, his face pale and anxious, the hint of a bruise visible on his cheek from their last encounter. "What took you so long?" Sam asked, his voice laced with a mix of irritation and fear.

"Shut up," James snapped, kicking the door shut behind him. "Let's get this over with."

Sam hesitated for a moment, then nodded, prying up the floorboards to reveal the stash of stolen goods they had hidden away. The sight of the pilfered items made Sam's stomach churn. Each piece represented another step down the dark path he had been led on, a path he was desperate to escape.

"Come on, hurry up," James barked, his patience wearing thin. He grabbed a few items, shoving them into a worn-out backpack. Sam followed suit, his hands trembling as he stuffed bottles and cigarettes into another bag.

"We're taking this to Jock's?" Sam asked, though he already knew the answer. Jock was their only option for unloading the goods, the only one who wouldn't ask questions.

"Yeah, and don't screw it up this time," James said, his eyes narrowing. "If you mess this up, I swear—"

Sam bit his tongue, the words of defiance dying before they reached his lips. He was sick of James, sick of being under his thumb, but fear kept him in check. They finished packing up and left the shed, making their way through the backstreets to Jock's place.

Confrontation at Jock's Flat

Jock's flat was as they remembered it—dark and dingy, the air heavy with the smell of smoke and stale beer. The curtains were drawn tight, casting the room in shadows that danced menacingly in the dim light. As they entered, Jock was lounging on the sofa, his expression unreadable as he watched them with eyes that missed nothing.

The couple from before were gone, leaving an eerie silence that was only broken by the distant hum of traffic outside. "What've you got for me?" Jock asked, his voice a low rumble as he gestured for them to sit.

James dropped the bag onto the table with a thud, his bravado on full display. "Got some stuff for you, Jock. Should be worth a decent trade."

Jock raised an eyebrow, leaning forward to inspect the goods. He picked through the items with a practiced hand, his face betraying no hint of what he was thinking. Sam watched nervously, his heart pounding in his chest. He knew how these meetings could go—Jock was unpredictable, his temper as volatile as the drugs he supplied.

As Jock assessed the goods, James turned to Sam, his eyes narrowing with disdain. "You better not have screwed us over this time, Sam," he muttered, his voice dripping with menace.

"I didn't," Sam replied, though his voice was barely a whisper. He felt the weight of James's glare, the threat lingering in the air like a noxious gas.

"You sure about that?" James challenged, stepping closer. "Because if you did, I'll make you regret it."

"I said I didn't!" Sam's voice rose, a flicker of defiance finally breaking through. "I'm sick of this, James! I'm sick of you!"

The room seemed to hold its breath as the tension reached a boiling point. James's expression darkened, his hands balling into fists as he prepared to strike. He was about to lunge at Sam when Jock's voice cut through the air like a whip.

"Enough!" Jock barked, his Glaswegian accent thick with authority. He rose from the sofa, his towering presence filling the room. "Not in my place. Not now, not ever."

James hesitated, his anger momentarily checked by the weight of Jock's words. But the rage was too deep-seated, too ingrained to be easily quelled. He took a step towards Sam, his intent clear.

"I'm warning you, James," Jock said, his voice a growl. "You lay a hand on him, and you'll answer to me."

Sam stood frozen, like a rabbit caught in headlights, unable to move as James's fury burned hot and bright. He hated James with every fibre of his being, every ounce of his soul crying out for revenge. But fear held him captive, trapping him in a cycle he couldn't break.

James sneered; his defiance unwavering. "He's mine to deal with," he spat, though there was a hint of uncertainty in his eyes.

"Not here, he isn't," Jock replied, his tone unyielding. "Sam's under my protection. You hurt him, and you'll find out what real pain is."

The room was charged with tension, the air thick with unspoken threats and dangerous promises. Sam watched as Jock and James squared off, the two forces locked in a silent battle of wills. Jock stood firm, his presence a bastion of strength, while James bristled, unwilling to back down.

"You think you're so tough, Jock?" James challenged, his bravado faltering under the weight of Jock's gaze.

Jock didn't flinch, his eyes boring into James with an intensity that was impossible to ignore. "I don't think, James. I know. And you'd do well to remember that."

For a moment, time seemed to stretch, the world narrowing down to the small room and the three figures caught in a deadly dance. Sam's heart raced, his mind a whirl of fear and fury. He longed to escape, to be free of the chains that bound him to this life.

Finally, James relented, taking a step back, though his eyes promised retribution. "Fine," he muttered, his voice a simmering cauldron of anger. "But this isn't over." With that, James turned and stormed out, the door slamming shut behind him with a finality that echoed through the flat.

"He is beginning to piss me off, Sam," Jock said. "He thinks he is untouchable but he's not. He is coming here and behaving like that. If I get a knock on the door from the police, I'm going away for a long time. If that happens, James is a dead man. Come to think of it, he is a dead man walking."

Sam slumped against the wall, the adrenaline coursing through his veins leaving him drained and shaken. He couldn't bring himself to meet Jock's gaze, the shame of his situation heavy on his shoulders.

"Don't worry, lad," Jock said, his voice unexpectedly gentle. "You're safe here."

Sam nodded, though the words felt hollow. He knew the reality—he was trapped in James's world, a pawn in a game he couldn't escape. But in the back of his mind, a small flame of defiance flickered, a hope that one day, he might break free and reclaim the life that had been stolen from him.

For now, he was caught in a storm, but he vowed that one day he would rise above it, no longer the victim but the master of his own destiny. The flat was silent except for the muted sounds of traffic outside, a stark contrast to the chaos that had unfolded moments before.

Sam sat slumped against the wall, his breath coming in shallow gasps as he tried to steady his racing heart. The room felt cold and oppressive, the shadows stretching like fingers to envelop him in their grasp. Jock's presence was a comforting anchor, but it was not enough to dispel the fear that had taken root in Sam's chest.

Jock watched Sam with a concerned eye, his gruff exterior softened by a flicker of compassion. "You alright, lad?" He asked, his voice rough but sincere.

Sam didn't answer, his mind too wrapped in the memory of James's threats, the promise of violence that hung heavy in the air. He could feel himself trembling, each shiver a reminder of the danger he was in. Jock sighed, sensing Sam's turmoil.

"I'm cooking up," he announced, moving to the kitchen with a familiarity that spoke of long years spent in its cramped confines. The phrase was a well-worn expression among those who frequented Jock's flat, a casual declaration that he was preparing his next fix.

Jock pulled open a drawer, retrieving his kit with practiced efficiency. The tin clattered onto the counter, the contents spilling out like some macabre treasure. A small paper wrap nestled among the paraphernalia contained the poison he craved, a balm for the soul even as it corroded the body.

"Do you want some?" Jock called out to Sam, who looked up for the first time since James had stormed out.

Sam's eyes were hollow, the light in them dimmed by fear and despair. "Yes, please," he whispered, the words barely audible, a plea for escape from the pain that clung to him like a shroud.

Jock tossed him a tourniquet, the elastic band snapping in Sam's trembling hands. "Put this on," Jock instructed, turning his attention back to the task at hand. The flame of the lighter danced beneath the spoon, the liquid bubbling and swirling into a hypnotic dance that captivated Sam's weary gaze.

As Sam tightened the tourniquet around his arm, Jock drew up the hot liquid, the syringe filling with a dose of oblivion. He approached Sam, who offered his arm with the resignation of a man who had nothing left to lose. The needle pierced the skin, and Sam watched as the drug seeped into his veins, a warmth spreading through him like a lover's embrace.

The flat was a pit of filth, the kind of place where even the rats had given up and moved on, seeking better prospects elsewhere. But as the heroin took hold, the grime and squalor faded into insignificance, replaced by the gentle lull of sleepless dreams.

Sam's body relaxed, sinking into the worn cushions as the world around him blurred into nothingness. For a brief, blissful moment, he was safe, cocooned in the comforting embrace of his only true friend—the drug that whispered sweet promises of escape, of freedom from the chains that bound him. In his haze, he saw Jock as a guardian, a twisted saviour who provided solace in a world that offered none.

Elsewhere, in the Shadows

James was a tempest of rage, his mind a whirlwind of anger and hatred. Every fibre of his being screamed for release, for vengeance against Sam and anyone else who dared cross him. Jock had been an obstacle, a challenge to his authority, but James was nothing if not determined.

He replayed the confrontation in his mind, each blow he wanted to land on Sam's face adding fuel to the fire that burned within him. His steps were measured as he made his way back to Sam's summerhouse, the cool night air doing little to soothe the inferno raging in his chest.

The plan was simple—he would wait for Sam, confront him, and make him pay for his defiance. James was convinced that Sam had stolen from him, that the missing goods from the stash were proof of betrayal. The paranoia ate at him, feeding the beast within.

The summerhouse loomed ahead, its silhouette a dark shadow against the night sky. James slipped inside, the door creaking ominously as he settled in to wait. The silence was oppressive, the minutes stretching into hours as he stewed in his own fury.

Every creak of the floorboards, every rustle of leaves outside, was a harbinger of Sam's impending arrival, and James relished the thought of what he would do. The longer he waited, the more his anger simmered, boiling beneath the surface until it threatened to overflow.

He paced the small space, the walls closing in as his imagination conjured images of Sam's betrayal. The thought of Sam's perceived treachery was a knife twisting in his gut, each twist a fresh wound that demanded retribution. Nothing was going to stop James—not reason, not fear, not the whispered warnings of conscience that tried to claw their way to the surface.

He was a force of nature, a storm on the brink of breaking, and Sam was the target of his wrath. In the dark, James plotted his revenge, the twisted fantasies of violence and control spiralling into a fevered haze. He would make Sam pay; teach him a lesson he wouldn't soon forget. When it was done, when the storm had passed, James would stand victorious, his dominance reaffirmed.

***

The drugs began to wear off, and as Sam slowly regained his senses, a hazy contentment settled over him. He lay sprawled on Jock's worn-out sofa, blissfully unaware of the earlier chaos that had unfolded in the cramped flat. The dim light from a flickering bulb above cast a warm glow, wrapping him in a cocoon of false security.

It was late now. Jock, sensing the lingering tension in the room, leant against the doorframe of the kitchen and eyed Sam thoughtfully. "Listen, Sam," he said, his voice gruff but not unkind. "I don't think it's safe for you to head out just yet. James is probably lurking in the shadows, waiting to kick your head in."

Sam's eyes fluttered open, and Jock's words pierced through the fog in his mind, bringing back the violent confrontation with James. The memory flickered in his mind like a broken film reel, each frame sharp with the memory of James's rage.

"No," Sam replied, shaking his head as he tried to ignore the growing knot of fear in his stomach. "I'll go home."

"Suit yourself," Jock shrugged, pushing off the doorframe. "But if you leave, you're on your own, and in the dark. Stay on the sofa and head out in the morning. Whatever you do, just make sure you close the door on your way out. I'm going to bed."

With that, Jock retreated into his bedroom, the door clicking shut behind him. The silence of the flat swallowed Sam, leaving him alone with his thoughts. He glanced between the front door and the worn sofa, weighing his options. Jock was right, and Sam knew it.

Out there, James was waiting—a maniac, poised to strike. The sofa, though threadbare and uncomfortable, offered a sanctuary of sorts, a temporary refuge from the storm outside. Sam lay back on the sofa, his mind a whirlpool of confusion and despair.

How had things escalated so quickly? How had his life spiralled so far out of control? James was like an angry wasp trapped in a jar, and if freed, his sting would be felt by all. Sam knew he would never truly understand James's complexity, nor his unpredictable wrath.

His mind wandered down darker paths. He needed to change, but where could he start? He envisioned a life free from James, from the suffocating grip of drugs and the petty crimes that had become his existence. Could he reach out to his family, seek their help and forgiveness?

But his rap sheet painted a grim picture—petty theft, drug abuse, a break-in he hadn't yet been caught for but feared would eventually lead to his undoing. Anger bubbled up within him, thoughts turning to James and the fear he inflicted. Sam wanted him gone, out of his life forever, but how?

Sam was no criminal mastermind, just a petty thief with a drug habit. Yet, as he lay there, thoughts of retribution began to take root, tendrils of a plan that might one day bloom into action.

***

Meanwhile, James was waiting, crouched in the bushes near the summerhouse like a predator stalking its prey. The night air was cool, but a simmering rage burned within him. He could see the silhouette of Sam's aunt through the curtains of her house, watching the dark, unlit abode that Sam called home.

She checked her watch, seemingly unfazed by Sam's late-night habits, before drawing the curtains shut. James was restless, his skin crawling as the need for his next fix clawed at him. It had been hours since his last hit, and the familiar ache was setting in.

He faced a choice; wait for Sam and try to endure the withdrawal symptoms gnawing at his insides or retreat home and satisfy the unrelenting cravings that threatened to consume him. He spat on the door of the summerhouse, a gesture of disdain, and turned away.

His car was parked a hundred meters away, just around the corner. The short walk felt interminable, each step heavier than the last as his limbs trembled and his vision blurred. By the time he reached his car, his hands were shaking so violently, he struggled to fit the key into the lock.

Finally inside, he sank into the driver's seat, his heart racing as he fought to steady his hands. The short drive home was treacherous, the narrow lanes a blur as he navigated them with white-knuckled determination. Once inside his flat, James wasted no time. He prepared his fix with frantic precision, the ritual movements offering a brief respite from the chaos within.

As the heroin coursed through his veins, he lay back on the bed, his anger temporarily soothed by the numbing bliss. But deep down, James's fury simmered, waiting to erupt once more.

***

Sam woke early, around 6 am, and glanced around Jock's flat, but there was no sign of Jock. He walked over to the window and peered outside; he couldn't see James' car, but that didn't mean James wasn't lurking nearby. Gathering his courage, Sam decided to leave the sanctuary of Jock's flat.

As he approached the door, his eyes fell on a long screwdriver on a small table next to it. He hesitated for a moment before grabbing the tool and heading out. The journey home would take about 40 minutes on foot if he followed the road, or an hour through the farmer's fields.

Taking the bus wasn't an option—he had no money. Sam paused to gather his thoughts. It was still early, and James was never up at this hour, so the chances of running into him were slim. With the screwdriver as a precaution,

Sam decided to walk through the fields to the edge of the village, then cut through the churchyard and down the lane to the summerhouse.

The closer Sam got to home, the more his nerves frayed. Every rustle and creak seemed to herald James's arrival. Clutching the screwdriver tightly, he muttered to himself, "Come near me, and this is going in you."

Part of him hoped James would appear, giving him the chance to end things once and for all. Sam thought, *he has to go*. Whether he could actually go through with it, he wasn't sure. But one thing was certain, he was done taking anything more from James.

Sam arrived at the summerhouse, relieved that his journey home was safe. As he approached the door, he paused, casting a wary glance through the window to ensure James was nowhere to be seen. Satisfied for the moment, Sam locked the door behind him and set off down the path to the garden gate.

He reached for the top bolt and slid it shut, the metallic clang echoing in the stillness of the morning. Finally, he felt a modicum of safety. Returning to the summerhouse, Sam quickly pulled down the blinds, leaving a small gap at the bottom to serve as a lookout.

He sat heavily on his bed, the memories of the previous day weighing heavily on his conscience. The shop he had turned over weeks earlier loomed large in his mind, each detail of the crime vivid and relentless. Guilt gnawed at him, especially after seeing Ben, the shopkeeper, sweeping outside the shop as Sam left the church earlier.

Sam's heart ached with the desire to confess, to unburden himself from the secret that threatened to consume him. His mind raced, thoughts colliding in a tumult of fear and regret. Tears welled in his eyes as the weight of his choices pressed down on him, suffocating him with their consequences.

He longed for an ordinary life, free from the shackles of crime and addiction, but he felt trapped in the clutches of a bully, a man more powerful and ruthless than he could ever be. If he defied James, he knew James would extinguish his life without hesitation, snuffing out his flame like a candle in the wind.

The threat was always there, looming over him like a storm cloud, promising destruction if he dared to dream of freedom. Sam wiped his eyes, determined to find a way out, to reclaim his life from the darkness that had overtaken it. But as he sat alone in the dim light of the summerhouse, he felt the enormity of the challenge before him.

He was trapped in a vicious cycle, a prisoner of his own making, and the path to redemption seemed impossibly distant. Sam must have fallen asleep, because he awoke sometime later, disoriented and groggy. He blinked at the clock, which read 9:30.

He sat up slowly, the events of the previous day lingering in the corners of his mind. Today, he decided, would be the day he would try to start over. He stumbled to the small bathroom in the corner of the summerhouse, catching sight of himself in the mirror. A 36-year-old man stared back at him, but he looked closer to his late forties or early fifties.

His face was unshaven, his hair greasy and unkempt, his skin slick with sweat and grime. Sam grimaced and stepped into the shower, the first one he'd had in days. The water washed away layers of dirt and despair, and he let it run over him, feeling the weight of his failures swirling down the drain.

After the shower, he shaved his face clean, each stroke of the razor making him feel a little more human, a little more like the man he once aspired to be. He began to feel better, more awake, more alert, and determined to do something good for a change.

In the small chest of drawers, Sam found fresh clothes neatly folded. His aunt must have done his laundry, a small but significant gesture that filled him with gratitude. He dressed quickly, relishing the feel of clean fabric against his skin. Today, he decided, he would try to be a better man.

He knew that at some point, James would come looking for him, but with his trusty friend—a long screwdriver—tucked securely in his pocket, he felt a sliver of confidence. Stepping out of the summerhouse, Sam walked down the path, pausing when he saw his aunt watching him from the window.

Their eyes met, and for the first time in a long time, Sam smiled at her—a genuine smile that reached his eyes. His aunt, surprised but pleased, smiled back nervously and lifted her hand in a gentle wave. Sam stopped, raised his arm, and waved back, the simple exchange warming his heart.

He smiled to himself, a rare flicker of hope kindling within him, and continued down the path. Once outside the confines of the locked garden, Sam made his way towards the church. He wanted to see if there were any odd jobs he could help with, any way he could give back to the community he had taken so much from.

It was a long shot, but he needed to try. The determination to make amends, however small, spurred him forward, each step carrying him towards the chance of redemption. As he approached the church, Sam's mind whirled with possibilities.

What if he could turn his life around? What if he could break free from James and his destructive influence? The path to a better life was fraught with challenges, but Sam was ready to face them, one step at a time. Today was the first step on a long journey, and he was determined to see it through.

Sam reached the gates of the church and paused for a moment, his heart pounding in his chest. He pushed the gate open, its hinges creaking loudly in the still morning air. As he stepped inside, Reverend John emerged from the church, and their eyes met. Sam raised his arm in a tentative wave.

"Can I help you?" Reverend John called out, his voice calm and measured.

Sam hurried over, eager but nervous. "Hello, I'm Sam. I live just over there with my aunt."

Reverend John nodded, recognising him immediately but choosing not to reveal that he knew all about Sam's reputation and the company he kept. He wanted to hear what Sam had to say first.

"What can I help you with?" John asked, maintaining a neutral tone.

"I'm looking for work," Sam replied, his voice wavering slightly.

John shook his head. "Sorry, we don't have any work available."

"I don't want to be paid," Sam said quickly, a hint of desperation in his voice. "I just want to do something good. I want to—" He paused, catching himself before he revealed too much.

John picked up on his hesitation. "Go on," he encouraged, leaning in slightly. "What do you want to do? Tell me, it might help."

Sam felt the weight of the world on his shoulders, a heavy burden he was desperate to share. "Erm," he stammered, struggling to find the words. "I want to be useful, to feel useful. I want to prove to myself that I can be a good person."

Reverend John studied him closely, weighing his words. He knew this young man's history, the troubles that had plagued him. But there was something about Sam's earnestness that gave him pause.

"Really? Is that truly what you're asking?" John challenged, his voice carrying a hint of scepticism.

"Yes," Sam insisted, his eyes pleading. "I have a lot to offer."

John considered him for a moment longer, then nodded. "I think you have things on your mind, Sam. Would you like to share? I won't judge, and perhaps we can ask for God's forgiveness. It might help you on the path you wish to choose."

John's offer was strategic. He wanted to coax Sam into the confession box, to extract whatever information he might have about the break-in, the shop, and James. There was an urgency to John's enquiry, a quiet obsession to learn what James might have confided in Sam.

"I'll make you a bargain," John proposed. "If you come to confession with me, I'll introduce you to Henry, our gardener and handyman. He might be able to offer you something."

Sam hesitated, weighing his options. The chance to prove himself and earn redemption was tantalising, but the thought of confession was daunting. Still, it was a chance—perhaps his only one.

"Okay," Sam agreed finally.

John placed a reassuring arm around Sam's shoulders and led him into the church. They walked together in silence, the air thick with anticipation. As they approached the confession box, John opened the door and gestured for Sam to enter.

Sam hesitated on the threshold, anxiety gnawing at him. John gave him an encouraging nod and a gentle push, guiding him inside. The door closed behind him with a soft click, enveloping him in darkness. Reverend John made his way to the adjoining box, pulled back the curtain, and settled into his seat.

He took a deep breath and began to speak, his voice low and soothing, "Bless me, Father, for I have sinned. It has been too long since your last confession, but today, let us seek the light together. Speak freely, my son, for you are in a place of sanctuary. Whatever burdens you carry, lay them down here, and let us find the path to redemption."

The words hung in the air, a lifeline cast into the turbulent sea of Sam's conscience. Sam swallowed hard, his heart racing as he grappled with the decision to unburden himself.

"I don't know where to start," Sam admitted, his voice barely a whisper.

"Start with what troubles you most," John urged gently. "There is no judgment here, only understanding and the hope of finding peace."

Sam took a deep breath, steeling himself for what he was about to reveal. His mind was a storm of thoughts and memories, each one vying for attention. "It's about the break-in at the shop," Sam began, the words tumbling out in a rush. "And about James. I'm scared of him. I'm scared of what he might do."

The confession had begun, and with it, the possibility of salvation—or ruin. Reverend John listened intently, his mind whirring with the implications of Sam's revelations, knowing that every word brought them closer to the truth and the tangled web that bound them all.

Sam began to blurt out his confession, words tumbling over each other in a desperate rush to be freed. He described how James had forced him into turning over the shop, threatening him with violence if he didn't comply. Sam's voice trembled as he recounted how James had hit him several times, the blows leaving both physical and emotional scars.

Reverend John listened intently, his face a mask of calm, though inside, he was both furious and oddly satisfied. This was the information he had been hoping for, the confirmation of James's malevolence and his role as a puppet master pulling Sam's strings.

"James got me hooked on heroin," Sam confessed, his voice cracking with emotion. "He used it to control me, to keep me under his thumb. I've done things I'm not proud of, things I wish I could take back."

Sam's words painted a vivid picture of James as a manipulative force, a man who thrived on power and control. The reverend could feel his anger rising, a burning desire to see justice done for the pain James had inflicted on Sam and others in the village. And then came the bombshell John had been waiting for.

Sam mentioned that James had boasted about how nothing was safe from him—not even the church. Sam asked James what he meant by this, and James had merely grinned, a malicious glint in his eyes, and said it was far too easy. Reverend John's heart pounded in his chest.

This was the connection he needed, the thread that linked James to the church break-in. Sam described the shop, detailing where they had hidden the stolen items and where they were now. His fear of James was palpable, his words tinged with desperation.

"I'm scared," Sam sobbed, his shoulders shaking with emotion. "I'm scared of what he'll do if he finds out I've talked. I don't know how to get out of this."

John's initial anger was tempered with a deep sense of compassion for the broken man before him. He reached through the confessional screen and placed a reassuring hand on the wood, offering comfort and encouragement. "You've done the right thing, Sam," John said softly. "You've taken the first step towards redemption. You're not alone in this. I'm here to help you."

Sam wiped his eyes, trying to regain his composure. "I want to speak to the shopkeepers, to apologise for what I've done. I want to make it right."

John considered this, knowing the consequences of such an action. "If you do that, Sam, they will call the police. It would be better for you to go to the police yourself, to confess everything you've told me. They'll be more lenient if you come forward voluntarily. I can go with you, act on your behalf."

Sam looked at John, a glimmer of hope in his eyes. "You'd do that for me?"

"Of course," John replied. "I'll be with you every step of the way. Together, we can face this."

Their conversation continued, with Sam gradually opening up about the extent of his involvement and the grip James had on his life. Each revelation was like a weight lifted from Sam's shoulders, his soul unburdening itself in the sacred confines of the confessional.

For Reverend John, the conversation was both illuminating and sobering. He realised that beneath Sam's troubled exterior lay a man desperate for redemption, a man who had been trapped in a cycle of addiction and abuse. And in helping Sam, John saw a path to his own redemption, a way to confront the demons of his past while bringing a semblance of peace to the village.

Chapter 8
Beneath the Surface

Mrs Wilson was engrossed in her beloved garden, a sanctuary bursting with flowers and shrubs that flourished year-round. She took immense pride in her horticultural haven, having even founded the village garden competition, where she served as a revered judge.

As dawn broke, she was diligently watering the hanging baskets in front of her house when she noticed James strolling down the lane towards Sam's house. He was accompanied by a dog Mrs Wilson had never seen before. This peculiar sight immediately piqued her curiosity, for Mrs Wilson prided herself on knowing every detail of village life.

She hurried inside and scribbled a note in her A5 book, a faithful companion that rested on a small table by her window overlooking the lane. This book, filled with meticulous entries of dates, times, and observations, was her way of maintaining order in her world.

Today's entry was no different, though her perspective often skewed reality. "A man, approximately 5ft 10, wearing dark gym shorts and a scruffy grey t-shirt with writing on the front, white shoes, walking a brown dog with flecks of white. Dog appears to be a bull terrier, on a lead, heading towards Sam's house. Man identified as James Parsley."

Mrs Wilson's imagination ran wild. She concluded the dog must have been stolen and that its owner was desperately searching for it. She kept a vigilant eye on James as he approached Sam's house, pausing near the gate, and noted every detail in her book.

Her hand hovered over the phone, ready to alert the authorities. The gate was securely locked, as Sam had ensured before leaving for his visit to the church. James looked around, searching for a way in. Mrs Wilson, her curiosity mingled with a sense of duty, dialled Sam's aunt.

"Hello, it's Mrs Wilson. There's a strange man at your gate trying to get in. Shall I call the police?" She asked, her voice fraught with urgency.

Sam's aunt assured her she would investigate. Opening a side window, she called out to the man. James looked up, and after a brief conversation, he walked away, disappearing down the lane.

Mrs Wilson, ever the vigilant observer, called again. "Is everything alright?" She enquired, a mix of concern and nosiness in her tone.

"Yes, all is well. He was just looking for Sam. I told him he was out," replied Sam's aunt.

Relieved but still suspicious, Mrs Wilson recorded the encounter in her book and closed it with a decisive snap. Her world, once again, was meticulously catalogued and somewhat more secure.

Sam had left the house early that morning to assist Henry with jobs in the church grounds. The church stood as a prominent figure in the village, dating back to the 15th century, with gravestones in the churchyard bearing dates as far back as 1850.

Henry was making a cup of tea in the shed beside the church when Sam arrived. Approaching sheepishly, Sam knocked on the shed's side. "Hello, I'm Sam. Father Bailey told me to report to you."

"Yes, come in. Would you like a cup of tea?" Henry asked, filling Sam with a sense of pride.

He isn't judging me, just being kind, Sam thought. He didn't drink tea but accepted out of politeness. The pair managed small talk over tea until it was time to start work.

"It's going to be a busy day," Henry announced. "We have a wedding on Saturday, and we need to get everything looking sharp for the big day."

"Just tell me what you want me to do and I'll do it," Sam responded with enthusiasm.

Henry looked at Sam thoughtfully. "John told me you're looking for a second chance, and he sees some good in you. Don't let him down, don't let yourself down, and don't let your aunt down."

"She doesn't know I'm here," Sam admitted.

"She does, Sam. I told her. I've known your aunt for as long as I can remember. I saw her in the shop yesterday and mentioned I was looking forward to working with you. She was very proud. Don't let her down, Sam."

Feeling a mix of anxiety and determination, Sam and Henry picked up some gardening tools and walked around to the front of the church to start work. Sam's nerves buzzed, fearing that James might drive past and see him.

"Henry," Sam called out, "would you mind if I started at the back of the church? Just tell me what to do and I'll do it."

Henry, slightly confused, asked, "Is everything okay?"

"Yes," Sam replied, "but I'd prefer to be at the back." He hoped to hide between the trees.

Sensing something amiss, Henry relented. "Okay, go around the back and begin to pull the weeds from the path. Nothing else, just the weeds."

Sam nodded gratefully, retreating to the back of the church, trying to find solace among the ancient stones and the shadows of history. Sam worked diligently in the churchyard, pulling weeds from the path as Henry watched over him.

Henry's presence was comforting yet firm, a silent reminder of the support and expectations surrounding Sam's second chance. As the morning progressed, Sam felt a sense of calm wash over him, the rhythmic work proving therapeutic. Henry glanced up and saw a familiar figure walking into the churchyard.

It was Sam's aunt, her face glowing with pride. She approached Sam, who looked up, surprised and slightly anxious. "Hello, Sam," she said warmly. "I heard you were helping out here today. I just wanted to tell you how proud I am of you."

Sam's eyes widened, and he felt a lump in his throat. "Thank you, Aunt. It means a lot."

John arrived shortly after, his presence bringing an air of authority and encouragement. "Sam," he said, clapping him on the shoulder, "you're doing a great job. Keep it up. Everyone here believes in you."

Sam nodded, feeling a renewed sense of determination. "Thanks, John. I won't let you down."

Meanwhile, James was making his way back up the lane. Mrs Wilson, ever watchful, noted his return in her book with meticulous detail. James approached Sam's house again, attempting the gate only to find it still locked. Frustration etched on his face, he pulled out his mobile phone and called Sam. The call went to voicemail.

"Where the fuck are you? We have unfinished business. You ripped me off, and I want what's mine," James hissed into the phone. He was referring to items left in Jock's flat, stolen during the shop break-in. Not satisfied with just leaving a voicemail, James sent a similar text message to Sam. James continued his march towards the church, anger simmering just beneath the surface.

Henry, keeping an eye on the surroundings, noticed James's approach. He quickly walked around the back of the church to find Sam. "Stay here, Sam," Henry said firmly. "Your friend is near the church. John told me you don't want to see him."

Sam's face drained of colour, his hands beginning to shake slightly. "What should I do?" He asked, panic creeping into his voice.

"Come on, let's go inside the church," Henry suggested, guiding Sam towards the sanctuary.

The ancient walls and stained glass seemed to offer a haven from the troubles outside. As they entered the church, the heavy wooden doors closed behind them, muffling the sounds from the outside world. Sam took a deep breath, trying to steady himself, knowing that within these walls, he had allies and a chance to prove himself anew.

James, marching quickly with rage etched on his face, noticed Sam's aunt and called out, "Where is he? He has something that belongs to me."

She acknowledged James calmly and said, "He's out and won't be back for a few days. What does he have of yours?"

James's eyes narrowed with fury. "Tell him he owes me, and I want what's mine," he demanded, his rage becoming more apparent.

Inside the church, Sam could hear the aggressive tone and began to shake uncontrollably. "He's going to kill me. I'm not safe. You don't know what he's capable of," Sam whispered, his voice trembling. "He's a madman. He once told me he hit someone with an axe. I don't know if that's true or not, but it's the sort of thing he would do." Sam continued, recounting all the terrible things James had done.

He mentioned the teardrop tattoo under James's eye, filled in—a symbol that supposedly meant he had taken a life. "Was it true or bravado? No one knows, only James."

James eventually disappeared from sight, but moments later, the loud noise of his car revving could be heard from within the church. The sound grew louder as James sped past, the roar of the engine gradually dissipating as he drove further away, heading in the direction of Jock's flat.

Sam took a shaky breath, trying to regain his composure. The church's silence enveloped him, offering a temporary reprieve from the chaos outside. Henry placed a reassuring hand on Sam's shoulder. "You're safe here, Sam. We'll get through this together."

James was a storm of fury, his rage palpable as he drove recklessly, overtaking cars with a reckless disregard for oncoming traffic. The red mist clouded his vision, and his anger fuelled his aggression.

"I'll kill him," he muttered, pounding the steering wheel. "I'll fucking kill that prick. Ripping me off, taking my shit and keeping the money, he's fucking dead."

His tirade continued unabated until he reached Jock's estate. He skidded into the carpark, jumped out, and slammed the car door. His stride was a march of vengeance as he headed for the stairwell, ignoring the out-of-order lift. On the stairs, he shoved past two lads descending, their shoulders knocking together.

One of them barked, "Watch where you're going, pal."

"Fuck off, you prick," James snapped back, his eyes wild. The lads, sensing danger, didn't pursue the matter. James pounded on Jock's door. "Open the fucking door! You in there, Sam? I'm here for you, Sam. I want what's mine. You're fucking dead."

Jock swung the door open, fury etched on his face. He grabbed James by the hair and yanked him inside. With a swift punch to James's gut, Jock had him doubled over, gasping in pain.

"You cunt," James wheezed. "What the fuck did you do that for?"

Jock didn't relent. He grabbed James by the throat, pinning him against the wall with a strength borne of pure muscle and anger. "Sam's not here, and I told you yesterday, he's under my protection. You're a fucking bully and you need to be taught a lesson. You come banging on my door, bringing unwanted attention to my home. If the police sniff around, I'll put you in the ground."

James's eyes blazed with defiance. "I want my stuff that we left here yesterday unless Sam took it. Or the money if you bought it."

"I didn't buy it, and it's still there where you left it," Jock growled.

James demanded, "How much are you going to give me for this? There's about £700 worth."

"Fuck all," Jock spat. "Take your stuff and fuck off. Come back when you find your manners. If you see Sam, leave him well alone. If you lay one finger on him, you'd better disappear because if I catch you, this will be your last summer." Jock opened the door, grabbed James by the arm, and hurled him out. "Fuck off, James. Do one."

"Fuck you, Jock. You think you're something special, you're a joke," James taunted, but Jock slammed the door shut and stalked to the kitchen, his mind already spinning with contingency plans. Jock was worried about a potential visit from the police. He quickly made a call to another dealer.

"I've got a problem. Can you handle some of my clients while I take a short break? I'm expecting a visit."

The dealer agreed, and Jock gathered everything that could incriminate him, stuffing it into a shopping bag. He made his way to his friend's house on the other side of the estate. The friend, fully aware of James's reputation, listened intently as Jock explained the situation.

"Surprised he's still around. Plenty of people want him gone," the friend remarked. "But no one's done it yet. I won't deal with him. He's unpredictable and a fucking loon."

"Yeah, well, he's a good client," Jock admitted. "He always wants something and pays every time. But I fucking hate him, despise him. Someone should slit his throat and watch him die slowly and painfully."

The two men discussed the best ways to get rid of James for a few more minutes. Jock left his friend's house, his mind buzzing with dark ideas. Would he ever go through with it? Who knows? Jock had secrets, and no one knew much about him.

His past in Scotland was a mystery, but everyone suspected it wasn't pleasant. As Jock walked back to his flat, he contemplated the day's events. The confrontation with James had been inevitable, but the aftermath left him uneasy. He glanced around, wary of prying eyes and listening ears, wondering if James would return or if the police would come knocking. One thing was certain, Jock needed to stay one step ahead.

James made his way home, his rage still coursing through his veins, every step echoing with thoughts of revenge. He couldn't shake the humiliation of his encounter with Jock, completely disregarding the fact that his own behaviour had sparked the conflict. All he could think about was making Jock pay.

When he arrived at his flat, he was greeted by his dog, a brown Staffordshire bull terrier, who jumped up excitedly as he walked in. The dog, around six or seven years old, had no name; her previous owner, facing a likely prison sentence, had simply called her 'Dog'.

The arrangement between James and the owner was simple; look after her until he got out or was bailed. James was content with this setup. He had no one else he trusted—no real friends, just people he picked up and discarded along the way. For a moment, James's hard exterior softened as he bent down to stroke the dog, her enthusiasm chipping away at his anger.

"Who's a good girl?" He murmured, rubbing her belly and fussing over her. It was one of the rare moments where James showed any affection, and it was directed at the only living thing that seemed to care about him. As the dog's calmness began to seep into him, James felt the edge of his fury start to dull.

He headed to the kitchen, opened a tin of dog food, and filled her bowl. Then, he reached into the fridge and pulled out a large bottle of cider. With a practiced motion, he twisted off the cap and took several long gulps, finishing with a loud burp that startled the dog.

James laughed, a harsh, humourless sound, and took another drink. He wandered into the lounge, a sparse room with a single armchair and a small sofa. The TV hung on the wall, its cables dangling messily down to the plug. James slumped into the armchair, staring at the blank screen as he continued to drink, his thoughts still simmering with frustration and need.

The main reason for his visit to Jock had been to score, but after their altercation, it was clear Jock wasn't going to sell him anything. As James drained the bottle, the gnawing desperation in his gut grew stronger. His body was crying out for the drugs that usually kept the darkness at bay, and he knew he was running out of options.

He pulled out his phone and started dialling numbers, trying anyone who might help him out. But one by one, they all made excuses, claiming they had nothing to share. He considered cold calling a dealer he'd heard about but had never met—a risky move in his world, but desperation was making him reckless.

Finally, he called Billy, a mutual acquaintance. "Billy, it's James. Any chance you could sort me out? Can you introduce me to your man?"

There was a pause on the other end. Billy wasn't quick to answer. "I can't, James. He doesn't like strangers. Not even if I take you—he'd cut me off."

"Can you go for me? I'm desperate," James pleaded, his voice tinged with a vulnerability he hated showing.

Billy hesitated, sensing an opportunity. For once, James was at his mercy. "It'll cost you. I need something, but I'm skint."

James clenched his teeth, knowing he had no choice. "Fine," he agreed reluctantly.

They arranged to meet in the park in 15 minutes, but James ended up waiting closer to half an hour before Billy finally showed. Billy handed over a small wrap without ceremony, taking the cash James offered without a word of thanks. The power dynamic had shifted, and Billy relished it.

James hurried back to his flat, his hands shaking as he prepared his fix. He rolled up his sleeve, found a vein, and injected the drug. As the familiar warmth spread through his veins, his tension melted away, replaced by a euphoric haze.

"Oh, that's fucking good," he muttered to himself, sinking back into the chair as the drugs took hold, washing away the rage and fear—if only for a little while. But as the high settled in, a nagging thought lingered at the edge of his mind. The craving for revenge hadn't gone away, just dulled.

Jock had humiliated him, and James wasn't one to let that go. He stared at the ceiling, the haze thick around him, and knew that this wasn't over—not by a long shot.

***

It had been a relatively quiet day for John. He had conducted a morning service, visited several housebound parishioners, and made the obligatory stop at the hospital. Now, back in the quietude of his cottage, he was preparing for a peaceful evening when the phone rang.

John walked over to the table, picked up the receiver, and answered, "Hello, this is Reverend John Bailey. How can I help you?" There was silence on the other end of the line. John waited a moment, then spoke again, "Hello? Is anyone there?"

Still, the caller remained silent, their only communication a faint, unsettling sound of breathing. "Do you need help?" John asked, his tone shifting from polite to concerned. "Can you make a sound if you need assistance?" But there was no response. The line went dead.

John stood there for a moment, the silence of the room pressing in around him. *This was odd*, he thought. His first concern was that perhaps one of his parishioners had fallen ill or was in trouble. He reached for his phone book and began calling those he knew might require assistance.

Each call, however, brought the same answer; no one was in need, no one had called. The oddity of the situation gnawed at him. Who would call and not speak? A prank? Kids messing around? Or something more sinister? John couldn't shake the feeling that it wasn't random.

His thoughts spiralled, pulling him back into memories he had long tried to bury. He felt a creeping unease and instinctively moved to the back door, locking it. He did the same with the side door off the kitchen and finally, the front door. As he locked the front door, a thought occurred to him; he would go across to the church, sit there for a while, and see if anyone came looking for him.

His past was catching up with him, paranoia flaring up like a long-dormant ember suddenly fed with oxygen. If someone wanted to harm him, that was fine—John could handle himself. But not John—Lorcan.

Lorcan had been a hard man, a force to be reckoned with. John, the reverend, was a far cry from Lorcan, the man who had left a trail of fear and violence in his wake. But now, the boundaries between the two were blurring. John sat on a bench outside the church, watching his cottage, the road, and the people going about their business.

Most were just living their lives, but John's attention was sharp, his senses heightened. Out of the corner of his eye, he saw Mrs Wilson coming out of the shop. She waved at him, then made her way over.

"Good afternoon, John! How are you? What a lovely day," she said, launching into a conversation about her garden and a coffee morning she'd had with some friends. John nodded absently, not really listening. His mind was elsewhere, on the phone call, on the shadows of his past.

"Well, I can't keep you, John," Mrs Wilson finally said with a smile. "We could gossip all day if I let you!" She chuckled, oblivious to the tension radiating from John, who hadn't said a word in the ten minutes she'd been beside him. As she got up to leave, a car slowly approached along the road.

John's heart began to race as he recognised it—it was James. The car slowed as it neared John's cottage, and John's pulse quickened. Was this the man behind the call? Was this an attempt at intimidation? James stopped the car, stepped out, and walked towards the shop, glancing at the church and John's cottage.

John stood to walk Mrs Wilson to the gate. "Take care, Mrs Wilson," he said as he opened it.

"Thank you, John," she replied, closing the gate behind her as she made her way down the lane. John's eyes followed her, but his mind was elsewhere. *Where are you, you bastard?* He thought. *Was that you who made the call? What are you trying to achieve?*

James emerged from the shop, carrying a heavy bag, its weight pulling down on his arm. John could see a bottle inside, cheap cider no doubt, the kind that would get him drunk quickly.

"Hello, JOHN," James called out with a sneer. "How are you, JOHN?" His tone was mocking, dripping with disdain.

"Have you thought any more about coming into the church, seeking redemption, forgiveness? Why not come now? We can open the confession box." John's stomach tightened. There was something in James's voice, something that suggested he knew more than he was letting on.

James continued, "If we're opening the confession box, maybe *you* should pop in. You have something to tell, don't you?" He was teasing, but the tension in the air was palpable.

"James, you have the wrong end of the stick," John replied, keeping his voice steady despite the knot in his gut. "Sorry to disappoint you."

James laughed, a cold, smug laugh that sent a chill down John's spine. It was as if James held something back, something that could unravel everything John had built. James opened his car door, ready to leave, but not before dropping a bombshell.

"Have a lovely evening, Lor—" He paused, almost finishing the name before correcting himself. "John."

John's face remained impassive, but inside, his mind was racing. Their eyes locked, a silent battle of wills, before James finally got into his car, started the engine, and drove off. John stood there, rattled to his core. *What exactly does James know?* He wondered. *Had Shane spoken to him in prison?*

The thought that his past might be catching up with him, that the secrets he had buried deep were on the verge of being unearthed, filled him with a dread he hadn't felt in years. For the first time in his life, both as John and as Lorcan, he felt truly exposed. Something had to be done to ensure this threat didn't linger. Something permanent.

John made his way home, his mind replaying the unsettling encounter with James. The tension in his chest had only grown since their exchange. As he entered his cottage, he locked the door behind him and headed upstairs, trying to shake off the feeling of vulnerability that had taken hold of him.

He removed his clothes, opting for jogging pants and a t-shirt, and then pulled on a pair of gloves, the ritual calming his racing thoughts. On the landing, a narrow door caught his eye. It was almost hidden behind a dresser adorned with ornaments and a lamp.

Carefully, he moved the dresser aside, revealing the door that had remained untouched for years. With a firm shove of his shoulder, he forced it open. The smell of dust and aged wood hit him, filling his nostrils with the scent of the past he thought he had left behind.

A narrow staircase stretched before him, leading up to the attic. John ascended the stairs, each step echoing with memories. The fading sunlight filtered through a stained-glass round window, casting a dim, coloured light across the attic.

He pulled a cord, and two dim bulbs flickered to life, barely piercing the gloom. He walked over to an old trunk and pushed it aside, revealing a loose floorboard beneath. Kneeling down, he pried the floorboard open and reached inside, pulling out a tin box.

He stared at it for a moment, his hands steady despite the turmoil in his mind. With the tin in hand, he descended the stairs and made his way to the kitchen. Still wearing the gloves, John spread an old newspaper across the table and set the tin down.

He hesitated for a moment before opening it, the contents a stark reminder of a life he had tried to bury. Inside were letters, yellowed with age, newspaper clippings recounting events he'd been involved in, and a piece of cloth wrapped around something heavy.

He unwrapped the cloth carefully, revealing a gun—a Luger pistol, a relic from his time in Ireland. Alongside it was a magazine loaded with live rounds. The weight of the gun in his hand brought back a flood of memories, vivid and painful, of the days when he had been Lorcan, a man feared and respected, a man who had stood up for what he believed in, no matter the cost.

The flashbacks were intense—images of violence, of the loyalty he had once sworn, of the cause he had served with unwavering dedication. But as quickly as the memories came, he shoved them aside, placing the gun back on the table and wrapping it in the cloth once more.

What are you thinking, John? He chastised himself. *This life is over. You chose a new path, leaving this behind. Lorcan was left in Ireland. You are John now,* trying to convince himself as much as anyone else.

The encounter with James had shaken him, but not enough to make him consider using the gun. Not even to threaten him. The thought of returning to that life, of becoming Lorcan again, was abhorrent to him. John placed the gun back in the tin, his movements deliberate and controlled. He returned the tin to its hiding place beneath the floorboard, making sure everything was as it had been.

The gloves, now tainted with the residue of the past, were wrapped in the newspaper and placed in a bag. He would take them to the church later, where they could be burned—a symbolic act of purging the remnants of his former life.

As he stood in the kitchen, the weight of the day bearing down on him, he muttered to himself, "Pull yourself together, John. He's full of bravado, likes to think he's powerful, but he's not. Don't let him take your power."

He tidied up, restoring the kitchen to its usual order, and then settled in for the evening. The cottage, usually a place of peace, felt different tonight, charged with the tension of the day's events and the recent weeks. John tried to push it all out of his mind, but the encounter with James, the memories of Lorcan, and the weight of the choices he had made, lingered like a shadow over him.

As he sat in his armchair, staring into the quiet of the night, John knew he needed to stay vigilant. He couldn't allow the ghosts of his past to resurface, no matter the provocation. But for the first time in years, he felt the line between John and Lorcan begin to blur, and that terrified him more than anything.

There was one last thing John needed to do before he could finally settle in for the night—check on Sam. The day's events had left him uneasy, and though he tried to push the tension aside, his thoughts kept circling back to Sam. He knew Sam had been working in the church grounds with Henry, and John was curious to see how he was holding up.

John picked up his phone and dialled Sam's number. After a few rings, Sam answered, his voice carrying a tone of reassurance, a sense of worth that John had hoped to hear. "Hello, Sam. How are you? How are you feeling? Any issues today?" John asked, his voice calm, though his mind was far from it.

The two of them talked for about ten minutes, exchanging the usual pleasantries. John was careful not to bring up James directly, but he subtly guided the conversation in that direction, curious to learn if Sam had any news. He could sense the hesitation in Sam's voice when James's name inevitably surfaced.

"I've not seen James, not heard from him in a couple of days," Sam said. "I'm not worried about him, but I'm still worried about me." John offered words of comfort, trying to ease Sam's anxieties while carefully steering the conversation back to James.

"Has he ever spoken with you about his past? His time in prison? Anything else you might know about him?" John's tone was gentle, almost sympathetic, as he sought to extract more information without raising Sam's suspicions.

"Only that he's been to prison and got connected to a lot of people," Sam replied, his voice thoughtful. "Recently, he's been talking about a guy called Shaun, or maybe it was Shane—I don't remember exactly."

John's pulse quickened. "Was this during his time in prison or since his release?" He asked, trying to keep his tone neutral.

"I'm not sure," Sam admitted. "A lot of the time, James just makes things up to sound like he's been there and done it."

John nodded, even though Sam couldn't see him. "OK, thank you, Sam. Good night and stay safe. If you need anything, don't hesitate to call."

"Thanks, John. I appreciate it," Sam said before hanging up.

John sat there, the phone still in his hand, his mind racing. Was there anything to be concerned about? Did he need to worry, or was this just James being his usual braggadocios self? The mention of a man named Shaun—or Shane—nagged at him.

The name, combined with the vague connection to James's prison days, sent a chill down his spine. It could be nothing, just more of James's bravado. But John knew better than to dismiss it outright. His past had taught him to be cautious, to never underestimate the potential danger lurking beneath the surface.

As he finally settled into his chair, John couldn't shake the uneasy feeling that tonight's conversation had revealed more than it intended to. Whether it was a real threat or just the ghosts of his past stirring once again, John knew he had to stay vigilant.

The line between John and Lorcan had blurred slightly tonight, and he needed to ensure it didn't fade entirely. For now, though, he could only wait and watch, hoping that whatever storm was brewing would pass without forcing his hand. But deep down, he knew that if it came to it, he would have to confront his past once more. And this time, it might not be so easy to walk away.

Chapter 9
In the Shadow's Embrace

The next morning, John was jolted awake by the shrill ringing of the phone, cutting through the quiet of dawn like a knife. He reached for it, a sense of dread already pooling in his stomach. It was Sam's aunt, her voice trembling on the other end.

"Reverend, I'm so sorry to bother you, but it's Sam. He's been taken to the hospital. He's unconscious. We don't know what happened, but we think he was beaten up last night. The police are trying to trace what happened."

John felt his heart lurch. "This is terrible news. Where did this happen?" He asked, his voice calm but his mind racing.

"They found him outside the back gate this morning," she replied, her words shaky, barely holding back tears. "A lady walking her dog saw him lying there. She called the ambulance, and he was rushed to the hospital. The police called me shortly after."

John closed his eyes, trying to piece together what could have happened. "I'm so sorry. Which hospital is he at? Which ward?"

"St Bartholomew's," she said, her voice cracking with emotion. "He's still in A&E. They're waiting for a bed to take him to a ward, but I don't know what to do, Reverend. He's in a bad way. Either beaten up or hit by a car. Who would do such a thing?"

"It's going to be okay," John said, though he wasn't sure if he believed it himself. "I'm on my way." John hung up, his mind a storm of worry and anger as he hurried to get dressed. His thoughts kept circling back to James. Could he have done this? As much as he didn't want to jump to conclusions, everything pointed in that direction.

John dressed quickly and rushed out the door. The drive to St Barts was a blur, the 20-minute journey feeling like an eternity. His knuckles whitened as he gripped the steering wheel, his mind racing with scenarios, each one worse than the last. By the time he pulled into the hospital car park, his heart was pounding, a mixture of fear and fury coursing through his veins.

John found Sam's aunt in the waiting area, her face pale and drawn with worry. She looked up as he approached, her eyes pleading for reassurance. "Thank you for coming, Reverend," she whispered, her voice breaking.

John placed a comforting hand on her shoulder. "He's in the best hands now. Let's hope for the best." After a few moments of comforting Sam's aunt, John sought out a doctor he knew, hoping for some clarity.

The doctor, a tall man with a grave expression, recognised John immediately and ushered him aside, out of earshot of Sam's aunt. "John, Sam's injuries are severe," the doctor began, his voice low and steady. "He has multiple fractures—his jaw, three ribs, and his right arm are all broken. The bruising is extensive, and there's swelling around his left eye and temple. He was unconscious when they brought him in, which is our biggest concern right now. We need to monitor him closely for any signs of brain trauma."

John's stomach churned as he listened. "Is he going to be alright?"

"We can't say for sure until he regains consciousness," the doctor replied, his eyes serious. "He's stable, but these are significant injuries, John. They're consistent with a severe beating, not a car accident. We'll know more when he wakes up and we can assess his neurological state."

John nodded, his face a mask of composure, though inside, he was raging. "Thank you for being honest with me. I'll make sure his aunt understands, but gently." Returning to Sam's aunt, John softened the news, omitting the most graphic details. "He's stable for now, and the doctors are doing everything they can. They'll know more once he wakes up."

She nodded, clutching a tissue in her trembling hands. "Thank you, Reverend." Hours passed in agonising stillness. John and Sam's aunt waited in the sterile hospital corridor, the antiseptic smell filling the air, mingling with the tension and fear. John tried to keep the conversation light, but his mind kept returning to James. He couldn't shake the suspicion gnawing at him.

Finally, a nurse emerged from the ward, calling them over. "Sam's regaining consciousness," she said. "You can see him, but only briefly."

They followed the nurse to Sam's bedside, where he lay, his face a mass of bruises, his skin a sickly pallor. As they entered, a doctor was carefully removing a breathing tube, and Sam coughed weakly as it was taken out, the sound raspy and painful.

"Sam?" John whispered, leaning in close. Sam's eyes fluttered open, bloodshot and glassy, but there was recognition there. He tried to speak, but his voice was weak, barely a whisper. "Don't try to talk," John said softly, relieved to see even a glimmer of awareness. "Just rest. You're safe now."

A police officer John knew approached him quietly as they stepped back from Sam's bedside. The officer's face was solemn. "We don't have much, Reverend. No CCTV footage, no witnesses coming forward yet. We're still investigating, but it's looking like a dead end for now."

John clenched his jaw. "Nothing? No leads at all?"

The officer shook his head. "Nothing solid. But we're not giving up. We'll keep digging."

John thanked the officer, his mind swirling with anger and frustration. The lack of evidence only intensified his suspicions. As he watched Sam struggle to stay awake, he couldn't help but wonder if James was behind this, and if so, how much more damage he was willing to inflict.

The thought of it made John's blood run cold. As the day wore on, John remained by Sam's side, his heart heavy with the weight of uncertainty. The tension of the previous night was now a full-blown storm within him. James had pushed boundaries before, but if he was responsible for this, John knew the situation was far more dangerous than he had anticipated.

John would need to confront his past, and possibly James, head-on. The line between John and Lorcan was blurring further with each passing hour, and John knew that the time for decisive action was drawing near. But for now, all he could do was wait, his mind a maelstrom of worry, fear, and a growing, simmering rage.

A few hours later, after a series of tests and scans, the doctors confirmed that Sam was fortunate—there was no internal bleeding or brain damage. Despite the severity of his injuries, it seemed whoever inflicted them either knew precisely where to land the blows or was incredibly lucky.

Sam had escaped what could have been fatal with just broken bones and deep bruising, but the pain and trauma were still very real. Sam was being transferred to a ward for continued care. John and Sam's aunt accompanied him, watching as the nurses made him as comfortable as possible.

Before long, the nurses advised them to go home and prepare a bag for Sam—PJ's, a toothbrush, some books. It was clear Sam would be in the hospital for several days. After saying their goodbyes, John and Sam's aunt left the hospital.

The car ride back was tense, filled with unspoken fears and assumptions. John couldn't shake the feeling that he knew more about what had happened than he wanted to admit, while Sam's aunt was left grappling with the horrifying thought of who could have done this to her nephew.

When they arrived home, John suggested he take her back to the hospital later that day when visiting hours resumed. In the meantime, she could pack some things for Sam. She nodded, still visibly shaken, and went to gather his belongings.

John decided to stop by the shop to pick up a few items—drinks, magazines, crossword puzzles—things that might help pass the time for Sam. As he shopped, he updated Ben, the shopkeeper, on the morning's events. Ben wasn't surprised.

"Given the company he keeps, it was only a matter of time," he said bluntly. "If he was involved in that break-in, then maybe karma has been served."

John stiffened at Ben's words, his mind racing. "Do you really think people deserve to be beaten senseless for petty crimes?" He challenged, careful not to reveal what he suspected.

Ben hesitated, realising the harshness of his words. "You're right, John. I'm sorry. That was out of line." He added another magazine to John's bag. "This one's on me."

The two men continued their conversation, but it was clear neither was fully engaged. Ben rambled on about his shop, the break-in, and the new security system he had installed, while John's mind kept drifting back to Sam, the possible connection to James, and the growing knot of anger in his chest.

"Any news on the break-in?" John asked, more out of obligation than curiosity.

"No," Ben replied with a shrug. "Case closed. Insurance paid out, but my premiums have gone up. I've got better security now, though. If they come back, the alarm will go off, and that thing," Ben pointed to a device on the wall, "will fill the shop with fog. They won't see a thing."

John nodded absently, only half listening. The conversation eventually wound down, and he left the shop with a heavy heart. Meanwhile, Sam's aunt had gone to the summer house to gather his things. The place was a mess, a reflection of Sam's chaotic state of mind. The smell was overwhelming, stale, and unkempt.

She rarely ventured into the summer house, preferring to keep it at a distance, both physically and emotionally. She changed the duvet cover, cleaned up as best she could, and packed some of his clothes and PJ's. As she worked, she couldn't help but frown at the state of the place, her heart breaking a little more with every piece of evidence of Sam's troubled life.

A few hours later, John knocked on the door, asking if she was ready to return to the hospital. The drive back was filled with tentative conversation, mostly centred around the same questions—how, why, who? Sam's aunt kept repeating how he was a good boy, insisting he had never hurt anyone, her voice filled with a desperate need to believe it.

"Have you contacted his parents?" John asked gently.

"Yes," she replied, her voice tight. "His mother—my brother's wife—will visit. But my brother, he won't come. Work is more important, it seems."

John said nothing, but his heart ached for Sam and the strained family ties that left him so vulnerable. When they arrived at the hospital, they made their way to the ward. The small talk they shared along the way felt forced, an attempt to fill the silence that threatened to drown them in their own fears.

As they entered Sam's room, they found his mother already there, sitting in a chair by his bed, quietly sobbing. She looked up as they approached, her face etched with grief. They exchanged greetings, but the conversation was strained, the air thick with the weight of the situation.

John took a step back, sensing the need to give them space. But before he left, he made a point to mention that Sam had been working in the church garden. The news brought a flicker of joy to his mother's tear-streaked face, a small comfort amidst the overwhelming pain.

Sam was awake, but barely. His face was a patchwork of bruises, his body connected to monitors, IV drips, and a morphine pump—carefully controlled due to his history of drug misuse. The pain was evident in his eyes, even though the haze of medication.

John approached him slowly, his heart heavy with emotion. "It's going to be OK, Sam," he whispered, his voice thick with suppressed anger and sadness.

Sam struggled to speak, his voice a raspy whisper, "I didn't do anything wrong; I promise."

John forced a reassuring smile, though inside, a storm was brewing. "I know, Sam. I know."

As he stepped outside, the rage he had been holding back began to bubble to the surface. John clenched his fists, his mind racing with the certainty of who was responsible for Sam's condition. It was James—there was no doubt in his mind.

The signs were all there; the targeted violence, the lack of concern for life, the ruthless intent. James had made it clear that he was a threat, not just to Sam, but to everything John had tried to build in his new life.

The line between John and Lorcan was disappearing fast, and John knew that if he didn't act soon, the past he had tried so hard to bury would come crashing back, bringing with it a violence he thought he had left behind. But this time, it wasn't just about him.

It was about protecting Sam, protecting the life he had built, and ensuring that James never had the chance to hurt anyone else again. John knew what had to be done, but the thought of it filled him with a dread he hadn't felt in years. It wasn't long before the news of Sam's brutal beating spread through the village, and eventually, it reached Jock.

The details were sparse, but they were enough to turn his stomach. Sam—a man with no fight in him, someone who barely had the strength to defend himself—had been beaten so severely that he was now lying in a hospital bed. For Jock, this was beyond unacceptable.

Jock had seen plenty of action in his time, particularly during his days in Scotland, where crossing him was considered a fool's errand. But despite his reputation, Jock had a strict code. His words were his weapons more often than not, and he only resorted to violence when absolutely necessary, when there was no other choice.

Now, if this was James's work, Jock knew he had been crossed in the worst way. He made a few phone calls, reaching out to his network to see if anyone could shed light on what had happened. But it was as if a wall of silence had been erected.

No one knew anything, or if they did, they weren't talking. The lack of information only fuelled his anger. He realised there was only one way to get answers—he would have to confront James directly. This was a bold move, even for Jock, but he had to flex his muscles and show that he wasn't someone to be ignored.

Grabbing his keys, helmet, and phone, he left his flat, still drug-free and still expecting a visit from the police. He made his way to the basement garage, where his motorbike was locked up. He swung his leg over the bike, revved the engine, and began the journey to James's house, the roar of the motor drowning out his thoughts.

A short time later, he arrived. He parked the bike, slid his arm through his helmet—a comfortable way to carry it, but also a makeshift weapon if the need arose. He approached James's front door with the same deliberate pace he used in all matters of business.

He wasn't here to negotiate; he was here to make a statement. Jock banged on the door, four heavy thuds that echoed through the quiet street. "Who's there?" A voice came from inside.

"Open the door and find out," Jock said in his thick Glaswegian accent, his voice carrying a threat of violence.

"Fuck off, Jock," James called out sarcastically from behind the door. "Go play somewhere else."

"Open the fucking door, I want a word with you," Jock demanded, his patience wearing thin.

"I've got two words for you: 'Fuck' and 'You'," James shot back, his voice dripping with contempt.

Jock's eyes narrowed. "What do you know about Sam?" He asked, his tone deadly serious.

James laughed; the sound muffled through the door. "I know enough."

The argument continued, a back-and-forth through the closed door, neither man willing to back down. Jock could tell that James wasn't going to open the door, but he had one more card to play, and it was a big one.

"Did you know he was beaten up last night?" Jock said, his voice cold. "Some dirty bastard knocked ten tons of crap out of the wee man."

James laughed again, but there was a bitter edge to it. "I'd shake the hand of the bloke who did it," he sneered.

"Why don't you show me your hand, James?" Jock insisted, his voice low and menacing. But James was careful not to give anything away, not to show his hand, literally or figuratively. Jock decided to drop his bombshell. "Whoever beat him will be facing a murder charge. He died in the hospital this morning," Jock lied, his voice carrying the weight of finality.

There was a pause, and then James's voice, now tinged with worry, came through the door. "What the fuck?"

"Someone gave him a kicking," Jock continued, pressing his advantage. "The wee man took a beating that killed him. I'm asking again, what do you know about it?"

Silence from the other side. Jock continued to bang on the door, but James had gone quiet. He wasn't laughing now. Jock leant down and shouted through the letterbox; his voice deadly serious, "James, you're next." With that, Jock turned on his heel, leaving James to stew in the fear he had just instilled.

The thought that Sam might be dead was now lodged firmly in James's mind, even though Sam was very much alive in the hospital. But James didn't know that. Back inside, James's mind raced. If Sam was dead, he needed to get out of town before the police came for him.

He began packing a bag, his movements frantic and unsteady. He couldn't afford to stick around, not with the threat of a murder charge hanging over his head. After throwing together some clothes and essentials, James got in his car and drove to the place where the fight had happened.

He needed to see for himself, to confirm that Jock wasn't just screwing with him. When he arrived, he was surprised to find the area exactly as he'd left it. There were no flowers, no police tape, and no sign of anything unusual. James's fury boiled over.

Either Jock had got it wrong, or he had deliberately fed him false information. He sat in his car, gripping the steering wheel tightly, his mind a mess of anger, fear, and confusion. If Jock was lying, then what game was he playing? And more importantly, how was James going to deal with this?

He couldn't afford to let his guard down, but he also couldn't let Jock's threats go unanswered. One thing was certain, this wasn't over. Not by a long shot. James knew that the next move was his, but what that move would be, he wasn't sure yet. For now, all he could do was get as far away from the scene as possible and figure out how to regain control of the situation.

Chapter 10
The Edge of Darkness

Sam was recovering well in the hospital. He was eating and drinking on his own, and if he continued at this pace, he'd be discharged soon. His ribs, however, caused him the most discomfort—each breath, cough, and movement brought a sharp reminder of his injuries.

Still, he knew he was lucky; things could have been much worse. The police came to see him, as hospital policy required. Sam insisted he couldn't remember anything about the night of the attack. His aunt had spoken with them too. Although she couldn't be certain, she suspected James was involved somehow.

The police promised to pursue this lead but didn't seem overly hopeful. A few days later, Sam was released from the hospital. John Bailey had driven his aunt to pick him up and take him home.

"Sam, you look awful," she said, taking in his appearance. His eye was blackened, a few cuts marred his face, and his leg and wrist were in plaster casts.

"I'm okay," he replied with a wince. "I'll be fine."

John found a hospital wheelchair to take Sam from the ward to the car. Though Sam could walk, this was the easiest way to get him there. As his aunt spoke with the doctor, John and Sam were left alone.

"Do you have any idea what happened, Sam?" John asked, his voice gentle but probing.

"No, I can't remember anything," Sam replied, avoiding John's gaze.

"Are you sure? Are you certain you don't remember anything? I'm not going to tell the police—I just need to know if we should be keeping an eye on you. They might come back if they think this isn't over." John pressed on, trying to gauge Sam's reaction. There was something about Sam's denial that felt too rehearsed, too controlled.

"I didn't see anyone—it was dark, and I was jumped," Sam insisted, his voice tight.

"Your aunt mentioned hearing voices the night it happened. She said you left the house with someone—someone stocky, as tall as you. Does that jog your memory?" John asked, though it was clear he was grasping at straws. He was making it up, but Sam wasn't sure if he was telling the truth.

Just then, Sam's aunt returned. "Are we ready?" She asked.

"Yes, let's get home," John replied, casting one last glance at Sam, who was staring out of the window, lost in thought.

As they left the hospital, Sam replayed the conversation in his mind. Did they know what had happened? How could they? It was dark, and he didn't remember seeing his aunt at the window. The car ride home was torturous for Sam. Every bump in the road sent jolts of pain through his battered body, his broken ribs a constant, agonising reminder of the night that had left him in this state.

Each jostle of the vehicle felt like a sharp stab, causing him to wince and clutch at his side. The journey, though not long, felt endless, as Sam counted down the minutes until he could be still again. When they finally arrived, his aunt was quick to leap out of John's car. She hurried around to the front passenger seat where Sam sat, clearly in pain, his face drawn and pale.

"Don't worry, Sam," she said softly, "you'll be inside shortly."

They walked up the garden path to the front door, Sam moving slowly, each step measured and careful. Suddenly, he paused, confusion clouding his features. "Where are we going?" He asked, looking at the house with a frown.

"Home," his aunt replied gently.

"What do you mean? I live in the garden," Sam said, referring to the summerhouse where he had been staying.

"For now, you'll be living inside, where I can keep an eye on you. While you're like this, you're in my care," she explained, her tone firm but caring. "I will look after you, cook for you, and make sure you get your medication when you need it."

"You don't need to look after me, Auntie," Sam protested weakly, the effort of speaking taking more out of him than he expected.

"And when I don't, things like this happen," she replied, gesturing to his injuries. "You've been discharged from the hospital under my care. I've given them assurances that I'll be looking after you. You can't do this on your own. In a few days, if you want to and you're feeling better, you can move back to the summerhouse."

Sam was touched by her words, a swell of emotion rising in his chest. For all their differences, his aunt was stepping up to care for him in a way he hadn't expected.

"You'll have three meals a day, you'll shower—I'll help you if you need me to. And one thing is clear; no smoking, no drugs, and no alcohol. Do you understand?" She said, her voice leaving no room for argument.

Sam was still puzzled at her offering to assist him with the shower but nodded nonetheless. She continued, "While you're like this, I'll look after you, but I'm not going to be your servant. Breakfast will be at 9 am, tea at 11 am, lunch at 1:30 pm, and dinner at 6 pm. We won't be having anything after that."

John watched the interaction from a few steps behind, thinking this was going to be a tough few days. But he could see that she was doing this from the heart. He was glad Sam was in capable hands, though the circumstances were far from ideal.

John said his goodbyes, telling Sam's aunt that if she needed anything, she should call, day or night. He then left, driving the short distance back to his cottage. As he drove, John's thoughts lingered on Sam's expression when he'd questioned him about the night of the attack. Sam knew exactly who was responsible, John was sure of it. But why hadn't he said anything?

Back at his aunt's house, she was fussing over Sam, trying to make him comfortable. She fluffed the cushions on the couch, brought him tea, and even offered biscuits. But Sam was too tired to eat, only managing to express that he wanted to nap.

"Where will I be sleeping?" He asked, his voice barely above a whisper.

"I've made up the bed in the guest room," she replied. "It's upstairs, but you'll be able to manage the stairs. It's a very comfortable room, and it's right next to the bathroom, so you won't have any trouble getting there. I can also leave a bowl under your bed if you think that would be better?"

His aunt didn't have any children of her own and was finding this situation oddly satisfying. For her, it was a chance to care for someone in a way she hadn't before, though Sam found her attention a bit overwhelming.

Sam struggled to his feet, every movement a new reminder of his injuries. The stairs were a challenge—each step felt heavier than the last, each ascent more laborious, stealing his breath. His aunt stayed close behind, offering encouragement.

"Turn right," she called out as they reached the top. "It's right in front of you. That's it, go on in. Sit on the edge of the bed, and I'll help you." Sam wasn't sure what was going on. Was she planning to keep him prisoner? He chuckled to himself at the thought.

"Now, if you swing your legs onto the bed—there, that's it. Just like that, good boy," she said, with the tone one might use with a child. "Now, let's get you out of these trousers and top and into bed. Come on, quickly."

Sam, feeling increasingly uncomfortable with the situation, stopped her. "Can you leave the room while I get undressed?"

"Don't be silly, Sam," she said, brushing off his discomfort. "Come on, let's get these off."

It was clear she wasn't leaving. Sam, too exhausted and in too much pain to argue, gave in. Soon enough, she had removed his trousers and top and tucked him into bed.

"Now, you go to sleep for an hour. I'll come up and bring you tea." Sam was exhausted, not just from the physical strain, but from his aunt's relentless insistence. It was too much. He lay back, closed his eyes, and began to drift off to sleep.

Chapter 11
Sam's Descent

The days following Sam's discharge from the hospital were a blur of pain, both physical and emotional. Each breath sent a sharp reminder through his broken ribs, but the pain in his chest was nothing compared to the seething hatred that had begun to fester in his mind.

James Parsley—the man who had beaten him to within an inch of his life—was out there, free, unpunished, and Sam couldn't bear it. At night, Sam would lie awake, staring at the ceiling of his aunt's guest room, the darkness pressing in on him like a suffocating shroud.

Every creak of the house, every rustle of the wind outside, made him flinch, expecting James to appear in the shadows, ready to finish what he had started. But James never came. And that was what tormented Sam the most—the knowledge that James was out there, living his life without consequence.

The more Sam thought about it, the more the idea took root in his mind: James needed to be stopped. Not just for what he had done to Sam, but for the terror he had brought to the village. For the way he had manipulated, bullied, and destroyed lives without a second thought. And if no one else was going to do anything about it, then Sam would.

At first, the thought of revenge was a distant, half-formed notion, something that flitted through his mind in the dark hours before dawn. But as the days wore on, it became an obsession, consuming his every waking moment. He found himself going over different scenarios, trying to figure out how he could rid the world of James without getting caught.

He remembered the crowbar he had used during the break-in at Ben's shop—the way it had felt in his hands, solid and cold. It would be easy enough to get his hands on it again, to wait for James in a dark alley and use it to bash his skull in. The thought sent a thrill through him, a surge of adrenaline that made his pulse quicken. But then reality would crash in—blood would be everywhere, too much evidence, and too much noise.

Sam knew he wasn't clever enough to get away with murder. The idea of cutting the brakes on James's car came to him one evening as he watched the sunset from his aunt's living room window. He imagined James speeding down the road, only to find his brakes useless, the car careening out of control before smashing into a tree or a wall.

It would be poetic, Sam thought, for James to die in a twisted wreck of metal and glass, just as he had left Sam broken and bleeding in the dirt. But again, doubt gnawed at him. Sabotage was risky—too many things could go wrong, too many ways for it to be traced back to him.

One particularly dark night, the idea of burning down James's flat surfaced in Sam's mind. He pictured the building engulfed in flames, the heat so intense that it would warp the very bricks, reducing everything inside to ash. James would be trapped, with no way out, his screams drowned out by the roar of the fire.

Sam shuddered at the thought, a part of him recoiling from the horror of it, while another part revealed in the imagined satisfaction. But he dismissed the idea as quickly as it had come—arson was too unpredictable, too chaotic. The fire could spread, innocent people could get hurt, and again, it would be too easy to trace back to him.

Sam's thoughts kept returning to the idea of an overdose. It was clean, quiet, and most importantly, it was something he could control. James had a well-known habit, a dependency on drugs that made him vulnerable. All Sam had to do was find a way to give James a dose that was just a little too strong.

It wouldn't take much—just a little extra in the syringe, and James would drift off, never to wake up again. There would be no struggle, no blood, and no noise. And when they found him, it would look like just another junkie who had pushed too far, who had finally met his end in a dirty, forgotten corner.

The more Sam thought about it, the more it seemed like the perfect solution. He knew James's habits, knew where he scored, where he used. He could wait, bide his time, find the right moment. He could even mix something lethal into the heroin—fentanyl, perhaps—something that would guarantee an overdose, something that would make sure James didn't survive.

The thought of it made Sam feel powerful, for the first time in what felt like forever. He imagined James lying there, his body cold and lifeless, and for the first time in days, Sam felt a sense of calm wash over him. This was something he could do, something he could control. And it was justice—pure and simple. But then, as quickly as the calm came, it was replaced by doubt.

Could he really go through with it? Could he really take a life, even one as vile and destructive as James's? The thought made his stomach churn, but the hatred, the need for revenge, was stronger. It whispered to him in the dead of night, soothing his fears, reminding him of the pain, the fear, the humiliation that James had inflicted on him.

It told him that this was the only way to end it, to make sure that James could never hurt anyone again. Days turned into weeks, and Sam's resolve hardened. He began to plan in earnest, thinking through every detail, every possible outcome.

He knew where to get the drugs, Jock, of course, how to prepare the syringe, he had a drug habit, how to administer the dose without drawing attention. He thought about how he would get close to James, how he would make sure that James trusted him just enough to let him near, to let him help him with the needle.

Sam even practised, in the privacy of the summerhouse, drawing up water into a syringe, pretending it was the deadly dose he would one day give to James. He imagined the weight of the needle in his hand, the moment when he would press the plunger down, knowing that he was sending James to his death.

Each time he practised, it became a little easier, a little less terrifying. The fear was still there, but it was muted, overshadowed by the burning need for vengeance. One night, as Sam lay in bed, the final plan began to take shape in his mind.

He would approach James under the guise of making peace, offering him a chance to use in peace, away from the prying eyes of the village. He would bring the drugs and offer them to James as a gesture of goodwill. James, arrogant and overconfident, would never suspect a thing. And when it was done, when James was gone, Sam would simply walk away, leaving no trace behind.

It would be quick, clean, and no one would ever know. But as the plan solidified in his mind, so too did the weight of what he was about to do. Sam felt the darkness closing in around him, the line between right and wrong blurring until he could barely tell the difference.

He was stepping into a place he had never been before, a place where there was no turning back. In the quiet of the night, as the wind howled outside and the shadows seemed to press in closer, Sam made his decision. James Parsley had to die, and Sam was the one who would do it.

He could feel the hatred burning in his chest, a fire that refused to be extinguished, a fire that would only be satisfied with James's death. And so, with a heavy heart and trembling hands, Sam set his plan into motion, knowing that once he started down this path, there would be no return.

The darkness was all-consuming, and Sam knew that when it was over, he might not recognise the man he had become. But for now, that didn't matter. All that mattered was ending James, ending the fear, and taking back the control that had been stolen from him.

Sam knew he would be crossing a line, a line that once crossed, would change him forever. But he also knew that this was the only way to make sure that James could never hurt him—or anyone else—again. And so, with the weight of his decision pressing down on him like a heavy stone, Sam steeled himself for what was to come.

The night of the final confrontation was fast approaching, Sam had decided on a date, a time and a place, and could feel the tension building, a storm gathering on the horizon. He had made his choice, and now, all that was left was to see it through to the bitter end.

In the darkness of his room, Sam whispered a final prayer, not for forgiveness, but for the strength to do what needed to be done. For once, he wasn't asking for help—he was asking for the courage to follow through, to finish what James had started.

As he lay there, the plan running through his mind like a mantra, Sam felt a cold resolve settle over him. This was it. There was no turning back. James Parsley would die, and Sam would be the one to make sure of it. Sam lay on his bed, the weight of the upcoming confrontation pressing on his chest like a physical burden.

His heart was racing, his mind bouncing between excitement and fear. He picked up his phone and typed out the message, the screen glowing in the dim light of his room.

Hey James, how are you?

He hesitated for a moment, his thumb hovering over the send button. Once he hit send, there would be no turning back. This was his only shot at ending things. He exhaled slowly, his fingers trembling slightly as he pressed *send*. The phone screen darkened as he placed it on the bedside table. His plan was now in motion. Despite his racing thoughts, exhaustion crept in, and Sam finally drifted off into a fitful sleep.

The Next Morning

Sam awoke with a start, his body drenched in sweat. His heart still pounded in his chest, though he wasn't sure if it was from the nightmares or the lingering anxiety from the night before. His fingers fumbled for his phone on the bedside table, and when the screen lit up, his heart nearly stopped. Messages. All from James. His stomach churned as he opened the first one.

Why the fuck are you messaging me, Sam? Didn't you get the message the last time?

Each message that followed was just as abusive, filled with venom and aggression.

You still a little bitch, Sam?

Think you can just crawl back now? Fuck off!

Sam's hands grew clammy as he read through the barrage of insults. His pulse quickened as his mind raced with how to respond. The rush of adrenaline made him feel alive, the cold sweat mixing with the thrill of having James's attention. This was it—his only chance.

His window was small, but he had to take it. He wiped his sweaty palms on the bed covers and began typing his reply, his heartbeat pounding in his ears. *Hi James, sorry for getting in touch. Just wanted to say no hard feelings. It would be good to see you.*

His thumb hovered over the send button for a second before he hit it. The phone fell silent again. Minutes stretched into hours, but Sam felt no impatience. He knew this would take time. It always did with James. Finally, a ping broke the silence. His pulse surged. He opened the message from James.

You're a fucking loser, Sam. Why would I want to see you?

Sam smirked. It was working. He could feel it. He typed his response carefully, knowing this was the angle he had to play. *We used to have fun getting on it. You remember those days, yeah? Think about it—when you're free, come to my place.*

There. That was the message that would get him. Sam watched the screen for a long time, his nerves buzzing. He knew James couldn't resist the offer, not with heroin involved. The phone remained silent for what felt like forever.

Then came the reply.

Maybe.

Sam stared at the single word. That was all he needed. The game was now in play, and James was taking the bait. Three days left. The countdown began. Sam's aunt left for her sister's house every Thursday evening at 5:30 pm, like clockwork. It was the perfect window.

He would have four solid hours to put his plan into action. The next few days passed in a strange, surreal blur. Sam worked in the church garden as usual, pulling weeds and tending to the plants, but his mind was elsewhere, constantly replaying his plan.

Every time he thought about what was to come, a strange mix of excitement and guilt twisted inside him. He would feel a pang of doubt, but it would disappear just as quickly as it came. James needed to be dealt with. There was no other way.

He glanced around at the churchyard, wondering if anyone in the village could see the storm that brewed behind his eyes. The villagers were cautious but clueless. They had no idea what he was preparing for.

Two Days Left

Sam stood in the summerhouse, going over the plan once again. Everything had to be perfect. He couldn't afford a single mistake. The syringes were ready, hidden in the small cabinet under the table. He could almost feel them, like a loaded gun waiting to be fired.

His hands trembled as he worked. He hadn't felt this way since the early days of his recovery—like a man on the verge of breaking. He hadn't touched heroin in months, but the pull of it lingered in the air now. Could he resist the urge when it came to it? Could he stand by and watch James destroy himself without giving in to his own demons? His phone buzzed with another message from James.

What time on Thursday?

Sam swallowed, feeling his throat tighten as he typed his response.

7 pm at my place. I'll have the beers on ice.

James didn't reply right away, but when he did, it was simple, a thumbs up emoji. That was it. The trap was set. Now, all Sam had to do was wait.

One Day Left

The day before everything would come to a head, Sam found himself pacing the house, unable to sit still. His aunt noticed the tension in him, but she didn't ask. She assumed it was just residual stress from the beating and his recovery. Sam kept himself busy in the church garden again, hoping the physical labour would quiet his thoughts, but the anticipation gnawed at him like a hungry beast.

He replayed the plan in his head over and over, making sure every detail was perfect. He couldn't afford any slip-ups. James would arrive. They would shoot up together—or so James would think. Sam would be in control, and when the time came, James wouldn't even know what hit him.

The Countdown Was Nearly Over

Sam couldn't tell if he was excited or terrified anymore. All he knew was that the storm was about to break, and he was the one who had summoned it. Sam wiped the sweat from his brow as he crouched beside the rows of freshly planted bulbs.

His hands, covered in soil, moved with precision and purpose, but his mind was a chaotic storm. Beside him, Henry, his elderly colleague, worked methodically, humming quietly to himself. The old man had become something of a fixture in Sam's routine at the church garden—steady, reliable, and always ready with a bit of advice, whether Sam wanted it or not.

It was peaceful in the church yard, a place where Sam often found solace in the mundane rhythm of digging and planting. But today, the peace didn't reach him. His heart raced as the weight of what was to come settled on his chest. The time was drawing near.

"I've been thinking," Sam said, breaking the silence between them. His voice was low, almost hesitant. "You ever done something you didn't want to do? Like something you knew was wrong, but it felt like the only way out?"

Henry glanced over at him, his eyes narrowing with concern. Sam could feel the older man studying him, weighing the meaning behind the question. Henry had always been perceptive, often noticing when something wasn't quite right before anyone else did.

"I'm not sure what you're getting at, Sam," Henry replied slowly, setting his trowel down. "But I've lived a long life, and I've learned that doing the wrong thing, even if it feels like the only way, can come back to haunt you."

Sam bit his lip and shifted, feeling the soil give way beneath his knees. He avoided Henry's gaze, focusing on the dirt between his fingers. "But what if it's not that simple? What if it's the only way to fix things, to make things right?"

Henry's eyes softened with sympathy. "Sam, I know you've had your troubles. We all have, in our own way. I remember when people wouldn't give you the time of day, when they crossed the street just to avoid you. But look at you now. You've turned your life around. Those same people who used to avoid you, they're happy to see you. You've earned their trust back."

"I know," Sam muttered. "It's not about that. I'm just—just asking, have you ever done something you're not proud of?"

Henry was quiet for a long moment, the weight of Sam's words hanging in the air between them. Then, with a sigh, he nodded. "Yes, Sam, I have. I've done things I'm not proud of. Things that kept me up at night, made me wonder if I'd ever be able to look at myself in the mirror again." His voice was softer now, almost reflective.

"But life goes on. You learn to live with it, make peace with the choices you've made. And, over time, the things that seemed unbearable, they stop hurting as much."

Sam's chest tightened. He glanced up at Henry, searching the old man's face for something—maybe reassurance, maybe absolution. But all he saw was a man who had weathered his own storms, who had lived long enough to know that some things couldn't be fixed, only endured.

"I just." Sam hesitated, struggling to find the right words. "I feel like I don't have a choice."

"You always have a choice, Sam," Henry said gently. "Sometimes, it's hard, and sometimes, it doesn't feel like it, but you always do."

Before Sam could respond, the familiar figure of Reverend John Bailey appeared at the edge of the garden, his dark robe swaying slightly in the breeze. He waved as he approached, his usual calm demeanour wrapped in a cloak of quiet authority.

"Afternoon, gents," John greeted them, his voice warm but edged with concern. He had noticed the tension in Sam's stance, the way he kept avoiding eye contact.

"Afternoon, Reverend," Henry replied, wiping his hands on his trousers. "Sam's been working hard today. A lot on his mind, though."

Sam straightened, feeling the weight of John's gaze on him. He shifted uncomfortably but decided to ask the question that had been gnawing at him, unable to stop himself.

"John," he began, his voice cautious, "you ever done something you weren't proud of? Something you had to do, even though you knew it wasn't right?"

John blinked, clearly caught off guard by the question. For a moment, he didn't respond, his eyes flickering between Sam and Henry. Then, with a sigh, he folded his arms and looked directly at Sam.

"We've all done things we're not proud of, Sam," John said, his voice steady. "It's part of being human. But what matters is what you do after. How you live with those choices, how you make amends—if you can."

Sam put his hands in his pockets, his stomach twisting. "But what if it's something that can't be undone? Something that's permanent?"

John's eyes darkened with understanding, though he didn't push for details. "Then you need to ask yourself if you're prepared to live with that. If it's something that'll eat away at you, or something you can justify. But be careful, Sam. The line between what you can live with and what you can't—it's thinner than you think. Once you cross it, it's hard to go back."

Sam stared into the distance, his thoughts a turbulent storm, clashing with the calm exterior he struggled to maintain. He wanted to tell John everything, to unburden himself of the weight he had been carrying for too long. But he also knew that speaking the truth would make it real, and once it was real, there would be no escaping the consequences.

"I've crossed it already," Sam whispered, his voice hoarse with guilt. "I just don't know how to come back."

John didn't say anything for a moment, letting the silence between them stretch. It was the kind of silence that was filled with understanding, with shared experiences too painful to voice. He finally spoke, his voice steady but soft.

"You don't come back the same," John said. "No one does. But you can still decide what you want to be from here."

Sam swallowed hard, the enormity of the decision pressing down on him. "And if I can't?"

John's gaze was unwavering. "Then you live with it. But don't think you're the only one who's ever had to. We all have our scars, Sam. Some are just deeper than others."

The words hit harder than Sam expected. He looked down at his hands, feeling the weight of every choice he had made, every action he had taken. He had been so certain he was doing the right thing at the time, but now, with the consequences unravelling in front of him, he wasn't so sure.

"What would you do?" Sam asked, his voice small, vulnerable in a way he hadn't allowed it to be in a long time.

John sighed, rubbing a hand over his face. "I can't answer that for you. No one can. But whatever you decide, make sure it's something you can live with. That's the only advice I can give you."

Sam nodded, though the answer didn't bring him any closer to peace. The road ahead felt longer and darker than ever, and the way forward was anything but clear. John walked away, his gut tightening with unease. Sam was slipping, and he knew it.

As he entered the church, the cool air and faint scent of incense greeted him, grounding him for a moment. But his thoughts remained heavy, swirling around Sam's troubled expression. He needed to keep a close eye on him—something wasn't right.

A few minutes later, John emerged, his face composed but his mind still whirring. He called out, "Sam, come over here. I've made some tea. Let's talk in the vestry."

They settled inside, the small room dimly lit, with the soft clink of teacups breaking the silence. John leant forward, his voice calm but steady, the tone of a man who had seen too much and cared too deeply.

"Sam, whatever's going on, you have a choice. Don't let it overwhelm you. Talk to someone—your aunt, Henry, me. Write it down, read it back to yourself, say it out loud if you need to. Sometimes, getting it out of your head is the only way to make sense of it."

Sam stared at his cup, his fingers tracing the rim, clearly avoiding John's eyes. The weight of the words hung between them. John pressed on, his voice softer now. "You've come a long way. A few months ago, you opened up to me, and look at the progress you've made. If you're struggling—if you're relapsing—we can help. You don't have to do this alone."

Sam shook his head. "It's not that, John," he muttered.

John frowned. "Then what is it? Does this have anything to do with James Parsley?"

Sam froze for a moment, hesitation flickering in his eyes. "Yes and no," he said finally. "He's been in touch. Wants to meet." Sam deliberately phrased it carefully, not wanting to raise suspicions.

John's expression hardened, his voice cutting through the tension. "Stay away from him, Sam. He's trouble, and you know it. If I could make this choice for you, I'd tell you not to get involved. You've come so far—don't throw it away now." Sam swallowed, the words sinking in deeper than he wanted to admit.

"I trust you, Sam," John continued, his voice low but stern. "But if you go down this road with James, I'm not sure where that leaves us. You have to decide—your future or his chaos. But know this; you're at a crossroads, and there's no turning back once you make your choice."

Sam's heart raced as he sat across from John, the room suddenly feeling too small. His fingers trembled slightly as he gripped the edge of the table, the weight of what he was about to confess settling deep in his chest.

"John," he began, his voice barely a whisper. "James, he has a hold over me. I can't shake it. He's sorry for what he did, and I want to forgive him. I *need* to."

John's face remained unreadable, but he slowly looked up at the cross on the wall behind Sam. The room seemed to still as John made the sign of the cross, his movements deliberate.

"Sam," he said quietly, "some people are beyond change, beyond saving. And when that happens, we have to let them go." The words landed like a hammer, their finality sharp and cold. Sam felt the sting, knowing deep down John was right. But still, he couldn't let go. Not yet.

"Can I be honest with you?" John's voice broke the silence again, now more direct, more pointed.

Sam nodded, his throat tight. "Yes, of course."

John leant forward, his eyes locking onto Sam's with a fierce intensity. "If you go near James Parsley, you're finished. Your life—the one you've rebuilt with so much effort—it'll crumble. You'll lose your comfortable home. You'll be thrown back to where you were—sleeping in that garden shed like before."

John's voice sharpened, intentionally emphasising the word 'shed' instead of 'summerhouse', driving the point home. "And your job—do you really think I could let you keep working here? Knowing what you're getting yourself into?"

Sam flinched as the harsh reality settled in. The gravity of John's words pierced through the fog of loyalty and guilt he felt towards James. He had worked so hard to claw his way back, to earn the trust of the people around him. The idea of losing all of it—his home, his job, the fragile peace he had finally found—was terrifying.

John leant back, his gaze never wavering. "The choice is yours, Sam. But I'm telling you, don't make the wrong one. Don't lose everything you've built. Don't throw away your future for someone who will drag you back into the dirt."

Sam swallowed hard, the bitter taste of truth settling on his tongue. He knew John was right. Every instinct screamed at him to walk away, to heed the warning. But something inside him wouldn't let go of the idea of facing James, of confronting the man who still held power over him.

He wasn't sure if it was about forgiveness, guilt, or something else entirely—but he had to see this through. John watched Sam closely, seeing the battle waging inside him. "Think about it, Sam," he said, his tone softening just a little. "You don't have to go down this road. You've made it this far. Don't undo everything."

Sam nodded, but the tension didn't leave his body. He knew John's words made sense. They were logical, rational. But none of that mattered. Not right now.

"I understand," Sam finally said, his voice steady but hollow. "I'll think about what you said."

John studied him for a long moment, his eyes full of doubt. "I hope you do."

As Sam stood up and left the vestry, his mind was already elsewhere. He wasn't turning back. He had to cover his tracks, get ready for what was coming. The next 24 hours before the meeting with James was going to be long, and the decisions he made from this point on would shape more than just his future—they might well decide his fate.

Chapter 12
On the Edge of Control

Sam woke earlier than usual, his body buzzing with an anxious energy he couldn't shake. His hand instinctively reached for his phone, his pulse quickening as he fumbled to unlock it. Eyes still heavy with sleep, he checked for messages.

Nothing. No new notification, no word from James. He exhaled shakily, the nerves setting in like a slow-burning fire. Today was the day. Today, James would meet his maker, and whether Sam liked it or not, he was part of the plan. His fingers hovered over the screen, scrolling through old messages between him and James.

Each text, each word felt heavier now, like the final notes of a song coming to an end. Should he send something? Just a quick message to check in, to confirm? But it was too early. He didn't want to seem too eager, didn't want to show that he was unravelling inside.

James had a way of sensing weakness, and Sam couldn't afford to show any right now. Not today. He dropped the phone onto his bed and sat there for a moment, staring at the ceiling, his thoughts tumbling over each other. The weight of the day loomed large, pressing down on him like a thick fog.

Get up, he told himself. *Just get on with it.* He forced himself out of bed and into the shower, the hot water doing little to ease the tension in his muscles. His routine felt mechanical—shower, coffee, breakfast—but it was grounding, familiar, and right now, Sam needed that.

He had to pretend it was just another ordinary day. As he sat down to breakfast, his aunt shuffled into the kitchen, her usual warmth filling the room. She smiled at him, her hands busy preparing tea, her chatter light and soothing.

"You know, Sam, I'll be seeing your mother this evening. She's been asking about you. Why don't you come along with me? It'd be nice for us all to catch up."

Sam's stomach flipped. He hadn't expected that. He could feel his heart race again, the calm he had been trying to manufacture crumbling instantly. "Uh, I already told John I'd help him at the church tonight," he stammered, the words slipping out with more haste than intended.

He hated lying, but he couldn't see his mother tonight. Not with everything hanging over him. His aunt paused, her eyes narrowing just slightly, as if sensing something wasn't quite right.

"Oh, alright," she said with a smile that didn't reach her eyes. "Maybe another time then."

Sam nodded, too nervous to push the lie further. His mind scrambled for a distraction. "So, what are your plans for today?" He asked, eager to change the subject.

"Oh, the usual," she said, stirring her tea. "A bit of cleaning, some laundry, and I'm meeting Mrs Wilson for coffee later this morning. Nothing too exciting, I'm afraid."

They drifted into small talk, but Sam's thoughts were elsewhere. He felt the ticking of the clock in his bones, the weight of what the night held gnawing at him. Eventually, breakfast ended, and Sam began clearing the table, his hands moving on autopilot.

He glanced at his aunt, who was already getting started on the dishes, her back to him. Before he left, he hesitated. Something inside him twisted, a strange urge he couldn't ignore.

"Aunt," he said softly, his voice breaking the gentle clatter of plates, "thank you. For everything. Since I came here. You've done so much for me."

His aunt turned, a puzzled expression crossing her face. Sam wasn't one for these kinds of sentiments. "Oh, Sam," she said warmly, drying her hands on a towel. "You don't have to thank me. You're family. That's what we do."

Sam gave her a small smile, but inside, the unease only grew. He felt the pull of guilt, the weight of the things he had done and the people he had hurt. There was so much left unsaid, so much he couldn't explain. And tonight. Tonight might be his only chance to make things right—or see them spiral beyond control.

He left the house and made his way towards the village shop, his feet moving faster than his mind. The temptation gnawed at him. Irene and Ben—the shopkeepers—they were good people. And he had wronged them, been part of something that had shattered their trust in this small, close-knit community. The break-in still haunted him, gnawing at the edges of his conscience.

Sam pushed open the door to the shop, the familiar bell jingling as he stepped inside. Irene greeted him with her usual bright smile. "Good to see you, Sam! You're looking well these days."

"Thanks," he said, his voice tight. He picked up a pint of milk from the fridge, trying to shake off the anxiety. They exchanged small talk, Irene's kindness only making Sam feel worse. He wanted to confess, to tell her everything— but he couldn't.

It would shatter the fragile peace he had built. He wasn't ready to face that. Not yet. He paid, thanked her again, and hurried out of the shop, his chest tight with guilt. He had been so close to blurting it all out, but the consequences would be too great.

He couldn't afford to unravel now. Not with everything on the line. By the time he arrived at the church, the tension was still coiled tightly within him. Henry was already there, his broad frame hunched over a cup of tea.

"Morning, Sam," he said, his voice gruff but friendly. "Ready for the day?"

Sam nodded, trying to shake the fog of nerves clouding his thoughts. "Yeah. Ready as I'll ever be."

They sat for a moment, sipping tea and making idle conversation about the day's work ahead, but Sam's mind kept drifting back to the night ahead, to James, to the decisions he had to make before it was too late. Across the street, in the cottage opposite the church, John stood at his window, watching the scene unfold.

His brow furrowed with concern, his mind still turning over yesterday's conversation with Sam. Something was off. He could feel it. Sam was hiding something, and John wasn't sure how long he had before whatever it was came to light.

The previous day's conversation weighed heavily on John's mind. Sam's words had been vague, yet filled with an underlying tension that unsettled him. John didn't need to know every detail to understand one thing—James Parsley was bad news, and if Sam got mixed up with him again, everything Sam had worked for could come crashing down.

John had seen it before—men like James played dirty games, manipulating and pulling people down into their chaos. He didn't want that for Sam. Not now, not ever.

Standing at his window, John considered his options. A part of him wanted to find James himself, to tell him to stay far away from Sam. But another part of him knew better than to interfere directly. James thrived on confrontation, on twisting people's actions to suit his own ends.

A confrontation might only make things worse. Still, the idea of doing nothing made John's stomach churn. He had been down that road before, standing on the side-lines while someone he cared about made the wrong choice. It had cost him dearly. He cared about Sam. That was the problem.

Sam wasn't just another troubled soul passing through the village. He had potential, a real chance at redemption. John had seen him grow, watched as he rebuilt his life from the shattered pieces. And now, it felt like Sam was slipping again, walking too close to the edge, and John wasn't sure if he could pull him back this time.

"What did he mean, crossing lines?" John muttered to himself. The conversation played on a loop in his head. Why had Sam been so cryptic? Why now, when things were finally stabilising? John paced the small room, his mind racing.

He couldn't shake the feeling that Sam was involved in something far more dangerous than he let on. And it all circled back to James. As the morning light grew brighter, John made a decision. He couldn't sit idly by and watch Sam fall into the same trap again. He would confront Sam at the church, face to face.

He needed to understand what was going on, even if it meant pushing Sam harder than he wanted to. John grabbed his coat and headed towards the door, his mind set. Today, he would get answers. He had to. Before it was too late. At the church, John met Sam and Henry working steadily in the churchyard.

He watched Sam for a moment, something gnawing at the back of his mind, before calling out, "Sam, come and join me inside for a minute." John made his way into the vestry, waiting quietly as Sam followed behind, wiping his hands on his jeans.

"Can I help you, John?" Sam asked, his tone casual.

"Please, take a seat," John replied, his voice steady but serious. Sam hesitated for a second, but then sat down, folding his arms across his chest as if bracing himself. "I've been thinking about yesterday," John began, watching Sam's reaction closely. "About you meeting with James—"

"Let me stop you right there, John," Sam interrupted, his voice firm, almost rehearsed. "I've decided not to see him. You were right. Letting James back into my life would be a huge mistake. Yesterday's talk helped me get some clarity. I appreciate it."

John's eyebrows lifted slightly. The words were what he wanted to hear, but there was something in Sam's delivery that didn't sit right. He was too certain, too quick to cut the conversation off. John had spent years around people who kept secrets—he knew when someone was playing a role.

"I'm glad to hear that, Sam," John said slowly, his gaze steady, searching. "It takes strength to recognise when you're on the wrong path and turn back."

Sam nodded, flashing a brief, tight smile. "Thanks, John. I mean it. I needed that push."

But John wasn't convinced. He could feel the tension radiating off Sam like an electric charge. It didn't add up. But for now, he let it go, not wanting to push too hard too fast.

Sam stood abruptly, excusing himself. "I'd better get back to it. Henry's probably wondering where I've gone."

John watched him leave, a knot forming in his stomach. He couldn't shake the feeling that Sam was hiding something. He knew the look of a man trying to convince himself, and Sam wore it like a mask.

Outside, Sam's frustration simmered beneath the surface. He'd dodged John's questions, but the interference grated on him. What right did John have to meddle in his life? Sam's mind raced, the weight of the evening's plans pressing down on him.

He needed to focus, to stay in control. But he couldn't shake the growing agitation that John had somehow thrown a wrench into everything. After a few more hours of work, Sam pulled out his phone, typing a quick message to Jock, the local dealer he hadn't needed in a while.

Hi Jock, it's been a while. Can I pop up and see you later? Thanks, Sam.

It was code. Jock would know exactly what it meant. Sam's heart pounded as he waited for the reply. Within minutes, his phone buzzed. He opened it, expecting the usual short confirmation. Instead, the message was stark and cold.

No.

Sam blinked at the screen, reading the word again. He frowned and typed back quickly. *Why not?*

A few moments later, Jock replied, his message blunt: *You're off the team. You've got friends that don't want you to play anymore. Enjoy life, Sam.*

Sam's stomach lurched. His dealer—someone who had drained him of more money than he could count over the years—had cut him off. Just like that. No more supply. Who would do that? The answer came to him almost immediately. One name. John Bailey.

"What a cunt," Sam muttered under his breath, fury rising in his chest. "The interfering, self-righteous prick."

He paced in the churchyard, hands clenching into fists, his mind scrambling for an alternative. His plans for the evening were crumbling, and with Jock cutting him off, he had nowhere to turn. Sam pulled up his contacts, scrolling desperately, but there was nothing. No names, no numbers.

The realisation hit him hard—his phone had been scrubbed. Probably while he was in the hospital. He hadn't even noticed until now. Sam was furious, but also at a loss. Confronting John was out of the question. He couldn't exactly march up to him and say, *Hey, I can't score anymore, any idea why?*

He needed a new plan, something to regain control. He couldn't afford to be stuck without a way forward. Not tonight. As the weight of his frustration settled over him, Sam took a deep breath. The night ahead wasn't going to play out the way he'd hoped, but he wasn't ready to back down yet.

He'd just have to find another way to deal with James and the mess he'd got himself into. John had made his move—but Sam wasn't done. Not yet. Sam's mind churned as he stood in the churchyard, his pulse pounding in his ears. The weight of John's interference pressed down on him, turning his frustration into something darker, sharper.

He glanced back towards the vestry, where John was likely still inside, unaware of the storm Sam was wrestling with. It wasn't just about James anymore—it was about control, about Sam's need to take charge of his life, his choices. And right now, everything felt like it was slipping out of his hands.

He shoved his phone into his pocket, gritting his teeth as he considered his options. There had to be someone else, some way to make tonight happen. He couldn't just let John's meddling shut everything down. Not when things were already in motion.

He took a deep breath, forcing himself to focus. The day was ticking by, and he had to get through the next few hours without raising any more suspicion. If John suspected he was still planning to meet James, things could escalate quickly.

Sam didn't need John hovering over him or trying to pull any more strings behind the scenes. With one last glance towards the church, he walked back to where Henry was still working. He'd keep his head down for now, play along. But his mind was already racing, searching for an alternate plan.

The rest of the morning passed in a blur, the usual tasks at the churchyard feeling distant and unimportant. Sam's thoughts kept drifting back to James, to the night ahead, to the uncertainty of what would happen now that his lifeline to Jock had been severed.

When the clock struck 1pm, Sam made his excuses to Henry, mumbling something about needing to pop home for something. Henry barely looked up, too absorbed in his own work to notice Sam's unease. As Sam walked away from the church, his mind was working overtime.

He needed to find someone—anyone—who could help him get what he needed for tonight. But every contact, every avenue he thought of led to a dead end. He found himself walking towards the village shop again, his earlier visit with Irene still fresh in his mind.

The idea of confessing to her what he'd done, of owning up to the break-in, tugged at him. Maybe it was guilt, maybe it was his desire to clear his conscience before things potentially went sideways tonight—but something inside him was pushing him towards the idea.

As he approached the shop, his phone buzzed in his pocket. His heart leapt for a moment, hoping it was Jock, but when he pulled it out, it was James. He hesitated, his finger hovering over the screen before finally opening the message.

I'll meet you at yours at 8pm.

A knot formed in his stomach. It was happening. Tonight, everything would come to a head. He had no idea how things would play out—James was unpredictable, dangerous even—but Sam couldn't back out now. Not after everything that had already been set in motion.

He shoved the phone back into his pocket and turned away from the shop, his mind racing again. The back of the church. It was out of the way, secluded, the kind of place where things could go unnoticed. A meeting there could mean anything.

Maybe James wanted to talk, maybe he had something else in mind. Whatever it was, Sam had to be ready. But the problem still lingered. Without Jock, he was unprepared for whatever James might throw at him. He needed to think of something else—someone else.

There had to be a way to get through the night without falling apart. As he walked back towards his house, an idea flickered in his mind. Desperate times called for desperate measures. He hadn't wanted to go down this route, but if James was going to show up tonight, Sam needed leverage.

He needed to be in control, not vulnerable. And there was one person he hadn't contacted in a long time who might have what he needed. His hand hovered over his phone again, scrolling down until he found the number. He hesitated for a second, knowing what this could mean, knowing what kind of trouble it could drag him into. But with no other choice, he tapped the contact.

The phone rang once, twice, and then a familiar voice crackled through the speaker, "Sam? Haven't heard from you in a while."

Sam swallowed hard, trying to keep his voice steady. "I need a favour. Tonight."

There was a pause on the other end, followed by a low chuckle. "Still in the game, are we? What's the favour?"

"Meet me by the park at seven," Sam said, his voice quiet but firm. "I'll explain when we get there."

There was another pause, longer this time, and Sam could almost hear the gears turning in the other man's head. Finally, the voice spoke again, darker now, with a hint of something dangerous beneath it, "I'll see you there."

Sam hung up, his heart racing. He didn't know if he'd just made a terrible mistake or secured the one thing that could save him. Either way, the night was set. And now, all he could do was wait. As he made his way back home, his phone buzzed once more. A message from John, simple but sharp in its implication:

Remember what we talked about. I'm here if you need me.

Sam stared at the screen for a long moment, a bitter taste rising in his throat. He appreciated John's concern, but John had no idea what he was really up against. And tonight, Sam was on his own. Sam returned to work; his mind laser-focused on the plan unfolding in his head.

Every detail was lining up—he'd procure what he needed, set the trap, invite the victim, and that would be it. He'd call the police, report the overdose, and walk away. It felt like the only way to regain control, the only way to rid himself of the hold James still had on him.

The last few hours of fading daylight dragged on, each minute feeling agonisingly slow. Time stretched as if mocking him, the tension in his chest building as the evening drew nearer. Finally, when the workday was over, Sam said his goodbyes to Henry and John, who barely raised an eyebrow as he slipped away.

Everything was in motion now. As Sam arrived home, his aunt was busy gathering her things, preparing to leave for her visit with Sam's mum. She paused at the door, giving him one last opportunity. "Are you sure you don't want to come with me, Sam? It might do you good to see your mum."

Sam forced a smile, though his mind was elsewhere. "I'm quite sure. I told you, I'm helping John at the church this evening, remember?"

She hesitated, her eyes searching his face for a moment. It was clear she still wasn't convinced, she sighed and nodded. "Alright, Sam. I'll see you later, then." The moment she was out of the door, Sam's calm facade crumbled, replaced by a frantic energy.

He had time now, time to prepare the scene, but every second felt like it carried too much weight. He darted around the house, searching for the key to the summerhouse. He opened the drawer where it should have been—nothing. Panic set in. Where was it?

Sam yanked open drawers, pulling out their contents in a desperate search. He rummaged through cupboards, his frustration growing until his fingers finally brushed against something cold and metallic. He pulled out an old tin from the back of the cupboard, popping it open. The key.

He exhaled sharply, relief mingling with the anxiety coursing through him. There wasn't much time left. He checked his watch repeatedly, the pressure mounting with each glance. Key in hand, Sam made his way to the summerhouse, opening the door and stepping inside.

The air was stale, musty from disuse. It was just as he'd left it before his stay in the hospital, and the faint smell of decay in the air hit him hard. The mess, the grime—it all reminded him of the pit his life had become, and how far he'd fallen before he had tried to claw his way back.

For a brief moment, he stood there, surrounded by the remnants of his old life, disgusted with what he had let himself become. But he quickly snapped out of it, focusing on the task at hand. He surveyed the room, mapping out the evening in his mind. The layout was perfect.

"James will sit there," Sam muttered to himself, pointing to a spot in the corner where an old chair sat. "I'll prepare the junk over there." His eyes landed on a small table by the window, just the right distance from where James would be. "And he'll die there." The words echoed in the small space, and for the first time, the enormity of what he was planning hit him. *He will die there.*

It was a powerful thought, and it sent a strange surge of control through Sam. Finally, he had the upper hand. For years, James had manipulated him, dragged him into the mud, but tonight, Sam would be the one in control. As he went about setting up the scene, his phone buzzed.

His heart jumped as he saw James's name flash across the screen. *I might be late. Gotta do something first.* Sam's pulse quickened with frustration. He hated how James always seemed to be the one in control, even now.

How late? He quickly texted back.

A few moments later, the reply came: *When I fucking get there.*

Sam's hands shook with anger as he read the message, the casual disrespect igniting something deep inside him. "I hate this man," he muttered to himself, his voice trembling with barely restrained rage. "I fucking hate him."

He wanted to scream, to smash something, but instead, he gripped the phone tightly and forced himself to calm down. He had to stay in control. He couldn't let James get under his skin, not now. He took a deep breath and texted back one word: *OK.*

It was all he could do to stop himself from exploding. He had to keep his cool, to play the game until the final moment. And when James finally walked through that door, Sam would be ready.

Chapter 13
The Return of Lorcan

The ancient wooden door of St Mary's groaned as it swung open, the sound reverberating through the hollow, silent church like the mournful toll of a distant bell. James Parsley stepped inside, his eyes narrowing as they adjusted to the dim light.

Flickering candles cast long, sinister shadows across the cold stone floor, and the darkness that pooled in the corners seemed to pulse with a malevolent life of its own. John Bailey, standing near the altar, felt the oppressive presence before he heard the footsteps.

He was arranging hymnals, his hands moving with the precision of a man whose life depended on order and routine. But as the sound of approaching steps echoed through the nave, he stilled, his body tensing instinctively. He didn't need to turn around to know who it was; the very air seemed to grow thicker; the atmosphere charged with the malice that trailed behind James like a dark cloud.

"Evening, Reverend," James drawled, his voice cutting through the stillness like a blade, dripping with a malicious glee. "Or should I say Lorcan?"

The name struck John like a blow to the gut. His hands gripped the edge of the pulpit as he took a slow, measured breath, forcing himself to turn and face James. His expression remained carefully neutral, but inside, a storm was brewing.

"What do you want, James?" His voice was calm, steady, but there was a cold fury behind his eyes.

"What do I want?" James repeated, a slow, poisonous smile curling his lips as he sauntered forward. The sound of his boots striking the stone floor echoed like a countdown, each step bringing them closer to an inevitable collision. "I think you know exactly what I want."

John's eyes hardened, but he held his tongue, letting James play out his hand. "I know who you are," James continued, his tone thick with triumph. "Or should I say, who you were—Lorcan McNally, the man with a past as dark as this godforsaken church. You've been living a nice, quiet life, haven't you? But that can all change. Unless, of course, you make it worth my while."

John's jaw tightened. "You're wasting your time, James. I have nothing for you."

James let out a harsh, barking laugh, the sound bouncing off the cold stone walls, amplifying the tension between them. "Don't play dumb with me, John. I'm not just some thug you can scare off with a sermon. I know all about your past, about the people you hurt, the lives you ruined. And I'm willing to keep that information to myself, for a price."

John felt his patience snap, the thin veneer of control he had carefully maintained for years beginning to crack. "I told you, I have nothing for you. You don't know what you're playing with, James. You should leave well enough alone."

The sneer on James's face grew more pronounced as he stepped closer, the smell of stale tobacco and sour alcohol wafting off him in waves. "Oh, I know exactly what I'm playing with," he hissed, his voice dropping to a menacing whisper.

"You think you're safe here, hiding behind that collar? You're wrong. I can destroy you. One word from me, and your whole life comes crashing down. You've got nowhere to go, John. You're on the ropes, and I'm the one calling the shots."

John's hand clenched into a fist at his side, his knuckles turning white. He could feel the anger rising, an old, familiar rage he had spent years trying to bury deep within himself. His heart pounded in his chest, and when he spoke, his carefully cultivated English accent slipped, the harsh, biting lilt of his Irish roots breaking through.

"Don't push me, James," John warned, his voice cold as death. "You don't know who you're dealing with."

James's eyes widened slightly at the slip, a spark of triumph flickering in them. "There it is," he said softly, leaning in closer. "There's the real you, Lorcan. You can't hide it anymore. You're just as trapped as I am."

The tension in the air thickened, the flickering candles casting erratic shadows as the two men stood toe to toe. The church, once a place of peace, had transformed into a battleground, and both men knew that only one would walk away from this unscathed.

"Get out," John demanded, his voice trembling with barely controlled fury. "Get out of my church."

"Make me," James taunted, his grin widening into something monstrous.

In that moment, something in John snapped. Without thinking, he reached out, grabbing James by the scruff of his neck. He tried to shove him towards the door, but James resisted, his body twisting as he shoved back. The two men grappled, their movements awkward and desperate, driven by a primal need to dominate the other.

James, fuelled by arrogance and a lifetime of bullying, swung his fist, connecting with John's jaw. The impact sent a jolt of pain through John's head, but he refused to back down. The fight escalated quickly. Punches flew, wild and frantic, landing with dull thuds against flesh and bone.

James was stronger, his hits landing with brutal force, but John fought back with a ferocity he hadn't felt in years. Memories of his past, the violence he had tried so hard to leave behind, surged to the surface, fuelling his every move. James landed a hard blow to John's ribs, causing him to gasp for breath.

John retaliated with a vicious punch to James's jaw, sending him stumbling backward. James's eyes widened in shock as he lost his balance, his foot catching on the edge of the pew. As he fell, John lashed out again, his fist connecting with James's chest.

The force of the blow sent James reeling, his arms flailing as he toppled backward. His head struck the corner of the pew with a sickening crack, the sound echoing through the empty church. James's eyes went wide, the life draining from them as he crumpled to the floor, blood pooling beneath him, soaking into the ancient stone.

John stood frozen, his chest heaving with exertion, his mind struggling to process what had just happened. The flickering candles cast an eerie glow over the scene, illuminating James's lifeless body lying in a pool of blood. The church was silent once more, the oppressive darkness closing in around John as the weight of his actions settled over him.

***

Meanwhile, in the summerhouse, Sam's nerves were fraying by the minute. His plan, once clear and perfectly in place, was now disintegrating in front of him. James was late—far too late—and the longer Sam paced the floor, the more his thoughts spiralled out of control.

His hand hovered over his phone, itching to text James, to demand where he was. But he knew he couldn't. *Texting him would show weakness. He'd see right through me,* Sam thought, frustration building with each passing second. He'd met his contact, scored the gear—everything had been ready. But now? Now, it all felt useless.

Sam checked his watch again. His aunt would return soon, and if James didn't show up before then, the whole night would be a disaster. He couldn't afford this kind of failure, not with everything he'd risked. Time was slipping through his fingers, and Sam's chest tightened with a mix of panic and rage.

Finally, the dread became too much to bear. He left the summerhouse, abandoning the scene he had so carefully prepared. His steps were quick, frantic as he made his way back to the main house. Once inside, Sam hurriedly found the key to the summerhouse and returned it to its hiding place in the old tin tucked away in the cupboard.

His hands shook as he realised how quickly his plan had fallen apart. *What now?* Sam's thoughts raced as he rushed to the kitchen. The drugs he had procured felt like a weight in his pocket, reminding him of how badly this night had gone off course.

Without thinking, he ripped open the plastic bag and dumped the powder down the sink, watching as the water washed it away. It was over. His plan was ruined. The control he thought he had was gone, and in its place was the familiar bitterness of defeat.

Sam crumpled the empty bag and shoved it deep into the rubbish bin, making sure it was buried where no one would see it. He felt hollow. He checked his watch again. His aunt would be home any minute now. The day was done, and nothing had gone as he had planned.

***

Lorcan stared at James's body, his hands trembling, his heart pounding in his ears. The air was thick with the scent of blood, the coppery tang mingling with the cold, heavy stillness.

For a moment, time seemed to stretch, the reality of what he had done hanging over him like a guillotine blade. Then, slowly, another presence seemed to stir within him—an older, darker self. Lorcan McNally. John wouldn't be able to understand what to do next, but Lorcan would.

Lorcan had dealt with situations like this more times than he cared to remember, either first-hand or working alongside men from his unit. He was no stranger to blood, to bodies, to the grim calculus of survival. Lorcan's mind began to sift through the options, cold and calculating. The thought of calling the police flashed briefly before him, but it was dismissed just as quickly.

His swollen, bruised knuckles told a different story than self-defence, and the truth would only tighten the noose around his neck. The presence of the dead body was a glaring reason to involve the authorities, but there were countless others to avoid them. No, the police were not an option.

His thoughts churned with grim possibilities, each darker than the last. Lorcan weighed them with a practiced precision, the moral scales long since shattered. The right thing to do, or the necessary thing? There was no contest. He knew what had to be done, even if it sickened the part of him that still tried to cling to the remnants of John Bailey.

Lorcan glanced at the clock. It was 10:46 pm. Henry, the church's caretaker, would arrive in the morning, around 7 or 7:30. That gave him roughly six hours—a narrow window in which to erase every trace of James Parsley's existence from this place.

He couldn't afford any mistakes. The first task was to dispose of the body. Lorcan's thoughts turned to the freshly dug grave in the churchyard, a grim memory of the funeral John had presided over just days before. The thought of desecrating the grave gnawed at him, but the pragmatic side of Lorcan silenced any protest.

It was the perfect solution, abhorrent though it was. Remove some of the dirt, dig down four feet, drop James in, and refill the grave. A disgraceful plan, but one that left no loose ends. Any excess dirt could be scattered around the grounds, blending into the earth.

Other options flickered through his mind like shadows in the dark. Dump the body in the churchyard to be discovered by a passer-by? Too risky. Drive the body out of town, torch the car with James inside? A good plan but flawed. Where would he go? How could he be sure no one would see him?

The fire might cleanse the scene of his presence, but it would leave a burnt corpse—a trail that could still lead back to him. No, the burial was the better option. Bury him deep, and the problem would be solved. No body, no crime. Lorcan felt a sickening calm settle over him as he moved with purpose, his body guided by muscle memory and a grim sense of duty.

He approached the lifeless body of James, his mind calculating the necessary steps with a precision honed from years of practice. He fumbled through James's pockets, finding the phone. The signal would place them both at the church, a damning piece of evidence. He quickly unlocked the phone using James's face, his eyes flicking over the screen.

A series of unread messages greeted him, a litany of threats from an unknown number. *Where is my money? I want my money, you owe me. Pay what you owe, or we will break your legs.*

Lorcan's lips curled into a grim smile as he typed a reply, *No, I'm not paying you. Go fuck yourself.*

The conversation was kept alive, a distraction to buy him more time, to give the appearance that James was still very much alive and defiant. Lorcan read the messages between Sam and James.

"Stupid boy," Lorcan said. "Well, he's not coming to see you tonight."

The night air was thick and oppressive as Lorcan set about his task. He moved to the grave, shovelling away the freshly turned earth. Each thrust of the spade was accompanied by a whispered prayer, not for the dead man at his feet, but for the soul of the innocent buried below, whose grave was about to be defiled.

These were John's prayers, desperate and pleading, but Lorcan was too busy planning, calculating, ensuring that every step he took was precise and without error. An hour passed, maybe more. The grave was deep enough now. Lorcan fetched a black sack from the shed, wrapping James's body in it and securing it with tape.

The body, once vibrant with life, was now just dead weight, another obstacle to be dealt with. He placed the body in a wheelbarrow, the creak of its wheels the only sound in the stillness of the night. Every few steps, he paused, scanning the shadows for any sign of movement.

The village was silent, the night a cloak that hid his deeds from prying eyes. He tipped the wheelbarrow, and James's body slumped into the grave with a dull thud. John whispered a prayer for the man he had killed, but it was Lorcan who set about filling the grave, each shovelful of earth another step towards covering up his crime.

The blood on the stone floor was the next task, but before he could begin, another message pinged on James's phone. *Are you fucking stupid, Parsley? Pay me. Answer your fucking phone.* The threats came with increasing frequency, the calls unanswered.

Lorcan ignored them, focusing on scrubbing away the blood, every drop a damning piece of evidence that had to be eradicated. The stone was unforgiving, and the work was slow, but Lorcan was methodical. He had done this before, in different places, under different circumstances, but the principles remained the same.

The car. Lorcan had taken the keys from James's pocket along with the phone. He returned to the cottage, stripping off his bloodied clothes at the door and stuffing them into the washing machine. He set the dial to the hottest setting, letting the machine do its work as he changed into dark sweatpants, a grey hoodie, and a baseball cap—clothes that James might have worn, a disguise to blur the lines between them.

The village was a maze of silent streets as Lorcan walked towards the car, his steps careful, deliberate. The stillness of the night pressed in on him, every creak of the floorboards in nearby houses, every rustle of leaves making his heart pound in his chest.

He found the vehicle parked where James had left it, slipped inside, and started the engine. He drove with purpose, the car loud enough to be noticed, but not so much as to draw undue attention.

As he drove, Lorcan's mind raced. He could almost feel the eyes of unseen watchers on him, a paranoia that gnawed at the edges of his resolve. He shook it off, focusing on the task at hand. He drove the car into a dimly lit car park on the edge of Jock's estate, slipping out of sight into an old, abandoned garage.

The only signs of life were the occasional shadows of drifting junkies, seeking refuge in its forgotten corners, sending a few more texts to the unknown number before powering down the phone, removing the SIM card, and dropping it down a drain.

Before leaving, he wiped the car clean, erasing any trace of his presence. The walk back to the church was long, the path Sam had taken weeks earlier now trodden by Lorcan. The clothes he wore were the last link to the crime, and he removed them as soon as he was back in the vestry, locking them away in a cupboard, out of sight and out of mind.

A glance at the clock told him it was 4:26 am. Lorcan took a final sweep of the church, ensuring that everything was in order. The blood was gone, the body buried, and the evidence disposed of. Satisfied, he left the church and returned to the cottage.

A long, hot shower and a stiff whiskey awaited him. Lorcan stood under the scalding water, letting it wash away the night's exertions, the water running red as it mixed with the remnants of his crime. The whiskey burned as it went down, a welcome numbness spreading through him. But sleep would not come.

The adrenaline was still coursing through his veins, his mind racing with the events of the night. Lorcan lay in bed, staring at the ceiling, knowing that the darkness he had tried so hard to escape had found him once more. The shadows of his past were back, and they would not let him rest. Not tonight. Not ever.

As Lorcan lay in bed, the events of the night played over and over in his mind like a film on a loop. He felt the adrenaline slowly ebbing away, leaving behind an icy clarity. He had done what needed to be done—there was no room for remorse or second-guessing. John Bailey might have been tormented by guilt, but Lorcan McNally was a man who understood survival above all else.

The soft creak of the old cottage settling was the only sound in the room as Lorcan's thoughts raced. He had taken every precaution, cleaned every trace of blood, and buried the body where it would never be found. But something gnawed at him, a feeling he couldn't quite shake.

The messages on James's phone, the threats, suggested that James had been involved in something far more dangerous than he had let on. Whoever had been hounding James wouldn't just give up when their calls went unanswered. Lorcan turned on his side, trying to ignore the unease that tugged at his mind. But deep down, he knew this was far from over.

James might be dead, but his troubles had just begun. The first light of dawn began to filter through the curtains, and Lorcan knew sleep would not come. He pushed himself out of bed, his body aching from the night's exertions. The whiskey had done little to calm his nerves.

He needed to be ready for whatever was coming next. He dressed in his usual clerical garb, the familiar weight of the collar a strange comfort, a mask he wore with ease. It was almost 6 am, and the village would soon begin to stir. He had an hour, maybe less, before Henry arrived to begin his duties at the church.

Lorcan moved through the cottage, making himself a cup of strong black coffee. As he sipped it, his thoughts turned to what he would say if anyone asked about James. He needed to be prepared, to have a story ready that would hold up under scrutiny.

James had been troubled; everyone knew that. Perhaps he could suggest that James had gone away, fled his debts, or had simply disappeared in the night. It wasn't uncommon for men like him to vanish when the pressure became too much. But even as he crafted his alibi, Lorcan couldn't help but wonder if it would be enough.

The men who had been after James wouldn't be so easily fooled. They'd look for him, and when they didn't find him, they'd come to Lorcan for answers. He needed to be ready for that, to be two steps ahead at all times. The church bells began to toll softly in the distance, signalling the start of another day.

Lorcan finished his coffee, set the cup down with a determined clink, and grabbed his keys. He couldn't stay holed up in the cottage, not today. He needed to be visible, to go about his routine as if nothing had happened. The less suspicion he aroused, the better.

As he stepped outside, the early morning air was crisp, the sky a pale wash of light. Lorcan breathed it in, feeling the cold fill his lungs, grounding him. He walked with purpose towards the church, the weight of the night's events heavy on his shoulders, but his resolve steeled.

By the time he reached the church, the village was beginning to wake. He could see a few early risers heading to their jobs, oblivious to the darkness that had taken place just hours before. Lorcan unlocked the church doors, stepping inside the now-cleaned space.

The scent of cleaning agents still lingered faintly in the air, but the blood was gone, and the church appeared as it always had—a place of peace and sanctity. Lorcan went to the vestry, checking the time. Henry and Sam would arrive soon, and the day's work would begin. But Lorcan's mind was already racing ahead, thinking of what would come next.

He needed to be vigilant, to anticipate the questions that might arise, the suspicions that might form. And most of all, he needed to be ready to deal with anyone who came looking for James. As he stood there, the familiar weight of the collar around his neck, Lorcan knew one thing for certain, he could never let John Bailey resurface.

The man who had fought so hard for redemption was gone, replaced by Lorcan McNally, a man who would do whatever it took to survive. And with that thought, Lorcan prepared himself for the day ahead, knowing that this was only the beginning.

The darkness had returned to his life, and he would need all his wits, all his strength, to keep it at bay. But Lorcan had survived worse. He would survive this too.

***

Sam woke to the familiar sound of his alarm, but instead of the usual grogginess, a wave of frustration washed over him. The events of the previous night replayed in his head, his stomach churning with a mix of annoyance and confusion.

James had let him down—again. Not that Sam was entirely surprised. He should have expected it. After all, James had a knack for disappointing everyone around him. But this time, it stung more than usual. Sam had been prepared, the plan set, but in the end, nothing had come of it.

He swung his legs over the side of the bed, rubbing his face with both hands, trying to shake off the bad taste of the evening before. His mind was spinning. Part of him felt relieved that he hadn't gone through with his plan. It would have been a disaster—he could see that now. But another part of him, the part that wanted control, was still angry.

He had been ready to take matters into his own hands, to end the grip James had on him, but instead, he was left with nothing but frustration. Sam dressed quickly, his thoughts jumbled, trying to make sense of where things stood now. It was over, wasn't it?

He hadn't done anything wrong. Yet, that lingering disappointment gnawed at him, keeping him on edge. James was still out there, still a problem waiting to explode. By the time he arrived at the church, the cool morning air had done little to settle the storm inside him.

He saw John near the entrance, looking worn and pale. Sam forced a smile, stepping closer. "Morning, John," he greeted, trying to sound upbeat.

John turned towards him, his face drawn, dark circles under his eyes. He managed a small nod. "Morning, Sam."

"You look tired. Everything alright?" Sam asked, a sliver of concern in his voice.

John waved it off, his tone firm but polite. "Didn't sleep too well last night. Wasn't feeling myself, but I'm fine now. Thanks for asking."

Sam hesitated for a moment, sensing something beneath John's calm exterior. "Anything I can do to help?" He offered.

John shook his head. "No, no, I'm alright. Just one of those nights." His response was final, his tone suggesting no more discussion on the matter.

Sam nodded and moved on, though the exchange left him with an odd feeling. Something was off, but he couldn't quite put his finger on it. He tried to brush it away as he went about his tasks, but his thoughts kept returning to his phone, hoping for a message from James. He checked it frequently, his nerves prickling every time there was no response. He hated that James still had this power over him.

The morning drifted by in a haze, Sam barely focused on his work. He was too wrapped up in the silence from James and the gnawing sense that something wasn't quite right. At one point, John called him over, his voice cutting through the quiet, "Sam, come here a moment."

Sam wiped his hands on his jeans and made his way towards John, who was standing near the door to the church, watching him closely. "Everything okay, Sam?" John asked, his voice low, filled with concern. "We talked yesterday about the dilemma you were facing. I just want to make sure you're alright."

Sam blinked, surprised by John's sudden directness. He hesitated, not wanting to delve into last night's failures. "Yeah, I'm fine," he lied, forcing a smile. "Thanks again for your concern yesterday. It helped me put things in perspective."

John studied him for a moment, his expression unreadable. "I'm glad to hear it," he said softly, though there was a flicker of doubt in his eyes. "If you need anything, you know where I am."

Sam nodded, grateful for the concern, but also eager to get away from the conversation. He couldn't afford to let John see how rattled he still was. As the day wore on, Sam kept his head down, forcing himself to stay busy, though his thoughts were far from the tasks at hand. Every time he pulled out his phone to check for a message, his frustration grew. What was James playing at?

Meanwhile, John had retreated into the church, his movements slow and deliberate as he made his way to the altar. The weight of the secret he carried pressed down on him, each step heavier than the last. Once at the altar, he stopped, looking up at the crucifix that loomed over him.

His fingers traced the sign of the cross across his chest, his lips moving in a whispered prayer. The guilt clung to him, thick and suffocating, but he couldn't allow it to consume him. Not yet. Outside, the village moved along, its people going about their daily routines, blissfully unaware of the darkness that lurked beneath the surface.

To the world, it was just another ordinary day. But John knew better. He could feel the tension in the air, the weight of what he had done hanging over him like a storm cloud, waiting to break. And he wasn't the only one with something to hide. The village was holding a secret.

John carried the weight of his actions, haunted by the choices he had made. Sam was tangled in his own turmoil, uncertain whether his relief or frustration was stronger. And then there was Derek, resting in peace beneath the churchyard soil, now sharing his final resting place with a man whose life had been anything but peaceful.

Derek's grave was a quiet witness, holding a truth that no one in the village could ever know. Each of them—John and Sam—kept their silence, bound by the unseen threads of the secret they shared. But secrets, no matter how deeply buried, had a way of clawing their way back to the surface.

Echoes of Absence

Autumn had settled over the village of St Mary's with a gentle, golden touch. The trees that lined the churchyard had begun to shed their leaves, a mosaic of amber and crimson carpeting the ground. The air carried a crispness, a promise of colder days ahead, and the scent of wood smoke from distant chimneys mingled with the earthy aroma of the fallen leaves.

Sam arrived at the church early that morning, his breath misting in the chill air as he exchanged a nod with Henry, who was already tending to the grounds. The two men shared an easy camaraderie, built over months of working side by side.

Their conversations were often light, filled with small talk about the weather or the changing seasons, but today, there was a subtle tension that neither could ignore. As Sam worked, his thoughts wandered. He couldn't help but notice how quiet things had been lately.

He hadn't seen James Parsley around. The absence of James, once an unavoidable nuisance in the village, was like a missing piece in a familiar puzzle. It was unsettling, even for someone who had never cared much for the man. When John arrived at the church, dressed in his usual clerical black, Sam greeted him with a smile that was warm but tinged with something else—concern, perhaps, or curiosity.

They stood together in the churchyard, the morning sun casting long shadows as they talked. "Father," Sam began, his voice soft, almost hesitant, "I know you've probably noticed too. James hasn't been around for a while."

John's eyes remained steady, though his mind was anything but. He nodded, his expression composed. "Yes, I've noticed," he said, his tone calm, inviting Sam to continue.

Sam shifted his weight, glancing down at the ground as he spoke, "I mean, I didn't think much of it at first. The man was always causing trouble, and to be honest, I don't think anyone's really missing him. But something feels off."

John listened intently, aware of the implications behind Sam's words. Though James had been a thorn in many sides, his sudden absence was impossible to ignore. He knew he had to say something, to offer an explanation that would both reassure Sam and deflect any suspicion.

"James was always one to get himself into trouble," John said thoughtfully, choosing his words with care. "It wouldn't surprise me if he had done something that forced him to leave in a hurry. Perhaps he crossed the wrong person, or maybe he's been arrested, remanded in custody for something from his past. It's more plausible, considering his history. But don't worry, Sam. He'll turn up eventually, one way or another."

Sam nodded slowly, his brow furrowing as he considered John's words. "Yeah that does make sense," he agreed, though his tone was uncertain. He paused, glancing around as if to make sure they were alone, then looked back at John with a more serious expression. "But there's something else, Father, something that doesn't quite add up."

John's pulse quickened, but he forced himself to remain calm, his gaze steady on Sam's. "What is it?" He asked, the question slipping from his lips with the same composed tone.

Sam hesitated for a moment before speaking, his voice dropping to a near whisper, "James's car, it's still at Jock's house. I thought maybe he'd taken off, but Jock hasn't seen him. And the strangest part? Jock can't even remember when he saw him last. It's like he just vanished."

The words hit John like a blow, his mind racing as he processed what Sam had just said. The plan had been flawless—remove the body, erase the evidence, and make sure there was no trace left behind. But the car, how had he overlooked the car? It was a loose end, one that could unravel everything.

John forced a nod, masking the turmoil inside him. "That is strange," he said slowly, carefully keeping his tone neutral. "But maybe Jock's just mistaken. People often lose track of time, especially with someone as unpredictable as James. Still, it's something to keep an eye on. If the car is still there in a few days, we might need to look into it."

Sam seemed to accept this, his worry easing as he nodded. "Yeah, you're right. I guess I'm just overthinking it. James always was a wildcard."

John offered a reassuring smile, but inside, his thoughts were a storm of possibilities and potential threats. He had to find a way to deal with this new complication before it became a bigger problem. The clock was ticking, and he couldn't afford to let his guard down now.

As Sam turned back to his work, John remained standing in the churchyard, the crisp autumn air biting at his skin. He watched as the village carried on its routine, unaware of the darkness that had settled over it. But John knew—knew that the calm was only temporary, that the shadows of his past were drawing closer with each passing moment.

As he stood there, the weight of his decisions pressing down on him, John realised that this was far from over. The disappearance of James Parsley was just the beginning, and he would need all the cunning and resolve of Lorcan McNally to navigate the dangers that lay ahead.

The conversation with Sam lingered in John's mind like an unwelcome guest, a burning unease that refused to be extinguished. The more Sam had spoken, the tighter the knot in John's stomach had grown, the edges of his carefully constructed facade fraying under the strain.

But he knew he had to let it go—had to stop obsessing over the details and treat this like any other problem that needed to be dealt with and nothing more. Worry would only draw attention, and attention was the last thing he needed. John retreated to his vestry, the small, dimly lit room offering a sanctuary where he could finally think.

Outside, he could hear the sounds of the two men working hard in the churchyard, their voices muffled by the walls. The bonfire they had started was roaring fiercely, a controlled blaze that crackled and spat as it devoured the dead wood and autumn leaves.

John's eyes drifted to the cupboard, where the bag with the clothes from that night was hidden away. It was time. He couldn't afford to keep anything that tied him to the events of that evening—nothing that could come back to haunt him. With a steadying breath, John opened the cupboard and removed the bag. He hesitated for just a moment before unzipping it, his fingers brushing against the rough fabric of the hoodie.

The memories of that night surged back, but he forced them down, reminding himself that this was simply a task to be completed. Nothing more. He took out the hoodie, leaving the rest of the bag's contents inside, and carefully closed the cupboard again.

The weight of the fabric in his hands felt heavier than it should, a tangible reminder of the line he had crossed. John left the vestry, the hoodie concealed under his arm, and made his way outside. The air was crisp and filled with the scent of burning wood, masking the acrid smell of anxiety that clung to him.

The two men were busy at the front of the church, engrossed in their work, oblivious to his presence. This was his chance. He hurried to the back of the church, where the bonfire blazed high, the flames licking hungrily at the air. Without hesitation, John fed the hoodie into the fire, his gaze fixed on the flames as they began to consume the fabric.

The fire crackled louder, almost as if it recognised the significance of what it was being given. John stood there, watching intently as the hoodie began to dissolve into ash, the fibres curling and blackening under the intense heat. His heart pounded in his chest, but he remained outwardly calm, forcing himself to see this through.

As the flames licked higher, John reached for more dead wood, carefully placing it on top of the burning hoodie, ensuring that it was completely covered. He couldn't risk any part of it remaining intact—there could be no evidence, no trace left behind.

The fire roared on, a living thing that greedily devoured everything it was fed. John stayed until he was certain that nothing remained of the hoodie, the flames slowly dying down as the task was completed. It was only when he was sure that the evidence was nothing more than ash that he allowed himself to breathe a little easier.

Even as the fire settled into embers, the unease within him did not. The clothes were gone, the immediate danger averted, but the echoes of that night still haunted him. The truth of what he had done, of what he had become, was not so easily burned away.

With a final glance at the smouldering pile of wood, John turned and walked back to the front of the church. The two men barely noticed his return, still deep in their work. But John's mind was far from calm. He had dealt with this, but the weight of his actions would continue to follow him, a shadow that no fire could ever truly erase.

As he walked back to the vestry, the relief he had hoped for remained elusive, slipping through his fingers like smoke. John gazed over at the grave where James lay, a quiet weight pressing against his chest. The memory of that night flickered briefly in his mind, but this time, he didn't linger.

His eyes moved over the grave, then quickly away. The ground was beginning to settle, the earth gradually blending in with the surrounding soil, as if it harboured no secrets beneath its surface. The grave no longer stood out; it was just another patch of earth, indistinguishable from the others.

It should have filled him with unease, but instead, John felt a surprising sense of calm. The worst was behind him, and with each passing day, the evidence of his actions was being erased, absorbed into the landscape of the churchyard. But as his gaze swept across the grave, it wasn't James that held his thoughts—it was the man sharing that final resting place.

The thought of disturbing another man's peace for this dark necessity had gnawed at him, more than he had expected. So, standing there in the cool autumn air, John murmured a small prayer, not for James, but for the man whose grave he had desecrated.

He asked for forgiveness, for understanding, even though he knew the dead could not grant absolution. The wind whispered through the trees, carrying away his words, leaving the graveyard in its serene, deceptive stillness.

John's eyes returned to the settling earth, noting how it was beginning to level out, the tell-tale signs of recent disturbance fading into the past. The grave was becoming what it was meant to be—just another plot in the churchyard, no more suspicious than any other.

John took a deep breath, feeling a growing sense of contentment and confidence. The danger seemed to be slipping away, just like the autumn leaves that fluttered to the ground around him. But there was one final task to complete before he could fully allow himself to relax. The trousers and shoes.

They were still hidden away, a tangible reminder of the violence that had taken place. He couldn't afford to leave them there, not after everything else had been dealt with so meticulously. They too needed to be consigned to the fire, turned to ash along with the rest.

John turned away from the grave, his steps purposeful as he headed back to the vestry. He opened the cupboard and retrieved the bag once more, pulling out the trousers and shoes. They felt heavier than before, weighed down by the memories and the significance they carried. But he was resolute. With the clothing concealed under his arm, John walked back to the bonfire.

The two men were still working at the front, oblivious to his movements. The fire had dimmed but was still alive, glowing with a fierce heat that welcomed the new fuel. He stood over the flames, feeling their warmth against his face as he tossed the trousers and shoes into the fire.

They caught quickly, the fabric curling and blackening, the shoes melting and crackling as the flames consumed them. John watched, his expression calm, as the last physical traces of that night were obliterated, reduced to nothing more than embers and smoke.

As the fire roared back to life, John felt a deep sense of finality settle over him. The grave was blending in, the evidence was gone, and the past was becoming just that—the past. He had done what needed to be done, and now, with the fire's work complete, he could move forward.

He lingered for a moment longer, watching the flames dance and flicker, before turning away. The autumn air cooled his skin as he walked back to the church, leaving the fire and the past behind him, ready to face whatever came next with renewed confidence.

Chapter 14
Unseen Shadows

The morning air was sharp, biting through the thin fog that clung to the village like a shroud. St Mary's awoke slowly, the crispness of the autumn day seeping into the bones of the town, reminding its inhabitants that winter was not far off.

The tranquillity of the morning was disturbed, however, by the presence of police officers, their uniforms a stark contrast against the muted tones of the village. John sat in his cottage, the warmth of the fire doing little to quell the chill that had settled in his chest.

From his window, he noticed a police officer striding up the narrow path leading to Sam's house. Curiosity piqued, John leant closer to the glass, his breath fogging the pane as he watched the scene unfold. The door to Sam's house creaked open, revealing Sam's weary face.

He exchanged a few words with the officer before stepping aside to let him in. John couldn't hear the conversation, but the tension in Sam's posture was unmistakable. He remained at the window, his gaze fixed on the house as if trying to will away whatever trouble was brewing inside.

Fifteen minutes later, the door opened again, and the officer emerged, his expression unreadable. John's eyes followed the officer as he walked down the path and disappeared around the corner. Something was wrong, and it gnawed at John's insides like a relentless parasite.

Unable to sit still any longer, John decided to head to the church. He dressed quickly, his mind racing with possibilities, each one more troubling than the last. As he stepped outside, the cold air hit him like a slap, but it did little to clear his thoughts.

On his way to the church, John spotted another police officer exiting the village shop, his breath visible in the chilly air. Seizing the opportunity, John approached him, forcing a smile onto his face despite the unease gnawing at him.

"Good morning," John greeted the officer, his voice steady but with a hint of forced cheerfulness. "Cold morning, isn't it?"

The officer returned the smile, though his eyes remained serious. "Good morning, Father. How are you?"

"Quite well, thank you," John replied, though he could feel the lie of it in his bones. After a brief exchange of small talk, John couldn't contain his curiosity any longer. "Is everything all right? We don't often see police in the village."

The officer hesitated, then nodded slightly. "We're following up on a missing person's report. Someone who lived nearby hasn't been seen for between six to eight weeks."

John's heart thudded in his chest, but he forced himself to remain composed. "Who's gone missing?" He asked, feigning casual interest.

"A man by the name of James Parsley," the officer replied, his tone matter-of-fact. "I'm sure you've heard of him."

John nodded slowly, his mind racing. "Indeed, I have. His reputation lingers in the village like a bad smell."

The officer gave a faint smile at the remark but quickly returned to business. "Do you know anything that might help us find him? Any leads or ideas on where he could be?"

John shook his head, keeping his voice carefully neutral. "I'm afraid not. James wasn't exactly the sort of person I had much to do with. But I've heard he had a knack for getting himself into trouble."

"That's what we suspect," the officer said, a hint of frustration creeping into his voice. "He was reported missing by his mother. She couldn't get hold of him, which isn't unlike James, but she kept trying and eventually called us. We're treating this as a missing person case. Either he'll turn up and carry on as if nothing happened, or he's got himself into something he can't handle."

John nodded thoughtfully, though the officer's words sent a shiver down his spine. "Or he's dead in a ditch somewhere," the officer added bluntly.

John's stomach twisted, but he managed to keep his expression composed. "If I hear anything, I'll be sure to let you know."

The officer nodded, offering a polite smile. "Thank you, Father. Have a good day."

"You too," John replied, watching the officer walk away before he allowed his mask to slip. His heart was pounding, the fear of discovery settling like a stone in his gut.

John made his way to the church, his mind swirling with dark thoughts. He couldn't shake the image of James's lifeless body, buried in the earth, hidden beneath the surface. How long could he keep this secret buried as well? When he arrived at the church, Sam and Henry were already there, beginning their day's work.

John forced himself to focus, to appear normal, though the weight of his secret felt heavier with each passing moment. "Good morning, gentlemen," John greeted them, his voice steady but lacking its usual warmth.

"Morning, Father," Sam replied, though his tone was subdued.

John's eyes narrowed slightly as he studied Sam. "I understand from that young constable that your friend James is missing."

Sam nodded, a flicker of unease crossing his face. "Yes, the police came to see me this morning. They were asking when I last saw him and if they think the beating I took a couple of months ago was something to do with him."

As Sam sat across from the police officer earlier that morning, the familiar knot of anxiety tightened in his chest. They had asked about James, and though Sam had answered every question, he couldn't stop the flood of thoughts racing through his mind.

Why hadn't James been seen in weeks? Why wasn't he answering his phone? Sam had sent a few messages to James before that night, asking to meet. He had even planned to kill him—but the plan never unfolded. James never showed. But now, here Sam was, with the police asking pointed questions about the last time he'd seen him.

The words were innocent enough, but the implications pressed on Sam like a heavy weight. Did they suspect him? They had to, right? He had every reason to want James gone. He had a motive—a solid one at that. Years of being bullied, years of being used as James's personal punching bag.

Anyone in the village could attest to the hatred Sam felt towards him. But that wasn't the worst part. It was the fear creeping in, the gnawing thought that maybe the police already suspected him that they were simply waiting for him to crack.

Where was James? Who had he upset? What had he done that made him disappear like this? Sam's heart pounded in his chest as he forced himself to stay calm, to answer their questions carefully. The police didn't need to know about his plan, about the rage that had built inside him over the years.

He had done nothing—nothing, except dream about the day he could finally be free of James's shadow. But James had vanished, and now, it looked like Sam had a hand in it. His fingers twitched in his lap, betraying the nervous energy bubbling beneath his skin.

He was innocent, but the guilt still wrapped around him like a vice. He hadn't gone through with it, but that didn't matter to the police. They saw someone with a motive, someone who had tried to reach out to James before he disappeared. And that, Sam knew, was enough to make him look guilty.

The officers had left, but their questions lingered like shadows that clung to every corner of Sam's mind. Every word they'd spoken had stuck with him, heavy and oppressive, gnawing at the fragile edges of his composure. It wasn't over—he could feel it, a weight pressing down on his chest, tightening with each breath.

They would be back. He knew it. The silence they left behind wasn't comforting; it was suffocating. It felt brittle, like the air before a storm when the sky holds its breath, waiting for everything to break apart.

John's heart skipped a beat. "What did you tell them?"

Sam shrugged; his expression hardened. "I told them I don't know who jumped me and that I haven't seen James since before the attack. I said I don't care if I ever see him again. James leaving the village is the best thing that could happen. Let's hope he stays away."

John forced a smile, though his mind was racing. "I agree. The village could do without his kind of trouble."

Satisfied that Sam wasn't suspicious, John walked towards the back of the church, needing a moment to collect himself. He wandered through the churchyard, the cool air biting at his skin, as he tried to gather his thoughts. His eyes were inevitably drawn to the grave that carried his darkest secret.

The simple stone marker was nestled among the others, unassuming and blending seamlessly into the landscape. To anyone else, it was just another final resting place, but to John, it was a beacon of guilt—a constant reminder of the line he had crossed, the sin that could never truly be absolved.

He paused in front of the grave, his eyes tracing the words etched into the stone: *In Loving Memory of Derek Williams*. The name on the stone now shared its final resting place with James Parsley, though no one but John knew it.

The weight of that knowledge pressed heavily on his conscience, a burden that seemed to grow with each passing day. John murmured a prayer under his breath, his voice trembling slightly as he blessed the grave. He knew it was futile, that no amount of blessings could cleanse the sin buried beneath the earth. But he did it anyway, as if the act itself might bring him a fleeting sense of control in a situation that felt increasingly beyond his grasp.

As he turned to walk back to the church, John caught sight of Henry watching him from a distance. The older man's eyes were curious, his brow furrowed slightly as if trying to puzzle out what John was doing.

John offered a nod, masking his discomfort with a practiced smile, and continued back to the church. But the feeling of being watched, of being scrutinised, lingered long after he had entered the sanctuary.

The Vestry Confrontation

Later that day, as the sun began its descent, casting long shadows across the village, Henry knocked on the door of John's vestry. John, lost in thought, nearly jumped at the sound, but he quickly composed himself, calling for Henry to enter. "Ah, Henry," John greeted him, forcing a smile. "What can I do for you?"

Henry stepped inside; his demeanour polite but with an undercurrent of curiosity. "I just wanted to know if there are any services next week that I should prepare for, Father."

John nodded, opening his diary and scanning the pages. He listed off a couple of services, his voice steady as he tried to keep the conversation routine. But he could feel Henry's eyes on him, sensing that there was more to this visit than met the eye. After a moment of silence, Henry spoke again, his tone casual but probing. "Did you know Derek Williams, Father?"

John's heart skipped a beat, his pulse quickening. He looked up slowly, meeting Henry's gaze, trying to read the man's intentions. "What do you mean, Henry?"

Henry hesitated, then continued, his voice even, "I saw you this morning in the churchyard. It looked like you were blessing Derek Williams's grave. I thought perhaps you knew him."

John forced himself to remain calm, though his mind was racing. "Oh, Henry, it's something I do from time to time," he replied, his voice smooth, though his throat felt tight. "I bless all the souls in the graveyard, offering prayers for their peace. This morning, I must have been standing in front of Derek's grave when you saw me. Just a simple act of remembrance."

Henry nodded slowly, as if weighing John's words. "That's very thoughtful, Father," he said finally, offering a small smile. "I'm sure it brings comfort to many. Thank you for your time."

John returned the smile, though it didn't reach his eyes. "Of course, Henry. Let me know if you need anything else."

As Henry left the vestry, closing the door quietly behind him, John let out a huge sigh, the tension in his chest releasing slightly. He leant back in his chair, his head in his hands, feeling the weight of his secrets pressing down on him with renewed force.

"This isn't going to go away," he muttered to himself, his voice barely above a whisper. The secrets he had buried were beginning to rise to the surface, and he knew that no amount of prayers or blessings could keep them hidden forever. As the shadows lengthened outside, John was left alone with his thoughts, the once comforting walls of the vestry now feeling more like a prison.

The Discovery

The evening shadows deepened as the village settled into the quiet of another night, but the tranquillity that usually draped St Mary's was fractured by the hushed urgency of police activity.

Not far from the church, in the dingy, rundown car park near Jock's flat, a discovery had been made—James Parsley's car, abandoned, its once vibrant paint now dulled by weeks of neglect, was drawing unwanted attention.

A pair of uniformed officers stood guard by the vehicle, their breath fogging in the cool air as they awaited the arrival of the forensics team. The surrounding area, with its litter-strewn pathways and faded graffiti, seemed even more desolate under the harsh beams of their torches.

The car had been found just hours earlier, but already, it had become a focal point of the investigation. As the forensic van finally pulled up, its headlights cutting through the gloom, the officers exchanged grim looks. This was no longer just a routine check; it was the beginning of something far more serious.

The team began their methodical work, donning gloves and masks as they approached the car with measured steps. The air around them seemed to grow colder, the scent of decay hanging faintly as they prepared to delve into the secrets the car might hold.

The Discovery and the Call

As the sun dipped low in the sky, casting a golden hue over the estate, the police had already begun their investigation. The discovery of James Parsley's abandoned car had sent ripples of unease through the quiet village. For Jock, a local drug dealer, the sight of police on his turf was both anticipated and dreaded.

He'd been smart enough to clear out all traces of his dealings from the flat weeks ago, sensing that sooner or later, the law would come knocking. But this wasn't supposed to be about him—at least, not yet. The police, however, were systematic.

They combed through the car park with methodical precision, inspecting the car and its surroundings while it was still light. The dull, dirty exterior of the car only hinted at the secrets it might hold.

As the forensic team finished their initial sweep, the car was loaded onto a truck to be taken away for further examination. Officers continued to search the estate, their eyes sharp and inquisitive, but they found nothing of immediate concern.

The Knock on Jock's Door

Inside his dimly lit flat, Jock was a coiled spring of nerves. He had been watching the police from behind grimy curtains, his stomach churning with a mixture of fear and anger. He knew they'd come for him eventually, and he was ready to play it cool.

What he hadn't anticipated was the discovery of James's car right on his doorstep. A sudden knock on the door sent a shockwave of panic through him. Jock froze, the lukewarm can of lager in his hand almost slipping from his grip. His mind raced—had he missed something when he cleared out the flat? Was there anything left that could incriminate him? He'd been careful, meticulous even, but doubt gnawed at him as he approached the door.

"Who is it?" He called out, trying to keep the tremor from his voice.

"Police. Open the door, please."

Jock's heart sank. He knew better than to ignore them, and as much as he wanted to, there was no way out of this. He swore under his breath, steeling himself as he turned the handle and opened the door. Two uniformed officers stood on his threshold, their expressions serious, their eyes scanning him with suspicion.

"What do you want?" Jock growled, leaning against the doorframe, trying to appear nonchalant despite the dread churning in his gut.

"Good evening, Mr Davies," one of the officers said, his tone polite but firm. "We're investigating the disappearance of James Parsley. We'd like to ask you a few questions. Can we come in?"

Jock crossed his arms, his eyes narrowing further. "No, you can't," he replied bluntly. "Not without a warrant."

The officers exchanged a brief glance, their expressions hardening. The taller of the two took a step closer, his voice lowering to a more threatening tone. "You know how this works, Jock. We're not here for a raid, but if we suspect there's anything illegal in this flat, we can have twenty officers here in two minutes, and your place will be turned upside down."

Jock forced a bitter laugh, though there was little humour in it. "Flat's already trashed," he said, gesturing vaguely behind him. "Courtesy of my lack of desire to clean."

The officers didn't so much as crack a smile. Instead, they waited, the silence pressing down on Jock like a weight. He knew he had no real choice. With a grunt of resignation, he stepped aside and opened the door wider. "Fine, come in. But I'm not saying anything without a lawyer."

The officers stepped inside, their eyes scanning the flat with practiced efficiency. The room was as much of a mess as Jock had warned—cluttered and dirty, with an air of neglect that spoke volumes about its occupant. But the officers weren't there to critique his housekeeping. They were there for answers. They began with direct questions, cutting straight to the point.

"When was the last time you saw James Parsley?" The taller officer asked, his tone firm.

Jock shrugged, trying to appear indifferent. "I haven't seen him in weeks. Though he might've done a runner."

"Did you sell him any drugs recently?" The other officer asked, his eyes narrowing.

"No," Jock said firmly, shaking his head. "I've been keeping my head down. Haven't been dealing from here for a while."

The officers exchanged another glance, as if weighing the truth of his words. "How long has his car been parked outside?" The first officer continued, his voice pressing.

"Dunno," Jock replied, feigning ignorance. "Noticed it a few days ago. Didn't think much of it. Like I said, I mind my own business."

The second officer stepped forward; his tone more insistent. "Do you know where he might be? Did he mention anything to you about where he was going?"

Jock shook his head again, his frustration bubbling to the surface. "I told you, I don't know. He didn't say anything to me."

"Does he owe you money?" The officer probed, his gaze sharp.

Jock hesitated for a fraction of a second, but quickly masked it. "Yeah, but so what? James owes everyone money. Doesn't mean I know where he is."

The questions kept coming, each one more probing than the last. Jock's patience wore thin, and his responses became shorter, more clipped. Finally, he'd had enough.

"Look," Jock said, his voice hardening. "I don't know anything. If you want to question me further, arrest me and take me to the nick. We can talk there in front of my lawyer."

The taller officer narrowed his eyes, leaning in slightly. "This isn't just about you, Jock. We're investigating a missing person. It's crucial we find out anything you might know to piece this together and find James. If there's anything you haven't told us—anything at all—you'd better speak up now."

Jock met his gaze defiantly, though his stomach churned with unease. "I've told you everything I know. You've got nothing on me."

The officer stared at him for a long moment, then nodded curtly. "For now," he said, his voice laced with warning. "But don't think we're done here."

With that, the officers turned and left the flat, leaving Jock standing in the middle of his living room, his heart pounding in his chest. He let out a long breath, running a hand through his greasy hair. This was bad. Really bad. If the police were sniffing around James, it was only a matter of time before things got even more complicated.

Outside: The Forensic Investigation

As Jock tried to steady his nerves, the forensic team outside was meticulously combing through James's car. They worked in silence, their movements precise and methodical, as they photographed the vehicle from every angle, dusted for fingerprints, and searched for any signs of foul play.

The car itself was a grim sight—dirtied, neglected, and abandoned, with no indication of where its owner might be. The windows were fogged with grime, the tyres slightly deflated, and inside, the faint scent of stale tobacco and something sour lingered in the air.

One of the forensic officers opened the boot, his gloved hands moving carefully as he examined its contents. There wasn't much—just a few crumpled fast food wrappers, an empty water bottle, and a worn-out jacket. But even the smallest details could be significant, and the team treated every item with the same level of scrutiny.

The forensic officer paused, noticing something small and shiny wedged between the seats. He reached for it with a pair of tweezers, carefully extracting a tiny silver pendant, tarnished and scratched, as though it had been dropped in haste.

He held it up to the light, examining the intricate design—an angel, wings spread, with a tiny, barely visible cross at its centre. It was a strange and delicate thing, something that seemed out of place in the grimy surroundings. The officer bagged the pendant, marking it as evidence, and moved on to the rest of the car.

As they continued their search, the forensic team knew that whatever they found here might be crucial in piecing together the last moments of James Parsley's life—or, at the very least, in figuring out where he had gone. Every detail, no matter how small, could be the key to solving the mystery that had gripped this quiet village.

Back in the Village

The discovery of the car had not gone unnoticed by the villagers. Word had spread quickly, and now, as the evening drew on, small groups of people had gathered in hushed conversations, their faces etched with concern and speculation.

The once peaceful village of St Mary's was now abuzz with rumours, each one more outlandish than the last. John kept to himself; his mind preoccupied with the implications of the day's events. He had already known that the investigation would eventually touch upon James's disappearance, but the discovery of the car had escalated matters far more quickly than he had anticipated.

As he walked back to his cottage, John felt the weight of his secrets pressing down on him like never before. Every footstep echoed in the quiet streets, the sound of his shoes against the pavement a reminder that the facade of normalcy was slipping away.

The Rising Tension

That night, as the village settled into an uneasy silence, John sat in his study, staring at the flickering flames in the fireplace. The heat did little to warm him; the chill that had settled in his bones was far deeper than anything the fire could touch.

The discovery of James's car was a tipping point, a sign that the secrets he had buried so carefully were beginning to surface. He had always known this day would come, but the reality of it was far more terrifying than he had imagined. John had spent years hiding the truth, covering his tracks, and maintaining the facade of a pious man.

Now, with the police closing in and the villagers whispering behind closed doors, he could feel the noose tightening around his neck. He picked up his Bible, the worn leather cover cool against his fingertips, and opened it to a passage that had always brought him comfort.

As he read the familiar words, they felt hollow, their meaning slipping through his fingers like sand. John knew that his faith alone would not save him. The sins he had committed, the lies he had told, the lives he had destroyed—they were all coming back to haunt him. And there was no escape.

As the flames in the fireplace crackled and danced, John closed his eyes, a single tear slipping down his cheek. He was trapped in a nightmare of his own making, and there was no one left to save him.

The walls of the vestry, once a sanctuary, now felt like a prison, closing in around him. As the darkness of the night pressed in, John realised that the shadows he had spent so long hiding from, were finally catching up to him.

Chapter 15
The Weight of Suspicion

The crisp morning air hung heavily over St Mary's as the village began to stir. The low hum of conversation buzzed through the streets, with the discovery of James Parsley's abandoned car quickly becoming the talk of the town. But for Sam Taylor, the morning brought no such ease.

He awoke with a sense of foreboding, the knot in his stomach tightening with each passing minute. He had been expecting something like this, but when it had finally happened, it was far more terrifying than he had imagined.

The Knock at the Door

The knock at Sam's door was firm, authoritative—an unmistakable sound that instantly set his heart racing. He hesitated for a moment, his mind scrambling for a reason to delay the inevitable, but the knock came again, more insistent this time. When he finally opened the door, he was greeted by the stern faces of two police officers, their expressions giving nothing away.

"Sam Taylor?" One of them asked, though it was clear they already knew who he was.

"Yes," Sam replied, his voice barely above a whisper, his throat suddenly dry.

"We need you to come with us to the station. We have some questions about James Parsley."

The words hit Sam like a punch to the gut. His worst fears were being realised, and there was nothing he could do to stop it. He nodded, too stunned to argue, and allowed the officers to lead him out of the house. As they guided him to the waiting car, he caught sight of a few neighbours watching from their windows, their faces a mix of curiosity and concern.

The weight of their gazes felt like a noose tightening around his neck. Inside the car, Sam's mind raced, a whirlpool of dread swirling in his thoughts. Had they found something? Did they know about the break-in at the village shop? The memory of that night clawed at him, more vivid than ever—the way James had insisted, had practically forced him to go along with the plan.

Sam had wanted no part of it, but James had made it clear that he had no choice. They had stolen cigarettes and alcohol, trivial things in the grand scheme, but the guilt had gnawed at Sam ever since. He tried to keep his breathing steady, but the panic was beginning to take hold.

Every second felt like an hour as they drove towards the station, the reality of his situation closing in around him like a vice. His mind kept returning to the break-in. What if the police had connected him to it? What if they knew? He had worked so hard to rebuild his life, to earn the respect of the village after being just another troubled young man.

Now, it felt like everything was teetering on the edge of collapse. His hands trembled slightly as he clenched them into fists, trying to calm the storm raging inside him. The last thing he wanted was to confess, but the fear of being caught, of having his life unravel in front of him, made the temptation almost unbearable.

He had nearly let it slip during the interview, the pressure of the questions pushing him closer to the edge. But he knew that confessing now would destroy everything he had tried to rebuild. As the car pulled into the station, Sam felt a cold sweat break out on his forehead.

The officers got out, guiding him through the entrance and down the sterile, echoing corridors. His heart pounded in his chest, each beat a reminder that the truth he was hiding was too much for him to bear.

He didn't know what the police had on him—whether it was about the break-in or James's disappearance—but he knew one thing for certain; his life was hanging by a thread, and one wrong move could cut it short.

The Interrogation Begins

The interrogation room was small, stark, and cold—designed to unsettle, to strip away any semblance of comfort. The fluorescent lights buzzed overhead, casting harsh shadows on the bare walls. Sam was seated at a metal table, his hands trembling slightly as he gripped the edge.

Across from him sat Detective Inspector Harris, a seasoned officer with sharp eyes that seemed to miss nothing. Harris opened a thin file and began to speak, his tone measured but probing.

"Sam, we've been looking into James Parsley's disappearance. We understand you had an altercation with him not long before he went missing."

Sam swallowed hard, his mouth dry. "He attacked me," he said, his voice shaky but resolute. "Put me in hospital. But I haven't seen him since."

Harris leant forward, his gaze never leaving Sam's face. "We have a witness who saw James near his car the night he disappeared, not far from Jock Davies's flat. The description of the man with him fits you. Can you explain that?"

Sam felt the room closing in on him, the walls pressing down with invisible force. He knew denying it outright would make him look guilty, but admitting anything could be just as dangerous. His mind raced for an answer that would satisfy the detective without incriminating himself.

"I don't remember seeing James that night," Sam stammered, his voice betraying the fear bubbling beneath the surface. "It was dark, and I was still recovering. I didn't go near Jock's place."

Harris's eyes narrowed, his tone growing more insistent. "You've got a motive, Sam. He put you in the hospital. People have killed for less."

Sam shook his head vehemently, his desperation growing. "I wouldn't hurt him. I just wanted to stay away from him. I've got nothing to do with this."

The detective paused, as if weighing Sam's words, then opened the file in front of him. He began to read aloud, his voice steady, each word landing like a blow, "James Parsley was involved with some dangerous people, Sam. We found messages on his phone—threats, demands for payment. This wasn't just a fight between two men; this was something bigger. And you're caught up in it, whether you like it or not."

Sam's heart pounded in his chest. He knew James had been in trouble, but he hadn't realised the extent of it. "I swear, I don't know anything about his debts," Sam insisted, his voice barely above a whisper. "He kept that part of his life away from me."

Harris leant back, his gaze still fixed on Sam, unyielding. "Then tell me about the night he attacked you. Start from the beginning."

Sam took a deep breath, trying to steady himself. His hands were shaking now, and he clasped them together, hoping the detective wouldn't notice. "It was late," Sam began, his voice trembling. "James called me, said we needed to meet. He promised nothing would happen, said we just needed to talk."

Harris nodded, encouraging him to continue. "Where did you meet?"

"At my summerhouse," Sam replied, his eyes unfocused as he recalled the details. "That's where I was staying before the attack. My aunt, she let me stay in the main house after, so she could take care of me."

"And what happened when James arrived?" Harris pressed, his voice calm but insistent.

Sam hesitated; the memory of that night still vivid, still painful. "He lured me outside," he said slowly, his voice barely above a whisper. "He was calm at first, but when we left the garden, his mood changed. He grabbed me. His face twisted with anger. He said he was going to kill me."

Harris's eyes narrowed. "And then?"

"I tried to get away," Sam continued, his voice shaking. "But he was too strong. He punched me, and I fell. Then he just, he just kept hitting me. Punching, kicking. I couldn't fight back. I tried, but it was no use. The last thing I remember is him standing over me, and then, nothing. The next thing I knew, I was in the hospital."

The room fell silent for a moment, the weight of Sam's words hanging in the air. Harris studied him closely, searching for any sign of deception, but all he saw was fear—raw, unfiltered fear.

"Sam," Harris said finally, his tone softer but still probing, "if that's the last time you saw James, then where do you think he is now? Do you have any idea what might have happened to him after that night?"

Sam shook his head, his eyes filled with desperation. "I don't know," he insisted. "I haven't seen him since that night. I've been trying to put it behind me, trying to move on. But I swear, I don't know where he is."

Harris leant back in his chair, his gaze never leaving Sam's face. "You understand why we're asking these questions, don't you? You have a strong motive—James nearly killed you. And now he's disappeared. We have to consider every possibility."

Sam nodded, though the fear in his eyes was unmistakable. "I get it," he said quietly. "But I'm telling you the truth. I didn't do anything to him. I don't know where he is."

The detective sighed, closing the file in front of him. "For now, we're keeping you here until we can sort this out. You're not under arrest, but you're not free to leave, either. We need to look into this further."

Sam felt the floor drop out from under him. The weight of his situation pressed down on him like a heavy stone, and he felt a cold sweat break out on his forehead. He had told them everything he knew, but it wasn't enough. They didn't believe him. He was trapped.

The Church: John's Perspective

Across the village, John Bailey watched the events unfold with a mixture of concern and relief. He had seen the police arrive at Sam's house, watched as they led him away in handcuffs. The sight should have filled him with dread, but instead, he felt a strange sense of satisfaction.

The focus was shifting away from him and onto someone else, and for the first time in weeks, he felt a glimmer of hope that he might escape unscathed. As the police officers entered the house with a search warrant, John found himself watching from the safety of the church.

The familiar surroundings of the sanctuary offered him comfort, the weight of his collar a reminder of the role he played in this community. He had spent years cultivating an image of piety and respectability, and now, that image was his shield. But beneath the calm exterior, John's mind was racing.

He knew Sam was innocent of James's disappearance, but he also knew that the police wouldn't stop until they had a suspect. And Sam, with his troubled past and his violent history with James, was the perfect target. John found himself torn between the desire to help Sam and the instinct to protect himself.

He had buried James's body, hidden the evidence, and covered his tracks, but now, with the police circling, he couldn't afford to make a mistake. As he watched the police search Sam's house, John's thoughts drifted back to the night of James's death.

The memory of that night was still fresh, the fear and adrenaline still coursing through his veins. He had done what needed to be done, and he had done it well. But now, as the investigation intensified, he couldn't shake the feeling that he was standing on the edge of a precipice, one wrong move away from disaster.

The search continued for what felt like hours, the police combing through every inch of Sam's house, looking for anything that might tie him to James's disappearance. John watched from the shadows, his heart pounding in his chest.

He knew he should feel guilty, should feel some sense of responsibility for the situation Sam was in, but all he felt was a cold, calculated satisfaction. The more the police focused on Sam, the less they would focus on him. And that was exactly what he needed.

The Release

By the time the police finished their search and returned to the station, Sam was exhausted, physically and emotionally. He had been questioned for hours, his every word dissected, his every action scrutinised. And yet, they had found nothing—no evidence, no witness, no confession.

They had only his story, a story that was damning in its own way, but not enough to hold him. Harris sat across from him once more, his expression unreadable.

"Sam," he said slowly, "we're going to release you on police bail. You're not being charged with anything at this time."

Sam nodded numbly, too drained to argue. The words barely registered as he was led out of the station and into the cold night air. He was free, but the weight of suspicion still hung over him like a dark cloud. The village that had once been his home now felt like a prison, the eyes of its residents following his every move.

As he walked back to his aunt's house, the events of the day played over and over in his mind, each detail magnified, each word echoing in his ears. He knew the police were far from done with him, knew that this was only the beginning.

With each step he took, the fear that had been gnawing at him for weeks grew stronger, more insistent. He was caught in a web of lies and half-truths, and there was no way out.

The Police Discussion

Back at the station, Harris and his team gathered to discuss the day's events. The room was filled with the hum of conversation, the clatter of paperwork, the steady ticking of the clock on the wall.

"Sam Taylor is definitely hiding something," Harris said, his voice carrying a note of frustration. "His story is too neat, too rehearsed. He's been through hell, no doubt about it, but I think there's more to this than he's letting on."

One of the other officers, a younger man named Collins, nodded in agreement. "We've got motive, we've got opportunity. But we're missing the connection. If he's involved in James's disappearance, where's the body? Where's the evidence?"

Harris sighed, running a hand through his thinning hair. "That's the problem. We don't have enough to charge him, but we can't let him go, either. We need to dig deeper, find out what he's not telling us. And we need to figure out who else is involved. There's no way he did this alone."

The room fell silent for a moment as the weight of the investigation settled over them. They were close—so close—but the missing pieces of the puzzle were still just out of reach.

"We need to keep the pressure on him," Harris said finally. "He'll crack eventually. People like him always do."

The others nodded in agreement, their resolve hardening. They had a suspect, but the case was far from closed. Until they found the truth, they wouldn't rest.

The Darkness Returns

As Sam lay in bed that night, staring up at the ceiling, the events of the day played over and over in his mind. He was free, but the fear that had taken root in his heart refused to let go. Every sound, every shadow seemed to carry a threat, and sleep eluded him.

In the darkness, he could feel the weight of the police's suspicion pressing down on him, could feel the eyes of the village watching his every move. He was trapped, caught in a nightmare that had no end.

Somewhere in the shadows, John Bailey watched, his mind racing with plans and contingencies. He had shifted the focus away from himself, but the danger was far from over. The shadows of his past were closing in, and he knew that sooner or later, the truth would come to light.

Until then, he would play his part, hiding in plain sight, protecting his secrets at all costs. For now, the darkness was his ally. But even allies could turn on you when you least expected it.

The Residents' Meeting

The afternoon sun filtered through the windows of the St Mary's Community Centre, casting a warm glow over the assembled members of the Residents'

Committee. The room, a modest space with pale walls and wooden floors, was filled with the low murmur of conversation as the meeting ended.

It had been a routine gathering, with discussions ranging from the upcoming village fete to the maintenance of the village green. As usual, John Bailey and Sergeant Mike Porter sat side by side, both men longstanding members of the committee.

John had been his usual composed self throughout the meeting, contributing to discussions with his typical calm authority. The other members of the committee respected him, not just as the village vicar, but as a voice of reason and stability.

Mike, too, had played his part, offering updates on community safety and addressing concerns about recent incidents of petty theft. As the meeting wound down, the chairperson, Mrs Wilkins, thanked everyone for their attendance and reminded them of the next meeting's date.

Chairs scraped against the floor as the committee members began to gather their belongings, exchanging pleasantries as they prepared to leave. John, however, lingered behind, his mind working over the events of the past few days. He knew this was an opportunity he couldn't let slip by.

As the room gradually emptied, he turned to Mike, who was gathering his notes. "Mike," John said casually, "have you got a minute?"

Mike looked up, offering a small smile. "Of course, John. What's on your mind?"

The two men waited as the last few committee members left the room, their footsteps echoing down the corridor. Once they were alone, John leant back in his chair, adopting a relaxed posture, though his mind was anything but.

"I was just wondering," John began, his tone conversational, "if there have been any updates on the investigation into James Parsley's disappearance. I couldn't help but notice the police presence in the village these past few days."

Mike's expression shifted slightly, a hint of weariness in his eyes. "It's been a tough case, John. We've traced James's car to the village, but there's still a lot we don't know. The team's working hard, but we're not getting the breakthroughs we need."

John nodded thoughtfully, as if considering the complexity of the situation. "I saw that Sam Taylor was arrested the other day. That must have been a difficult decision for the police. Sam's had a rough time of it, especially with James."

Mike leant forward slightly; his interest piqued. "What do you mean?"

John hesitated, carefully choosing his words. "I don't want to speak out of turn, Mike, but it's no secret that James wasn't exactly a model citizen. He had a reputation for bullying, and Sam was one of his main targets. We all know James was behind that terrible beating Sam took a while back. It was such a shame—Sam didn't even want to report it, never said who did it, but everyone knew."

Mike frowned slightly, the wheels turning in his mind. "James did have a history of violence," he admitted. "And Sam certainly had a motive. But we need more than motive, John. We need evidence."

John sighed, his expression one of genuine concern, though his words were carefully calculated. "I just hope this doesn't push Sam over the edge. He's been trying to get his life back on track, you know? It would be tragic if all of this dragged him back down."

Mike studied John for a moment, sensing the underlying tension in his words. He knew John was right—Sam had been through a lot, and the village had rallied around him after the attack. But the investigation wasn't about sympathy; it was about finding the truth.

"I appreciate your concern, John," Mike said finally, his tone measured. "But you know I can't discuss the details of the investigation. We're doing everything we can to piece this together, and we're keeping all possibilities on the table."

John nodded, a faint smile touching his lips. "Of course, Mike. I wouldn't expect anything less. I just thought it might help to understand a bit more about what's going on. The village is on edge, and people are talking. I'm sure you've heard the rumours."

Mike sighed, leaning back in his chair. "You're right about that. It's been a challenge trying to keep things under control. But we're doing our best. And if you hear anything—or if anyone comes to you with information—you'll let us know, won't you?"

John's smile widened slightly, his eyes calm and reassuring. "Absolutely, Mike. I'll do whatever I can to help. This village means a lot to me, and I want to see justice done, just like you."

Mike gave a small nod of appreciation. "Thanks, John. It's good to know we've got people like you looking out for the community." With that, the conversation seemed to reach its natural conclusion. Mike stood, gathering his notes and offering a hand to John. "I'd better get going. There's still a lot of work to be done."

John shook his hand firmly, his grip steady. "Take care, Mike. And let's hope we get to the bottom of this soon."

As Mike left the room, John remained seated for a moment, his mind racing. The conversation had gone exactly as he had planned. He had subtly planted the idea that Sam was a viable suspect, without directly accusing him of anything. It was enough to keep the police focused on Sam, at least for now.

The Police Discussion

Later that evening, Mike returned to the station and sought out Detective Inspector Stephen Harris. He found him in the incident room, surrounded by case files and reports, his expression one of deep concentration.

"Sir, have you got a minute?" Mike asked as he approached.

Harris looked up, his brow furrowed. "What is it, Mike?"

"I had a chat with John Bailey after the Residents' Committee meeting today," Mike began, lowering his voice slightly. "He mentioned Sam Taylor, said he wasn't surprised that we'd arrested him. Apparently, Sam and James had a lot of bad blood between them.

"James was a bully, and everyone knew he was the one who beat Sam up. John didn't exactly accuse Sam of anything, but he made it clear that Sam had motive."

Harris leant back in his chair, his eyes narrowing in thought. "Interesting. We've already got Sam in our sights, but we need more than just motive to bring him back in. Did John say anything else?"

Mike shook his head. "Not much, just that he's concerned about the village and what all this is doing to Sam. But it's clear that he thinks Sam could be involved."

Harris tapped his pen on the desk, considering this new information. "We've traced James's car to the village, and we've got footage showing it entering and leaving. But there's still a gap in the timeline. If Sam was involved, we need to figure out how."

Mike nodded in agreement. "We've got to keep the pressure on. If Sam knows something, he'll crack eventually."

Harris sighed, running a hand through his hair. "We're not getting the evidence we need from the fields or the CCTV. It's all circumstantial at this point. We need something concrete to tie Sam to James's disappearance."

The two men sat in silence for a moment, the weight of the investigation pressing down on them. They were close—so close—but without solid evidence, they couldn't make a move.

"Let's keep an eye on Sam," Harris said finally. "And see if we can't get more out of the village. Someone must have seen something. We'll keep checking CCTV, video doorbells, anything that might give us a lead. And if Sam slips up, we'll be ready."

Mike nodded, his thoughts still on his conversation with John. He couldn't shake the feeling that there was more going on than they realised, but for now, he had to trust the process.

"I'll keep you posted on anything I hear," he said as he stood to leave.

Harris nodded in return, already turning back to the case files. "Thanks, Mike. Let's hope something breaks soon."

As Mike left the station, his mind was a whirlwind of thoughts. John's words had been subtle, but the implications were clear. Sam was under suspicion, and the investigation was closing in. But as Mike replayed the conversation in his mind, he couldn't help but wonder if there was something more beneath the surface, something John wasn't saying.

John's Internal Struggle

Meanwhile, back in his study, John sat alone, the events of the day replaying in his mind. The conversation with Mike had gone exactly as he'd hoped, steering the investigation towards Sam while keeping his own involvement hidden. But the satisfaction he felt was tinged with something darker, a shadow that lingered at the edges of his thoughts.

Lorcan McNally was creeping back, that part of himself that could do whatever was necessary to survive, to protect his secrets. John had spent years keeping Lorcan locked away, buried deep beneath the persona of the respectable vicar. But now, with the investigation closing in, he felt Lorcan stirring, ready to do whatever it took to keep the past from resurfacing.

He took a deep breath, pushing down the memories of that night, locking them away in the recesses of his mind. He had to stay in control, had to keep

Lorcan at bay. There was too much at stake, too much to lose if he let his guard down now.

But as he sat in the quiet of the vicarage, the weight of his secrets pressed down on him, a constant reminder that no matter how much he tried to distance himself from his past, it was always there, lurking just beneath the surface. For now, he could maintain the facade, could keep the darkness at bay. But how much longer could he hold on before it all came crashing down?

Chapter 16
Buried Secrets

The small kitchen of Sam's aunt's house was filled with the warm, familiar scent of tea brewing. Sam sat at the kitchen table, his hands nervously wrapped around a mug, his mind racing with the weight of the confession he was about to make. He had rehearsed the words over and over in his head, but now, as the moment approached, his resolve began to waver.

His aunt, a stout woman with kind but sharp eyes, bustled around the kitchen, placing a teapot and two cups on the table before sitting down across from Sam. She looked at him expectantly, her hands resting gently on the table, as if sensing the gravity of what he was about to say.

"Auntie," Sam began, his voice trembling slightly. "I have a confession. There's something I need to tell you, something I'm not proud of." His aunt's eyes narrowed slightly, but she remained silent, waiting for him to continue. Sam took a deep breath, trying to steady himself.

"It was stupid, and I got myself into trouble with James Parsley. We broke into the village shop. I didn't want to do it, but James—he pushed me into it. We stole cigarettes, alcohol. Things we didn't need. And now, with everything that's happened, I've been thinking about it more and more.

"I've been working hard, trying to be a better man, and I need to make this right. I want to go to Ben and Irene, confess, and pay them back. It's the only way I can move on, the only way I can. Finally stand on my own two feet."

He looked up at his aunt, expecting shock or disappointment in her eyes, but instead, he was met with an expression that chilled him to the bone. She was smiling—a cold, knowing smile that sent a shiver down his spine. Before Sam could say another word, his aunt leant forward slightly, her voice calm and almost too soft.

"If you're going to tell me about the night you and that evil man broke into the shop, don't bother. I already know."

Sam's heart skipped a beat, his breath catching in his throat. "You know?"

"Oh, Sam," she said, shaking her head slowly, her eyes never leaving his. "I've known since the night you plotted it and broke in. I know where you hid the items, how long they stayed there, where you took them—I know everything. I know more than you could ever imagine."

Sam felt the blood drain from his face. His mind was reeling, struggling to comprehend how she could know so much. "But how? I didn't, I never told anyone."

"You didn't need to," his aunt replied, her tone almost mocking. "I see everything, Sam. This village is small, and secrets don't stay buried for long. Not from me, at least. I've watched you, watched you struggle, watched you try to cover up your mistakes. But you're not as clever as you think you are. And neither was James."

Sam's hands began to tremble. He set the mug down, afraid he might drop it. "Auntie, I'm so sorry. I didn't mean for things to get so out of hand. I just want to make things right."

His aunt's smile faded, replaced by an expression of cold indifference. "Make things right? Sam, do you really think that's possible now? You're tangled in a web far beyond your understanding, and the threads are pulling tighter every day."

Sam's confusion deepened. There was something in her voice, something dark and unsettling, that made him feel as though he was missing a crucial piece of the puzzle. "What are you talking about?" He asked, his voice barely a whisper.

His aunt leant back in her chair, crossing her arms as she regarded him with a calculating gaze. "I'm talking about the things you don't see, the things that happen in the shadows when no one is watching. I'm talking about the fact that there are secrets in this village that would make your blood run cold. You think you're the only one with something to confess, Sam? There are things you don't know. Things you wouldn't believe even if I told you."

Sam felt a chill settle over him. There was an edge to her words, a darkness that he had never seen in her before. "What do you mean?" He asked, his voice shaking.

His aunt tilted her head slightly, her eyes narrowing. "Let's just say that not all the secrets in this village belong to you. There are others who have buried things far deeper than you could ever imagine. And sometimes, those things don't stay buried."

Sam stared at her, his mind racing. The way she spoke, the certainty in her voice—it was as if she was hinting at something more, something connected to the very darkness he had been trying to escape. "Does this have to do with James?" Sam asked hesitantly.

His aunt's smile returned, a cold, knowing smile that sent another shiver down his spine. "Perhaps, Sam. Perhaps not. But remember this, the past has a way of coming back to haunt you, no matter how deep you bury it. And some stains can't be washed away with apologies or confessions."

Sam's heart pounded in his chest, his breath coming in shallow gasps. "Auntie, what are you saying? Do you know something about James's disappearance?"

Her eyes glinted with something that Sam couldn't quite place—something that made his stomach twist with fear. "I know more than you think, Sam. But that's not for you to worry about. What you should focus on is making peace with the things you can control. Go to Ben and Irene. Confess. Make amends. But remember, Sam, not everything can be fixed with good intentions. Some things are broken beyond repair."

Sam felt as though the ground was slipping out from under him. His aunt's words were like daggers, cutting through his resolve and leaving him with more questions than answers. He had come to her seeking comfort, seeking guidance, but instead, he found himself staring into an abyss that he had never known existed.

"I will," Sam stammered, barely able to find his voice. "I'll go to them. I'll pay them back. I'll do whatever it takes."

His aunt nodded slowly, as if satisfied with his answer. "Good. That's a start. But be careful, Sam. Once you start down this path, there's no turning back. And if you dig too deep, you might not like what you find."

Sam nodded numbly, his mind spinning. He had come to his aunt with a confession, but it seemed that she had secrets of her own, secrets that were darker and more dangerous than anything he could have imagined.

As he rose to leave, his aunt's voice stopped him in his tracks. "Oh, and Sam, one more thing. If you ever feel the need to confess anything else, remember this, not all sins can be forgiven. And some confessions are better left unspoken."

Sam turned to look at her, but the cold, calculating smile on her face sent a chill down his spine. He left the house without another word, the weight of her cryptic warnings pressing down on him like a heavy stone. As he walked through the village, the sun beginning to set on the horizon, Sam couldn't shake the feeling that he was being watched.

His aunt's words echoed in his mind, filling him with a sense of dread that he couldn't escape. He had thought that confessing his sins would bring him peace, but now, he felt more lost than ever. The darkness that had taken hold of his life was deeper and more insidious than he had realised, and as he made his way towards the village shop, he couldn't help but wonder if he was truly prepared for what lay ahead.

Somewhere, in the back of his mind, a new fear began to take root—a fear that his aunt knew far more about James's disappearance than she was letting on. A fear that the secrets she harboured could destroy them all.

The Watcher in the Attic

Sam's footsteps slowed as he replayed the conversation with his aunt in his mind. Her words, laced with an unsettling undertone, echoed in his thoughts, making it impossible for him to think clearly. The resolve he had felt just moments ago, the determination to make things right, was now clouded by confusion and doubt.

His aunt's cryptic warnings about secrets and the things she claimed to know gnawed at him. What had she meant when she said she knew more than he could ever imagine? The dark implications of her words had planted seeds of fear deep within him, and those seeds were quickly taking root.

As he neared the church, intending to seek counsel from John, his phone rang, cutting through his troubled thoughts. He fumbled to pull it from his pocket, the sudden noise jarring him.

"Hello?" He answered, his voice tense.

"Sam," came his aunt's voice, calm but with an underlying urgency. "Come back to the house. Don't go to see Ben and Irene."

"But—" Sam began, his resolve faltering.

"No," she interrupted, her voice firm and unyielding. "Your confession may not be what they want right now. I will speak with them on your behalf. Come back to the house, Sam. Come now."

There was no room for argument in her tone. Sam felt a cold sweat break out on his forehead. The certainty in her voice, the way she seemed to know his every move, sent a chill down his spine. He glanced around, half expecting to see her watching him from somewhere nearby, but the street was empty.

The decision was no longer his to make. Her command echoed in his mind, and with a heavy heart, he turned back towards the house. The church, and the solace he had hoped to find there, would have to wait. His aunt had made it clear that she was in control, and he wasn't sure he had the strength to defy her.

Sam's aunt stood in the dimly lit attic room, the air heavy with the scent of old wood and dust. The small space was cramped, filled with an assortment of binoculars, telescopes, and chairs strategically placed at different angles. Each one was pointed towards a different part of the village, giving her a panoramic view of the comings and goings of St Mary's inhabitants.

She peered through a set of binoculars, watching as Sam turned and began walking back towards the house. She noted the hesitation in his step, the way he looked over his shoulder as if sensing he was being watched. She allowed herself a small, satisfied smile.

With one hand still holding the binoculars, she reached for a notebook on the nearby table. The pages were filled with meticulous notes, each entry detailing the daily movements and interactions of the village residents. She flipped to a fresh page and began to write:

Sam confessed to breaking into the shop. He said he was going to talk to Ben and Irene, but instead, turned and walked towards the church. Perhaps he intends to tell John what I told him.

She put down the binoculars and allowed herself a moment to reflect on what she had just written. Sam was a good boy, misguided perhaps, but good at heart. Still, he was easily swayed, and she couldn't allow him to disrupt the delicate balance she had worked so hard to maintain.

As she moved to place the notebook back on the table, the pages fluttered in the draft from a small, half open window. The pages settled on an earlier entry, one made on the night James had beaten Sam so savagely. Her eyes narrowed as she scanned the words she had written that night, memories flooding back with each line.

James Parsley arrived at the summerhouse just after midnight. I watched as they spoke in the garden. James seemed calm at first, but his demeanour changed quickly. He grabbed Sam, dragged him into the shadows of the trees. I then saw James storming off into the night. I heard every grunt, every blow, I knew what was going on. I watched James walk off towards the car and disappear into the darkness.

She closed the notebook with a deliberate snap, her mind whirring with the implications of what she had witnessed that night. There were things Sam didn't know, things he could never know. Her gaze drifted to the church steeple visible in the distance, barely illuminated by the fading light of day.

John. The vicar who held so many of the village's secrets, who knew the darkness that lurked beneath its peaceful facade. Did he know, she wondered, just how deep the shadows ran? How much did he truly understand about the events of that night?

Her thoughts returned to the present, to Sam's aborted attempt to confess to the shop break-in. He wasn't ready to face the consequences, not yet. And if he went to John now, he might unravel the very fabric she had so carefully woven. But there was more at stake than just a simple confession.

She had seen things, things that others hadn't, things that needed to remain hidden. And she knew that blood had a way of leaving its mark, no matter how hard one tried to wash it away. She would have to speak to John, not as a confessor, but as a guardian of the village's secrets.

There were things he needed to understand, warnings she had to impart. She moved to the small mirror on the attic wall, checking her reflection, adjusting her appearance to one of composed authority. Yes, she would go to John. But not to seek forgiveness.

There were sins in this village that went far deeper than what Sam had confessed, and there were marks that couldn't be scrubbed clean with the tools of ordinary life. She took one last look through the binoculars, seeing Sam as he approached the house, his steps slow and hesitant.

She noted the way he paused at the gate, the way his shoulders sagged with the weight of his indecision. And then she turned, her decision made, and began to descend the stairs from the attic, her mind already crafting the words she would say to the vicar when they met.

She had watched over this village for years, seen things that no one else had seen, and now, it was time to ensure that the darkness stayed buried where it belonged. For as long as she was watching, nothing would be left to chance.

Chapter 17
The Silent Confessor

The morning light filtered softly through the stained-glass windows of the vestry, casting a mosaic of colours across the room. The air was cool, and the quiet hum of the village seemed distant, muffled by the thick walls of the church.

John Bailey sat at his desk, his fingers tracing the worn edges of a prayer book as he gathered his thoughts. He had just finished his morning prayers, the familiar routine offering him a brief respite from the weight that had settled on his shoulders in recent weeks.

A gentle knock at the door broke the stillness, and John looked up, surprised by the unexpected visitor. "Come in," he called, his voice steady but tinged with curiosity.

The door creaked open, and in walked Sam's aunt, her presence filling the room with a quiet authority. She was a woman of modest stature, but there was something about her—an air of confidence, of knowing—that commanded attention.

John stood, offering a warm smile as he gestured towards a chair near the desk. "Good morning," he said, his tone polite and welcoming. "How are you today? Please, do sit down."

She returned the smile, though hers was edged with something John couldn't quite place—something that set him on edge. "Good morning, John. I'm well, thank you." She took the offered seat, settling into it with a grace that belied her years. "It's kind of you to see me without notice."

"Of course," John replied, moving to the small table where a teapot and two cups sat waiting. "Would you like some tea? I've just made a pot."

"Yes, please," she said, her eyes following him as he poured the tea. There was a pause, a moment of silence that seemed to stretch, as if she were waiting for something.

John handed her the cup, his own curiosity growing. "What brings you here this morning?" He asked, keeping his tone light. "I imagine it's not just to share a cup of tea with me, though I do appreciate the company."

She took a sip of the tea, her eyes never leaving his. "Well, I did want to talk about Sam," she began, her voice calm, almost conversational. "He's been doing so well lately, hasn't he? It's been a long road, but he's finally getting clean, staying off the drugs, and you've been such a tremendous help to him."

John nodded, feeling a flicker of pride mixed with apprehension. "Sam has worked hard to turn his life around," he agreed. "I'm just glad I could offer him some guidance, a place where he could find peace and purpose."

Her smile widened slightly, but there was a weight to her words that made John uneasy. "It's more than that, John," she continued, setting her cup down on the table. "You've done more than just offer guidance. You've given him a new lease on life. When he first came to me, he was lost, vulnerable.

"His parents couldn't handle him, and frankly, I was worried that I wouldn't be able to either. But you," she paused, her eyes narrowing slightly as she studied him, "you picked him up when he was at his lowest. You found the faith to help him when no one else could."

John shifted slightly in his chair, the warmth of the tea suddenly feeling cloying in his throat. "I've done what I can," he said, his voice modest. "Sam has made incredible progress on his own. He's a strong young man, stronger than he gives himself credit for."

"Yes, he is," she agreed, her tone softening. "But let's not downplay your role in all this. You gave him work, John. You gave him a purpose. He loves working at the church, tending the garden, learning from Henry. He's found something that makes him feel useful, something that makes him feel like he belongs."

John nodded, though the unease in his chest was growing. "Sam has taken to the work with real dedication. He's become a credit to the community."

"And to you," she added, her gaze piercing. "You've changed his life, John. The ghosts that once haunted him—his past mistakes, the people he's hurt, the things he's done—those ghosts have been buried. He's becoming the man he was always meant to be."

The phrase caught John off guard, his heart skipping a beat. *The ghosts have been buried.* What did she mean by that? Was there something more behind her words, something darker lurking beneath the surface of this conversation?

She continued, seemingly oblivious to his discomfort, "It's not often that someone has provided my nephew with a purpose in life. I want to thank you for everything you've done for him. For making him become the person he should have been from the start."

"You're very welcome," John replied, his voice careful, measured. "It's been my pleasure to help Sam. He's a credit to you, and I'm blessed to know him."

She smiled again, but this time it didn't reach her eyes. "You've done so much for this community, John. You've brought people together, been a pillar of support. Not everyone has faith, but they know it's there if they need it. And your church, our church, is a place where people can come if they need something—a place to talk, to confess, or simply to find shelter."

John's heart was beating faster now, a growing sense of dread creeping into his thoughts. There was something unsettling about the way she spoke, the way she circled around the topic without ever quite touching it. It was as if she was leading him somewhere, drawing him into a conversation that he wasn't sure he wanted to have.

"Thank you," he said, his voice a little too stiff. "It's what I'm here for. To help, to offer support to those who need it." She took another sip of her tea, her eyes never leaving his. "Have you come here just to tell me I'm doing a good job," he asked, his tone light but with an undercurrent of tension, "or is there something else that you need?"

She set her cup down with a soft clink, folding her hands in her lap. "It's not often that someone has given my nephew such a purpose in life," she repeated, her voice low and steady. "I wanted to thank you, John, for everything. For making him the man he is today."

There was a pause, a moment that stretched on too long, and then she continued, "But there's one more thing I want to thank you for."

John's heart was pounding now, the air in the room feeling thick, suffocating. "And what's that?" He asked, his voice barely above a whisper.

She met his gaze, her eyes hard and unyielding. "For taking care of the real issue."

John's blood ran cold, his heart thudding in his chest as the words hung in the air between them. "What do you mean?" He asked, though he already knew the answer.

She didn't flinch, didn't break eye contact. "Don't be silly, John," she said softly. "For taking care of the biggest issue this village has ever seen."

He swallowed hard, his mind racing. "What are you talking about?" He asked, his voice trembling slightly.

"James Parsley," she said, her voice calm, almost casual. "For getting rid of him. For allowing my nephew to start again."

John felt the ground shift beneath him, his world tilting dangerously. She knew. Somehow, she knew everything. "This is fine, John," she continued, her tone soothing, as if she were discussing the weather. "You don't have to worry. I'm happy you were here to help."

He shook his head, his hands trembling. "I don't know what you're talking about," he protested, but the words felt hollow, empty.

She leant forward slightly, her voice dropping to a whisper, "Please, John. I saw everything. James arriving, standing in the doorway, going inside, closing the door. Then you, John, coming out in a different hoodie than you went in wearing. You driving off in his car, coming back through the church grounds an hour later. I'm not even going to ask about the shovel."

John slumped back in his chair, his breath coming in shallow gasps. There was no escape, no denial. She had seen it all. "What do you want?" He asked, his voice hoarse, defeated.

She smiled, a small, knowing smile. "Nothing," she replied. "Just to let you know that I know. I'm not going to do or say anything. I just wanted to shake the hand of the man who gave my nephew a brand new start in life."

He stared at her, disbelief and fear warring within him. "You're not going to say anything?" He repeated, struggling to comprehend.

"No," she said simply. "I don't want anything, I don't need anything, and I'm certainly not going to say anything."

"Does Sam know?" John asked, his voice weak.

She shook her head. "No. Only two people know. Unless you've told anyone else." He shook his head numbly, unable to form words. With that, she stood, smoothing out her skirt as she prepared to leave. "Thank you, John," she said, her voice calm and composed. "For everything."

He watched as she turned and walked towards the door, his mind a whirlwind of fear and confusion. As she reached the middle of the church, she paused, turning back to face him. She stood for a moment, right where James had died, and then, slowly, deliberately, she made the sign of the cross before turning back towards the altar.

John's breath caught in his throat as he watched her leave, the sound of her footsteps echoing through the empty church. He felt a shiver run down his spine, his heart pounding in his chest as he slumped back in his chair. She knew everything. And yet, she had said nothing.

The thought was both a relief and a terror, a double-edged sword that cut deep. As the church door closed behind her, John sat in the silence, his mind racing. He didn't know what to do, didn't know how to respond to this new, terrifying revelation.

All he knew was that Sam's aunt was far more than she appeared to be. And now, she held the power to destroy everything he had fought to protect. But for now, she had chosen silence. For now.

The Hidden Truth

The attic was as silent as a tomb, the only sounds the faint creaking of the old house as it settled into the night. Sam's aunt moved carefully through the dim space; her hands steady as she reached up towards the beams that crisscrossed the ceiling.

She knew exactly where to look, her fingers finding the familiar roughness of the torn page hidden between the wood. Gently, she pulled the folded paper free, her heart beating steadily as she brought it down to the table. The page had been hidden away for some time, but she hadn't forgotten it. Not a single detail escaped her meticulous mind, especially not something as significant as this.

She unfolded the page with care, smoothing out the creases on the worn surface. The words, written in her precise handwriting, stared back at her, a chilling reminder of the events she had witnessed.

James Parsley, back in the village—what does that evil man want? Oh, off to church, are we? At 10:15 pm, James is standing in the doorway, wearing dark clothes as usual. Probably going to burgle someone—hopefully not the village shop again. He's gone inside, and the door is closed. This is suspicious.

She remembered that night vividly, every detail etched into her memory like a scar. She had been sitting in her usual spot in the attic, her binoculars trained on the village below, when she had seen James. Her instinct had been right—there was something off about his return to St Mary's, something that didn't sit well with her. Her eyes moved down the page, recalling the sequence of events she had documented.

Fell asleep in the chair, woke suddenly. James is leaving the church—what was he doing in there all this time? Noticed James wearing a dark grey hoodie. I'm sure it was black when he went in. Examined the man more closely. That isn't James's walk. I recognise that walk, and that isn't James.

The memory of that realisation sent a shiver down her spine even now. She had been certain at the time—whoever had left the church that night wasn't James. The way he moved, the posture, even the way he carried himself—it was different, wrong. And then there was the change in the hoodie, a subtle but telling detail that had set off alarms in her mind. Her eyes narrowed as she read the next entry.

The man walked slightly out of sight. A few minutes later, saw James's car driving past. The man with the grey hoodie was driving. Documented that in my book. So, where is John!

The question, written with a sharp exclamation mark, seemed to leap off the page. She had known then that something was terribly wrong, and her suspicions had only grown stronger with what she had witnessed later that night.

She had stayed awake, her curiosity piqued, her mind racing with possibilities. The lights in the church had remained on for hours, a stark contrast to the usual stillness of the night. And then, finally, she had seen him—John Bailey, emerging from the church, his face set in a grim expression.

An hour or so later, the lights went off in the church, and saw John leaving. Wrote: Something has happened to James. I don't know what, but I do know that whatever it is, Reverend John Bailey is involved.

She sat back in her chair, the weight of the discovery pressing down on her. The page in her hand was more than just a record of what she had seen—it was evidence, proof that something dark and sinister had taken place in the village. And she was the only one who knew the truth, the only one who had seen the pieces fall into place.

Her thoughts turned to Sam, her nephew, who was on his way back to the house even now. She had warned him not to confess to Ben and Irene, knowing that the shop break-in was only a small part of a much larger puzzle. But there was more she hadn't told him, more that she wasn't sure he was ready to hear.

The secrets she kept went deeper than Sam could imagine. She had watched over the village for years, her eyes always alert, always vigilant. And in that time, she had seen things that would shake anyone's faith in the peaceful facade of St

Mary's. But now, the time had come to confront those secrets, to decide what to do with the knowledge she had hidden away for so long.

She had always been content to observe, to watch from a distance, but the events of that night had drawn her into the shadows, made her a part of the darkness that had seeped into the village. As she refolded the page and placed it back in its hiding spot, she knew that she would have to act soon.

John Bailey was a man of the cloth, a man trusted by everyone in the village. But she had seen a side of him that no one else had, a side that she didn't think could exist. She would go to John, but not as a confessor. She would go as a witness, as someone who had seen too much to stay silent any longer.

There were things he needed to know, warnings she had to give. And if he was as clever as she thought, he would understand the gravity of what she was about to reveal. She descended the stairs from the attic, her mind already crafting the words she would use when she faced him.

The time for watching was over. It was time to step into the light and confront the darkness head-on. As she reached the bottom of the stairs, she heard the front door open and close softly. Sam was back, his footsteps hesitant as he approached the sitting room.

She took a deep breath, steeling herself for the conversation to come. There were things he needed to understand, things that would change the way he saw the village, the way he saw her. And perhaps, in time, he would come to understand why she had kept these secrets for so long. But for now, she would guide him carefully, just as she had always done, watching over him as she had watched over the village.

As she did, she would make sure that the truth—her truth—remained hidden, buried deep beneath the surface where it could never be uncovered. Not unless she decided to bring it into the light.

**

John Bailey's hands trembled as he gripped the edges of his desk, the wood cool and solid beneath his fingertips. The room was quiet, too quiet, the silence pressing in on him from all sides. His gaze drifted to the simple wooden cross hanging on the wall opposite him, its presence both a comfort and a condemnation.

He had spent years preaching about sin and redemption, about the boundless mercy of God. But tonight, as the darkness gathered outside and within him, those words felt hollow, like echoes of a faith that was slipping through his grasp. His mind churned with memories—scenes from a life he had tried so hard to bury.

But like the past he thought he had left behind, those memories had a way of resurfacing, clawing their way back into the light, refusing to stay hidden in the shadows where they belonged. He was no longer John Bailey, the vicar of St Mary's. Not in these moments.

No, in these moments, he was Lorcan McNally, a man who had lived by a different creed, a man whose hands had once been stained with blood, whose soul had been blackened by the choices he had made in the name of survival. It was a name he hadn't spoken in years, a name he had tried to forget, but one that haunted him still, lurking in the corners of his mind.

The ghosts of his past whispered to him, their voices insistent, relentless. He could almost hear them now, could almost see their faces—those he had betrayed, those he had lost. They were the ones he had left behind in Ireland, the ones who had shaped him, broken him, made him into the man he had become.

Now, in the stillness of the church, they demanded his attention, dragging him back to the days when he had been someone else entirely. A sharp knock at the door jolted him from his thoughts, and for a brief moment, he considered ignoring it. But the knock came again, firmer this time, insistent.

With a deep breath, John pushed himself away from the desk and made his way to the door, each step heavy, as if the weight of his secrets had settled in his very bones. When he opened the door, he found Sam's aunt standing there, her presence as unsettling as it had been earlier in the day.

She stepped inside without waiting for an invitation, her eyes scanning the room as if she could see through the walls, through him. "Good evening, John," she said, her voice calm, almost soothing. But there was something in her tone that set John on edge, a subtle undercurrent that hinted at knowledge she should not possess.

John nodded, gesturing for her to sit. "Evening," he replied, his voice steady, though his heart pounded in his chest. "What brings you back?"

She didn't answer immediately. Instead, she took her time settling into the chair across from him, her gaze never leaving his. Finally, she spoke, her words measured, deliberate.

"I've been thinking about our conversation earlier," she began, her tone casual, as if they were discussing something as mundane as the weather. "And about Sam. He's been doing so well, hasn't he?"

John's throat tightened, but he forced himself to nod. "He has. He's made great strides."

She smiled, but it didn't reach her eyes. "Yes, thanks to you. You've given him a second chance, a new beginning."

John shifted in his seat, uncomfortable with the direction this conversation was taking. "I've tried to help him," he said carefully. "But Sam's strength comes from within."

She leant forward slightly, her eyes narrowing. "Does it? Or does it come from the removal of certain obstacles from his path?" The question hung in the air between them, heavy and loaded.

John's breath caught in his throat, and for a moment, he couldn't speak. He could feel the walls closing in around him, the weight of her gaze pressing down on him, demanding a response.

"What do you mean?" He finally managed, though he feared he already knew the answer.

She didn't reply right away. Instead, she reached into her bag and pulled out a folded piece of paper, worn and creased as if it had been handled many times. She placed it on the table between them, her hand lingering for a moment before she slid it towards him.

John hesitated before picking it up, his fingers trembling as he unfolded the paper. His eyes scanned the familiar handwriting, and as he read the words, his heart sank.

James Parsley, back in the village—what does that evil man want? Oh, off to church, are we? At 10:15pm, James is standing in the doorway, wearing dark clothes as usual. Probably going to burgle someone—hopefully not the village shop again. He's gone inside and the door is closed. This is suspicious.

John's breath quickened as he continued reading, each sentence like a blow to the chest.

Fell asleep in the chair, woke suddenly. James is leaving the church—what was he doing in there all this time? Noticed James wearing a dark grey hoodie. I'm sure it was black when he went in. Examined the man more closely. That isn't James's walk. I recognise that walk, and that isn't James.

The man walked slightly out of sight. A few minutes later, saw James's car driving past. The man with the grey hoodie was driving. Documented that in my book. So, where is John!

He looked up at her, his face pale, his hands trembling. "You saw all this?"

She nodded slowly, her expression unreadable. "I did. And I've seen more, John. Much more."

The implications of her words settled over him like a shroud. She knew. She had seen everything. The night James had died, the night Lorcan McNally had returned, if only for a moment. And now, she was here, confronting him with the truth he had buried so deep.

"What do you want?" He asked, his voice barely above a whisper.

She leant back in her chair, her gaze never leaving his. "I don't want anything," she said, her tone as calm as ever. "I just wanted you to know that I know. That your secret isn't as safe as you might think."

John's heart pounded in his chest, his mind racing. This was it. The moment he had feared, the moment he had prayed would never come. The ghosts of his past had caught up with him, and now, they were here, demanding retribution. But as he stared at the woman across from him, he realised something else— something that sent a chill down his spine.

She wasn't just here to confront him. She was here to remind him of who he had once been, to show him that no matter how far he had run, no matter how deeply he had buried Lorcan McNally that man was still there, lurking in the shadows, waiting for his chance to re-emerge.

"You're not going to tell anyone?" He asked, the words tumbling out before he could stop them.

She shook her head. "No, John. This is between us. But I think you should remember that not all secrets stay buried forever. Sometimes, they have a way of resurfacing when you least expect it."

John felt the weight of her words settle over him, the truth of them sinking in. He had spent years building a new life, a life where he could be someone else, someone better. But now, that life was hanging by a thread, and he had no idea how long it would hold.

As she stood to leave, she paused, looking down at him with an expression that was almost pitying. "Remember, John," she said softly. "I saw everything." With that, she turned and walked towards the door, her footsteps echoing in the quiet room. As she reached the threshold, she stopped, turning back to face him one last time. "Take care of Sam," she said. "He's been through enough."

And then she was gone, leaving John alone with his thoughts, his guilt, and the knowledge that his past was far from dead. John sat there for a long time after she left, the piece of paper still clutched in his hand. His mind was a whirl of thoughts, memories, and fears.

He thought of Ireland, of the life he had left behind, of the man he had been. Lorcan McNally. A name that had once struck fear into the hearts of those who crossed him, a name he had tried so hard to forget. But he couldn't forget. Not now. Not when the ghosts of that life had come back to haunt him.

He had tried to bury Lorcan McNally, just as he had buried James Parsley. But Lorcan was still there, just beneath the surface, waiting for his chance to rise again. John closed his eyes, his breath coming in shallow gasps as he tried to calm the storm raging within him.

He had built this life, this new identity, to escape the darkness of his past. But that darkness had followed him, clinging to him like a shadow, and now, it threatened to consume him. He knew he couldn't run from it forever.

One day, the truth would come out. And when it did, everything he had worked for, everything he had built, would come crashing down around him. But for now, he had to keep going. He had to protect Sam, protect the village, and protect the secrets that had been buried in the grave of Derek Williams. Because if those secrets were ever uncovered, they would destroy more than just him.

They would destroy everything. As the night wore on, John finally rose from his chair, the piece of paper still clutched tightly in his hand. He walked to the window and looked out at the village below, the darkness swallowing everything in its path.

He knew that this was only the beginning. The shadows of his past were closing in, and it was only a matter of time before they caught up with him. But until then, he would do whatever it took to keep the truth buried, to keep Lorcan McNally hidden in the shadows where he belonged.

Because as long as the truth remained hidden, as long as the darkness stayed at bay, there was still a chance—however slim—that he could find redemption. But as he stared out into the night, John knew that redemption was a distant dream, one that he might never reach.

Because in the end, the ghosts of his past were still there, waiting, watching, and one day, they would demand their due. And when that day came, there would be no escape. Only the cold, hard truth, and the price he would have to pay.

For now, the village slept, blissfully unaware of the shadows that lurked beneath its peaceful surface—hidden from sight, but always there, waiting. And John, the keeper of those shadows, felt their weight pressing in on him, a burden he could no longer share.

The innocent would remain in the dark—for their own protection, and for his. But he knew, deep down, that the truth was like a crack in a dam. Sooner or later, it would break through. He had no way of knowing when, or how, but one thing was certain.

The shadows were rising. And when they emerged, they would consume everything. How long could he keep the darkness at bay? How long until the ghosts of his past came for him, demanding their due? John didn't know. But as he stared out into the stillness of the night, a chill ran down his spine.

He only knew one thing for certain; when the truth finally surfaced, there would be no redemption. Only reckoning.